THE WHISPERING DARKNESS

BY

FRANK THAYER

A Sun Cross Publication
P.O. Box 3136
Las Cruces, NM 88003 USA

THE WHISPERING DARKNESS
By
Frank Thayer

ISBN # 0578409070

ACKNOWLEDGEMENTS

•Cover art by Graham Kennedy gkilius@aol.com
•Black and white 1978 photographs by Frank Thayer
•Vintage photographs of Mogollon 1914 and Wagon Train in Silver City printed courtesy of the Silver City Museum
•Mogollon map by Frank Thayer copied from an original published in Mogollon Diary by William Rakocy 1977
•Color photos of Mogollon 2018 by Frank Thayer

Book design by Pamela Porter

The characters and situations presented in this book are fictional, and any connection with people or events is purely coincidental or imagined. Locations are actual and accurate to the period in which the stories are set. Frank Triolo, the Chandlers and the Englishes were actual residents of Mogollon in 1978. All others are fictional characters.

This book is a Sun Cross Publication
Contact: Frank Thayer, Box 3136
Las Cruces, NM 88003 USA
gticruiser@aim.com

Dedicated to the tradition of classic literary horror. This volume is also dedicated to those who have provided inspiration and guidance during the development of this story, including Becky Smith, Sallie Thayer, Mary Kaschak, Pam Porter, and to John Pittsenbargar for our nostalgic trip back to Mogollon in 2018.

THE WHISPERING DARKNESS

BY

FRANK THAYER

An Introduction and Disclaimer

The Whispering Darkness is a work of fiction and must be seen from that perspective. The story's sense of reality can be found in settings as real as the period photographs displayed throughout the book. Set in the mining town of Mogollon, New Mexico, the story unfolds on real streets and in buildings that exist now or did exist in 1978. The other major setting is the town of San Vicente, whose real name will be instantly recognizable to anyone living in that community and which was the setting for supernatural horror tales in the author's previous work Terror Tales of the Southwest.

The mining town of Mogollon is often called a "ghost town," and that romanticized name is inspirational to a writer who wants to create a what-if story, and readers may wonder if there is any reality to the people who are portrayed in the story. For historical foundation in 1978, the author uses the names of the Chandlers and the Englishes, who operated the Mogollon Museum and the Mogollon Theater in those days, as well a respectful tribute to Frank Triolo, who was an honored long-time resident of the town. That being said, the major dramatis personae in The Whispering Darkness are fictional, though the author may be accused of using real people and giving them an avatar as they play their fictional roles.

Otherwise, the standard disclaimer applies: The characters and situations portrayed in this story are fictional. Any connection between these elements and real people or situations is coincidental or imagined, though locations may be recognizable to residents of Southwest New Mexico. Readers with 40-year memories may seek to connect the gallery portrayed with two real people, and those deductions must remain the stuff of rumor. The author readily admits that the Englishes did not have a dog named Sparky.

As for Mogollon, its reality is portrayed throughout the book with vintage photos taken in 1978, and each image confirms the author's familiarity with the town, its people, and its history. It was intended to present the reader with the names of current residents of the town and their work in keeping the town alive; however, despite a visit to Mogollon in May, 2018, and letters sent to proprietors of the Silver Creek Inn and the Mogollon Museum, it was not possible to obtain more information about the current state of a too-tough-to-die town that continues to maintain its identity through the respect and hard work of those who live there and love its unique location.

For those whose interest in Mogollon is awakened, a thumbnail sketch is in order. The town of Mogollon was established in the late 1880s at a time when Apache bands were still terrorizing settlers, and the town boomed as did many mining towns in the Southwest.

Buildings sprang up in Silver Creek Canyon, and the smelted gold and silver was taken down the mountains by wagon to Silver City, 78 miles away. The town was supplied by freight wagons often employing 10-and 12-horse, or mule, teams, and the yield was taken back to Silver City. A one-way trip by wagon was probably a three-day trek. So important was Mogollon in those days that the first single telephone line ran from Silver City to Mogollon in1908 to connect with the mine at a time when telephones were rare in the Southwest.

One of the better comprehensive histories of Mogollon and area is probably the 1977 Bravo Press publication by El Paso artist Bill Rakocy and his co-editor C.T. Jones, Mogollon Diary 1877-1977. In its 207 pages, the author/editors tell the story of the town, richly illustrated with copies of period photos, Rakocy's sketches and articles reprinted from Silver City newspapers to show how important Mogollon was at the turn of 20th Century New Mexico. Though disjointed and eclectic in nature, the book leaves the reader with a rich appreciation for the people who ranged through the mountains of the Southwest and who created towns and legends.

Rakocy once owned the stone building that later served as the gallery setting for The Whispering Darkness, and he erected the "ghost town" sign on the building that served him as his personal art gallery. His work is still known in the El Paso area in 2018. The 1978 photos published herein recall the days after Rakocy sold his workplace.

While many mining towns collapsed with the closure of their mines, leaving little but stone foundations, Mogollon was never completely abandoned, and this alone kept the ravages of vandalism from destroying the buildings. Even when it was the home of more than 1,500 people, Mogollon fought and survived raging fires and occasional floods of Silver Creek. In the 1960s, there were many vacancies along the main street, and this drew regional visitors to purchase buildings to restore and operate concessions or galleries to serve those who drove through on their way to forest locations such as Willow Creek. The solid structures of the J.P. Holland General Store, the Coats & Howard store, the Mogollon Museum, have all survived, with the latest catastrophe in 2013 being what is described as a 100-year flood that devastated the main street and brought federal government relief to restore and renovate the town site.

The Whispering Darkness is a tribute to Mogollon and its people, with a fictional horror tale and a portfolio of period photographs to serve as tribute to the town as it was (and might have been) in 1978. It was the author's privilege to spend many happy hours there.

Mogollon Ghost Town circa 1965

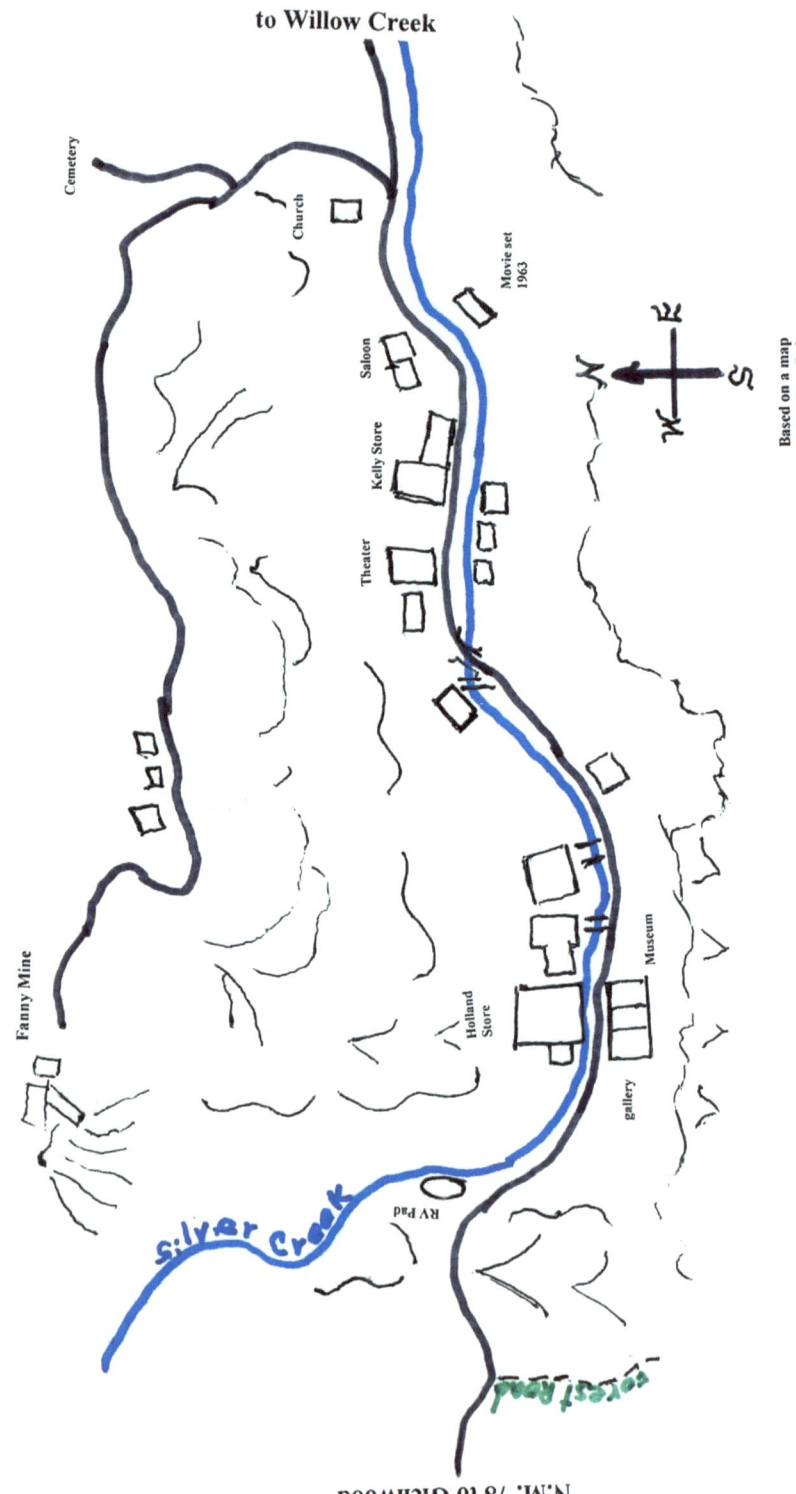

to Willow Creek

Cemetery

Church

Movie set
1963

Saloon

Kelly Store

Theater

Fanny Mine

Holland
Store

Museum

gallery

RV Pad

Silver Creek

forest Road

N.M. 78 to Glenwood

Based on a map
by William Rakocy

The J.P. Holland General Store

RickPhoto 1978

THE WHISPERING DARKNESS

I have seen the black universe yawning
Where dark planets roll without aim,
And they roll in their horror unheeded,
Without knowledge or luster or name.
—After H. P. Lovecraft
"The Haunter of the Dark"

1

A recent news feature described a discovery by the Hubble Space Telescope that has detected a galaxy 13.2 billion light years from Earth—an unthinkable distance and an unfathomable vastness. Along with encounters with varieties of human-like aliens, in the blackness of space exist entities so unspeakably loathsome and hostile that when they descend to Earth, only horror follows.

* * *

I confess that I was not entirely rational that May night in San Vicente, because I was still convulsed with dread after my wife Margo and I fled the New Mexico mountain ghost town of Mogollon* in blind panic two nights before, driving wildly the 78 miles to our home. That Monday afternoon I telephoned the authorities in Catron County, but they were non-committal, saying only that the road was being repaired on the mountain.

Margo was out on Monday night—her long-time friend Susan, the curator of the San Vicente Museum, had picked her up to allow her a few hours of normalcy. It was a good enough reason for Margo to leave me alone, but I also knew she would unburden herself as to my idiotic betrayal that would have torn our marriage apart had we not been overwhelmed by a hellish attack. Thus, I remained at home, thinking how I could begin to put frightening events into words. I had just written what I knew about the missing woman outside the town of Glenwood, and I had begun to approach a description of the drive up the mountain to the isolated canyon and its century-old structures.

The very act of typing seemed to ease my deep anxiety for a few minutes, and I do not remember hearing the front door open—surely I must have bolted it when Margo and Susan left for their girls' dinner and soul-baring confessions. An LP of Pachelbel's "Canon" was playing on the stereo as I sought to calm my nerves. I was hunched over my Royal Portable typewriter, fingers unsteady, halfway down a page. The room was brightly lit, with two floor lamps and the five-branch ceiling lights blazing underneath the six-bladed fan that stood idle. I wondered how I could put to words the screaming chaos of panic when all reason vanishes.

The night visitor was suddenly just—there, standing behind my shoulder. I know I started up from the chair, a clumsy grunt exploding from my chest. An electric bolt of shock went through me, and I seemed frozen, trying to focus. As I looked at the visitor, fear was grinding in my gut. I backed against the wall. I knew him! God help me, I knew him, and his presence stirred a loathing and fear as it would for an unknown terror.

The record playing on the stereo had finished, and the only sound in the room was the soft wheeze of Arthur Brunk's breath. His wrinkled blue shirt was buttoned to the neck, but

*Mogollon, New Mexico—a sparsely populated Old West mining town in southwestern New Mexico, built into a declivity of Silver Creek Canyon in the mountains of the Gila National Forest. Established in 1878, the town carries the name of the Spanish Governor of New Spain from 1712–1715 (pronounced MUH-GEE-YONE) and also given to the prehistoric culture of Native Americans who lived in the region before the coming of the Spanish. Still called a ghost town, it has survived fires and the occasional flooding of the creek that flows along the road through the center of the town.

one side was untucked, and his Docker slacks were soiled at the knees, leather shoes scuffed at the toes.

I recalled how tan his skin was when I first met him, but this night his face was a pallid mask, and his dark hair fell across his forehead, hanging to the left side of his face. That face was a mass of horrid pustules, dotted with dozens of raised lesions, almost like the curse of smallpox, but strangely alien. His dark eyes were narrowed, and they exuded malevolence unlike any earthly personality.

In my terror, renewed from the wild flight to escape Mogollon two nights before, my eyes would not focus properly. Was it human, or a shade risen from the grave? All these thoughts poured in a flash flood through my mind as I stood before an alien presence. Some of the pustules on that face were leaking a clear fluid in tiny rivulets down his cheeks and hideous in the aspect it gave him. Yes, he had disappeared into the mine two days before the final horror in the ghost town, and his wife had told me…no, I did not want to remember that part, but he–it–stood before me.

Brunk's voice emerged from lips twisted downward, not carrying his Texas twang, but sepulchral and hollow with menace. He did not call me by name, but his words were directed deep into my mind. The speaker's drone was chillingly familiar, re-awakening cold terror within me. I felt the perspiration of acrid fear, cold and damp under in my armpits. "You… saw… nothing," the voice almost buzzed in mechanical rhythm that was dreadfully recognizable. His arms were at his sides, the thumbs slowly squeezing the other four fingers, again and again as the arms seemed to roll back and forth on their axes.

My first impulse was to shout at him, but I was suddenly unable to speak, my throat dry with fear. My head was throbbing and my vision was hazy, my thoughts a welter of panic.

My mind was back in Mogollon and a buzzing, droning sound was coming from … from…from the thing hidden in the trees. Oh God! My memory suddenly returned. It could not be, but Arthur Brunk's voice had adopted a hellish similarity. "You…will not…speak of this…" Brunk looked slowly around the room and turned to fix me with a hypnotic, alien gaze: "Iä!" That word! That meaningless word! My world grew dark.

I was lying on the floor, my head throbbing as an acidic odor burned my nasal passages. With difficulty, I stood up and was assailed with vertigo. Arthur Brunk was no longer there, and I had a paranoid thought that he had become *their* agent, whatever that could mean. There was nobody in the room, but the front door stood open. I stumbled to the next room and retrieved my pistol, battling the assaults of dizziness, fear, and amorphous images in my head. I could not swallow as I returned to the front door, looking out into the night. There was nothing there. Once more the horror of Mogollon was so real that I knew I could never forget what had happened to us just days before. My sense of security crumbled as I tightened my grip on the .45 automatic, loading a round into the chamber. I was so grateful that Margo was away from the house. because she had been almost hysterical when we just barely escaped the whispering darkness, knowing better than to report it. For who would believe us?

When I remembered that I had been typing. I looked at my watch to see that almost a half hour had elapsed. I had typed several pages before the intruder entered, so I walked unsteadily to the desk where the typewriter sat. Again, vertigo made my vision swim. I looked down and saw the typewriter keys bunched against the carriage where a vicious hand had mashed the keys, and the typed sheets were gone, the page in the machine ripped out, leaving a torn scrap still pinned under the keys. I could not comprehend what had happened before I lost consciousness, but the sinister warning had frightened me to my core. The only thing more terrifying than that caricature of a person I knew was the cosmic horror encountered in the mountain ghost town.

As one hypnotized, I vowed to suppress what I knew. I cannot stop the nightmares though, and the hideous inhuman face of Arthur Brunk appears in my dreams when I least expect it, even now, 40 years later. That face is part of a larger vision of incomprehensible terror. Then, when I have that dream, I awaken in a cold sweat as I see a human face transmogrified into an alien mask.

One

At the Threshold of Horror

The demons of uncounted centuries must be as real as those documented visitors from outer space, I argued as we drove the two-lane highway from San Vicente toward the ghost town of Mogollon. It was a 78-mile drive from San Vicente, but a wonderful way to spend weekends in an Old West building we had bought in that rustic canyon town, sold to us by the eccentric El Paso artist Bill Rakocy.

Margo rolled her eyes as she grinned and shook her head, "No, you are contradicting yourself. You yourself told me that UFO researchers have uncovered a case over near Roswell, and that the alien bodies are human. Don't you think it makes sense that any intelligent beings, no matter where they are from, will have to be more or less human? Or is it that you have to make everything an unpublished horror tale." She punched me on the arm.

"OK, OK, I can't answer that, but history is full of monster and demon stories." On the long Friday drive from San Vicente to the ghost town, there was plenty of time for conversation and planning. The tires hummed on the late afternoon blacktop, the sun shining brightly through the driver's side window of the white 1971 Volkswagen bus, its engine almost reaching top end at 60 mph. The interior was packed with food and drinks for the weekend, framed photographs by me, and stained glass panels created by Margo.

The passing environment was always a treat for the eyes as U.S. Highway 180 unfolded north near the Arizona border. The 78 miles from San Vicente to Mogollon, snaked through the scattered hamlets and ranches to Cliff, Buckhorn, Pleasanton, Glenwood, before the turnoff at N.M. Highway 78, and seven miles up into the Gila National Forest to Mogollon. Just beyond the N.M. 78 turnoff was the tiny cluster of buildings named Alma.

To stay on Highway 180 past the turnoff, it is 25 miles to the intersection of N.M. Highway 12 and five more miles to the Catron County Seat at Reserve and then north to Pietown, Datil, and east to where it meets U.S. Highway 60 leading to Socorro. To stay on 180, the traveler continues west across the Arizona border where the road meets the north/south U.S. Highway 666 in Alpine, Ariz.

For those who say that superstition has been outdated by scientific and rational civilization, that latter road has since been re-named because of disturbing tales related to its diabolical association.

Passing the Leopold Vista, I always had the impulse to stop and take photos, but the results from my Nikon F were always disappointing when I knew that the view of the towering bluffs, canyons, and pines of the forest required attention from a 4x5 view camera such as my Rochester, N.Y., photography mentor, Dennis Adams, used.

When we passed the turnoff to the San Francisco Hot Springs south of Glenwood, Margo commented that it was a shame that the unspoiled geothermal waters of the small river had been taken over by hippies, and I commented, "Yeah, they have been co-opted." My words had a double meaning as I was suspicious of New Age food co-ops.

"Hey, you apologize right now. Some of our best friends shop at the co-op." Margo was baiting me.

I laughed and squeezed her thigh as we entered a straight stretch. Ahead was a car parked at the side of the road, warning lights flashing. "Rick, slow down. Maybe we can help." Margo strained over the high dashboard as we pulled in behind the Oldsmobile Toronado, easily recognized because of the TV commercial touting its leather interior and featuring movie actor Ricardo Montalban. It also had the characteristic vinyl top and was a metallic brown color. From my point of view its virtue was a 403 horsepower engine, but right now it obviously had a flat right rear tire.

As we got out of our van, a woman emerged from the driver's side of the Olds, stylishly dressed in skirt and jacket, with shoes not meant for hiking. Margo introduced herself and the woman gave her name as Ofelia Armendariz, on her way to visit family in Reserve.

I asked her to pop the trunk so that I could change her tire, and Ofelia exhaled audibly, shrugging, "You know, the spare is missing, and my husband was using the jack and tools back home in our garage."

"Well, we could take you into Glenwood. The service station there might help."

"That is really nice, but I hate to leave this car."

Margo volunteered, "We would be glad to drive in and get them to come out for you."

Mrs. Armendariz thanked us and got back into her driver's seat as we pulled around her to drive the few miles to Glenwood. When we pulled in, the New Mexico State Police cruiser was parked across the street at the Blue Front bar and café. We gave the service station manager the details, and then we also walked over and reported it to the State Policeman as well.

I said, "OK, Babe, good deed done. Let's get up the hill."

Margo thought for a moment. "No, it could take them a long time to get the service truck going. Turn around and go back so that we can keep her company until help arrives."

She made sense. Mrs. Armendariz could not be sure that we actually did what we promised, so we did what we hoped anybody else would do, and I pushed all 40 horsepower of the VW bus to the maximum. We had been gone a total of about 25 minutes, and when the Oldsmobile hove into view, I quickly made the u-turn and pulled in behind the listing Toronado. We had not seen a single vehicle during the round trip to Glenwood.

We climbed down from the high VW red leatherette seats to say hello to the stranded Mrs. Armendariz. The vehicle was empty—nobody in the driver's seat, the passenger seat, or in the rear of the car. We stared at each other, and Margo was shaking her head. "A woman dressed like that does not just walk away. She told us she wanted to stay with the car."

I felt helpless as I looked up and down the empty grey ribbon, and then we sat in our vehicle, waiting and staring at the luxury Oldsmobile and wondering. There had to be a simple answer, but with no traffic, no simple solution made any sense.

Twenty minutes later a service truck from the four-pump Texaco station came rolling down the highway, two yellow lights at the top of the cab alternately blinking, and followed a few hundred yards behind by the black New Mexico State Police cruiser.

The name of the station attendant's striped shirt was embroidered "BOB," and underneath was the color Texaco star emblem. The state cop did a vigorous u-turn and parked behind the tow truck. We climbed out of our vehicle as "Bob" scratched his head.

The officer peered into the driver's side window, turning back to us. "Key's in the ignition," as he made a wide 360-degree circuit of the Toronado. Wearing gloves, he opened the car door, removed the keys and went to the trunk. Margo put her face into my shoulder as the hollow click of the trunk opening seemed to be louder than the idling engines behind it.

Nothing.

The afternoon turned ominous, and it seemed to me that we all sensed something in the air. The state cop pushed his visor cap back on his head, chewing gum as he began writing vehicle information. He interviewed us but would not speculate on the disappearance. He took down our information and told us to go on to Mogollon.

We were uncharacteristically silent most of the way, punctuating our thoughts by voicing occasional ideas about why Mrs. Armendariz might have abandoned her luxury car as we passed through Glenwood again, reaching the turnoff to N. M. State Road 78 just before Alma. Everything seemed so familiar, and yet…

Margo looked at me, pushing her medium-length blond hair back as she did so . "I hope she's OK."

"So do I." I knew something had happened to the woman, but I had no idea what could explain what we had seen. I concentrated on the road whose initial stretch was deceptively straight before it began winding upward more than 1,000 feet, wrapped

The Mogollon Gallery   RickPhoto 1978

around the mountains, in places barely wide enough for two vehicles to pass each other. The most precarious curve was a hairpin turn that was impossible to see around. One side was a sheer cliff rising toward the sky, and the other side was a precipitous drop, hundreds of feet into a chasm beneath. The mountain road was originally hacked out with the indentured help of prisoners from as far away as San Vicente.

I had grown used to looking down that rugged drop because I always singled out the pale corpse of a white van that lay on its side at the bottom of the ravine. It had been there as long as I could remember, a warning to the reckless and the careless. The VW engine was straining, and the speed dropped to 30 mph on the steep grade. It was always a relief to see the other side of the hairpin and not see a descending vehicle coming at me. We negotiated the serpentine road successfully, with Margo looking as much at me as at the narrow road.

As we topped the mountain, the scattered pine trees grew more numerous, closing in on the road in the fading light of afternoon. The road seemed to wind almost endlessly down until we encountered a stretch where I noticed the man-made shallow rectangular 20'x30' pool off to the left side of the road. I was sure it was newly constructed, and it did not appear to be for cattle to use because there was a low screen fence around its perimeter and some kind of sign that I could not read, posted on the wire.

Then we turned two corners and eased into Silver Creek Canyon, suddenly greeted by the gaunt and venerable survivors of buildings from a century before. Buildings are lined in single rows on either side of the street, while the modest Silver Creek trickles along the north side of the street.

On the north side of the road is the two-storey cream-colored stucco building, the most imposing in the town for a century, and its bold name painted on the front "J.P. HOLLAND GENERAL STORE." The stucco was crumbling on the near side of the building, overlooking a wooden shed with a sloped tin roof attached to the lower part of the wall. A weathered board porch with a fence-like low railing stretched across the front of the building, and an additional sign tacked to its front announcing, "Gila National Gallery." The building was vacant.

Directly across the street lay a smaller two-storey rock building that was also a major mercantile establishment in frontier days. It was the Coats & Howard General store, built in 1885. It and the Holland store had survived fires, including the great conflagration of 1910, and periodic floods, for over a century, and the west wall of the rock Coats and Howard building presented two aging painted wood signs by the El Paso artist Bill Rakocy. One read "Art Gallery" and the other read "Ghost Town Mogollon." It was now our building, with a newly crafted and lacquered wooden sign emblazoned with the raised design of a pyramid with light rays emerging and named pretentiously "Enchanted Light Gallery." A parking area stretched west from the building side and along south side of N.M. 78.

I pulled the VW bus in front of the outhouse that was the only bathroom facility for the gallery, and we faced the unloading task. Across the street, the Holland store was dark and vacant. Even though the sky was still bright, shadows gathered early at Mogollon because it was enclosed in the canyon, the mountains rising on all sides, and almost vertically behind the buildings on each side of the road.

The Old Kelly Store   RickPhoto 1978

Stretching up the meandering street were stone buildings, wooden buildings, and a fake storefront and saloon constructed for the 1973 spaghetti western movie, "My Name is Nobody," starring Henry Fonda and Terence Hill. Most tourists probably took the set buildings as more appropriate to an Old West town than the true, original structures. At least a dozen people were year-round residents of the town, and the vintage occupied buildings included our gallery, a curio store, a museum across from the Holland store, the Mogollon Theater dating from 1915, the Old Kelly Store, and one other store selling miscellaneous trinkets and snacks.

At the east end of the town was a small boarded up church on the steep slope of a small hill, 100 feet above the trickling creek. Also at the east end of the town was the home of Mogollon's long-time resident Frank Triolo whose white hair befit him as the grand old man of the town at 81.

State Road 78 continues through town, the pavement ending as the road goes deeper into the forest, eventually emerging near the town of Datil far to the north. The road is impassible during the winter snow months. Before 78 disappears into the vastness of the Gila National Forest, another dirt track hooks to the left and up to the Mogollon Cemetery and around to the expanse of the Little Fanny mine that nurtured the community through its heyday. The mine dump covers the bottom half of a mountain, hanging down like a patriarch's giant grey beard against the slope.

Halfway up the mountain, a maze of cavernous sheet metal mine buildings from the

Movie Set Saloon from "My Name is Nobody"   RickPhoto 1978

turn of the century still wait for the next gold rush, and the head frame looms above everything like a monster's scaffold.

* * *

The late spring afternoon was pleasant, and when we unlocked the front door of the gallery, we felt the cold air retained by the building over the past week. At this 6,300-foot altitude, nights could be cold even in the summer. Perhaps a half dozen proprietors and weekend residents arrived any time between Thursday and Friday evening, departing again late Sunday afternoon.

With the ceiling lights on, light was already flooding through the tall, rectangular, four-pane windows, set back in their rock and concrete frames to reveal the thickness of the building walls. The upstairs windows were smaller, and it was necessary to access the upstairs by means of a heavy wooden stairway bolted to the west side of the building.

The ancient dark wood flooring echoed hollowly as we carried groceries and products inside. The walls were hung with stained glass suncatchers and panels as well as mounted photographs I exhibited. The steady spring tourist traffic promised to bring a moderate stream of gallery visitors during the day every weekend. A large wood stove sat toward one corner of the main gallery area, and a partition left a small area for a rudimentary kitchen.

I unlocked the rear door in the kitchen area to step outside and throw the switch to activate the well pump that would give us running water in the kitchen. Everything was in order, and I silently thanked the El Paso artist for putting a new roof on the building to assure that it would be weather tight. At the original store counter was our pride and joy, the cast metal silver filigree National Cash Register that was the center of attention in the gallery. I pressed "No Sale" to hear the bell ring as the oak-segmented cash drawer emerged.

At that moment, Arthur Brunk came through the door. "Howdy, Rick. Glad you made it up again this week." Brunk was my height, almost lanky, with a mild Texas twang. He remembered the years when Rakocy owned the gallery, and both he and his wife Matilda usually drove all the way from El Paso to operate their ghost town museum, even though Matilda had a brother living in San Vicente.

Both Arthur and his wife were personable and outgoing. Art usually flirted with Margo when the opportunity arose. For her part, Matilda called residents and visitors "Honey," or just "Hun," and there was a rumor that Nikki English had braced Matilda for being too familiar with her husband. That was amusing to me, because, though Matilda was socially assertive, she had an appearance I thought of as average and motherly, with neck length curled hair, comfortable clothes, and modest makeup. She sometimes exhibited an enigmatic smile as though she was contemplating something very interesting. Maybe it was the dark-framed glasses that tended to make her appear matronly, rather than an upper-middle-class car dealer's wife.

For some reason, when I once talked with her about the sources for some of the rare displays of firearms and American Indian pots in the museum, she had suddenly asked me to call her "Darouse," as though it was a personal favor. She said the name was French. It seemed an unusual request, because I knew that everybody's nickname for her was always "Mattie." I wondered if her husband knew about the avatar name she had given herself

Brunk himself was in his 40s, but he had an unusually smooth tan complexion and a narrow nose whereas most men in the Southwest developed a rougher skin in the arid, windswept expanses that beckoned many of us to the outdoor life. He twanged, "Gonna be at the Englishes' social at the theater tonight?"

"Hey, wouldn't miss it, Art." We shook hands, and he presented a strong grip. His dark hair was parted on the right and combed to his left side, threatening to drop a strand over his eyebrow at any moment.

"Where's Margo?" He asked loudly, even though he could hear activity coming from the kitchen area. His smile always seemed to be lifted on the left side of his mouth, and I always expected him to call me "pardner."

Margo had put on her heavily lined leather jacket because the gallery was chilly, and she bounced out from behind the partition, flashing her signature smile, the one that showed all her perfect teeth. "Hi, Art. How's Mattie?" Brunk's wife had undergone minor surgery earlier this year, and he had made the trip by himself for the past month.

"Nothing keeps her down, Marg." Brunk's dark brown eyes brightened as he used his pet name for her. He looked at Margo, smiled broadly, and jammed his hands into his jeans pockets; she either did not notice or just accepted it as a normal male reaction. "She's down at the shop organizing our Fanny mine photographs and relics."

"What's your plan for the weekend, Art?" I knew the answer to that one. Brunk was fond of the Little Fanny mine, and he spent a lot of time visiting Old Man Akeley who

The Mogollon Museum   RickPhoto 1978

lived at the mine entrance. Akeley was a crafty individual who was poorly educated and was rumored to have a considerable stash of money hidden at the mine somewhere.

In my few encounters with Akeley, he came across as caustic and suspicious, his bushy beard stained with tobacco juice and more facial hair than any man I knew. He always wore baggy denim coveralls, and it was rumored that he kept a hog leg Colt revolver hidden inside the spacious, baggy pockets. Though age had reduced his height to 5'7", he was legendary for never backing down. He had a decades-long feud with Frank Triolo, partially because Triolo was revered, and Akeley was only tolerated because he controlled access to the Little Fanny mine property.

I didn't wonder that Akeley and Brunk had found common ground, because Brunk owned the Lone Star Ford dealership in El Paso, and given a silver tongue when it suited him. I was certain Brunk had more than friendship in mind when he visited Akeley. I sometimes had an uneasy feeling about Art, but that may have been because of my protective feelings for Margo. There was just something about his posture, his smile, as he tilted his feet to the outside edges of his cowboy boots.

Margo came closer. She had an endearing spring to her step. "We'll get up the street to see Mattie either this evening or in the morning." Matilda had been absent for the past month, and her husband reminded us that she was recovering from minor surgery. She was a likeable woman, several years younger than her husband. She was almost as tall as her husband, and they had a son in high school who cared for the El Paso home most weekends, because there was nothing for a teenager to do in a ghost town of fewer than two dozen residents.

I had always noticed that Matilda-Mattie-Darouse had a well-kept figure, though she never seemed to accentuate her natural attributes. I thought she must have been very attractive when she and her husband married, but she had probably done what many married women do after preganancy, cutting her hair, dispensing with careful makeup, and preferring modest clothes that lent comfort and practicality. Because raising children is a taxing career, her evolution made sense.

Brunk himself was always solicitous and friendly, but I had reservations about his motives that Margo said were unwarranted. She should know, because she was certainly more successful than I was as she operated a major real estate office in San Vicente and supplied more than 50 percent of our general income. My office job with the school system was dependable but not lucrative, while photos and photo postcards in the gallery would not even keep a family pet alive.

After Brunk went back to his museum, twilight descended on Mogollon, and we prepared the gallery for a Saturday opening. We ate our dinner of meat burritos and soft drinks before walking outside and up the stairs to the living quarters.

The spacious upstairs looked more like an attic. Two partitions roughly defined the sleeping area, where comfortable futons were made up like beds, and empty crates served as bedside tables. Naked bulb ceiling lights were supplemented by a single table lamp sitting on one of the crates and two 6 volt flashlights in case the power from the Arizona Cooperative were to go out during the night. The nine-foot ceilings were only the aging rafters, while, beyond the partition, the vacant section of the upstairs was also the warehouse, with an ordered pile of 2x4 studs and a stack of white dry wall too short to reach the rafters. The air was warmer here, and we had everything necessary for a comfortable night except a bathroom.

The privacy and mountain silence was an aphrodisiac, and I took Margo in my arms, smelling the fragrance of her blond hair and feeling the slim perfection of her pliant body. What began as an affectionate naked embrace became an escalating frenzy that did not end quickly

When we switched off the table lamp, the darkness was profound, unlike the semi-darkness of San Vicente. We lay side by side in the dark, talking and wondering about the strange case of Ofelia Armendariz. We kissed good night and sleep came quickly. It was less than an hour later when we heard the noise in the rafters. Margo shook me.

"Ummm, was I snoring again?"

Margo was whispering, "Of course you were, but listen…" We both heard a scratching directly above our heads. "Is it a rat?"

I reached out in the darkness with my right hand and grabbed the handle of the powerful flashlight, figuring I could grab the .45 if it was something threatening. I pushed the switch and pointed the light into the rafters.

Two large eyes were looking down from the rafter above our heads, framed by a small raccoon-like head, and the plume of a bushy, black and white ringed tail hanging down. I was astounded. "Hey, it's a ringtail cat. I never saw one before. They are so shy!"

"Oh, he's darling. Can we take him home?"

"Yeah, right!" We knew better. Sometimes called the "miner's cat," the shy creature was known to become a nocturnal pet for hard-rock miners who sometimes slept in tents or in declivities in the rocks here in the canyon. I did not know how he got into the building, but it could take months to earn the little creature's trust. I knew Margo would find a way to leave food for him, whether I liked it or not. We watched the sleek animal staring down at us until he wandered back along his rafter to the blackness beyond the drywall partitions, and we settled again.

It could not have been more than ten minutes later when the darkness was split by a silent, blinding light, sending white shafts through the pair of windows that looked down onto the street. "Somebody's got a rack of lights on their truck," I blurted, knowing there was no sound from outside. The room was as bright as day, and we heard the ringtail cat scampering out of sight, perhaps behind the lumber. I started to say, "A helicopter?" but that was ridiculous on its face. There was no noise, and the brilliance seemed to be moving very slowly, the windows serving as searchlights whose beams were traversing from left to right. We sat up, squinting in the brilliance.

There was still no sound as Margo and I looked at each other, sensing that a strange afternoon had become a puzzling night. Looking at my watch, I saw it was 10:07. Then the light blinked out, just as suddenly as it appeared, and we were submerged in darkness, my retinas imprinted with the last image I saw. Margo reached out and turned on the table lamp, rocking the crate it was sitting on. We looked at each other in bemused silence.

"OK, that's enough entertainment for tonight. Let's invoke Morpheus."

Margo pursed her lips, "Easy for you to say. I need to go to the bathroom." She got up and pulled on her slacks, and stuck her feet into her canvas shoes, preparing to go outside, down the stairway to the outhouse.

I grinned, "Isn't this fun, Babe? Closest thing we can get to camping and still be indoors."

Margo wrinkled her nose and grabbed the flashlight, heading for the door.

"Be sure to check for black widows." I stretched out again.

"Rick! Get out of that bed and get your clothes on—right now!" When she used that tone, I knew there was no arguing, and so I got up, dressed, and led the way down the raw board stairway. I opened the outhouse door and made a show of pointing the flashlight into every corner, then took the standard issue broom handle and put it inside the round hole, sweeping out any spider web that might be setting a trap. Then I waited outside in the dark until Margo emerged.

We stood in the darkness, looking up at the clear night sky, stars and planets diamond bright. There was no noise aside from the faint barking of a dog inside a home down the street. "Is that Sparky?" Margo liked that dog.

I nodded, thinking only that there was no trace of the light that had turned the town to daylight a few minutes before. Behind the closed door of the Englishes' theater up the street, Sparky was still barking. We stood for a minute longer, and then Margo hugged me and said "Serves you right."

Margo went to sleep quickly, but I lay there for a long time, listening to the faint sound of Sparky. We thought of him as Mogollon's patrol dog. He was an Akita or close to that, and he had a corkscrew tail combined with a lovable inquisitive disposition. When our gallery was open, Sparky always paid a visit in the morning, and others said that he made the rounds of most of the businesses, starting at our end of the street and ending at Frank Triolo's house. That was where an extensive rock wall was the setting for a prominent stone inserted halfway up and chiseled with "ABRIL D.1900." Sparky's owners, Bill and Nikki English, proprietors of the Mogollon Theater, suspected Triolo of providing Sparky with snacks during the dog's daily patrol up and down the street. Come to think of it, Sparky's affectionate gaze often got a treat from Margo in our gallery as well.

Mogollon Rock Wall with 1900 date   RickPhoto 1978

Two

Whispers in the Trees

Saturday morning dawned clear and cool, and we organized the gallery to open no later than 9 a.m., but earlier if there were visitors parked in the parking area. Because gallery visitors were sporadic, Margo and I took turns acting as proprietors, and I took opportunities to walk through town with my Nikon loaded with Kodak Plus-X black and white film. After we ate a camp-style breakfast, I put in the first hour or more while Margo went up the street to greet Bill and Nikki English and was planning to stop in the museum to chat with Matilda Brunk, whose husband had probably gone out early on a long walk to the Little Fanny mine and to meet with its crusty overseer.

Today I was going in the other direction. The camera and a Gossen exposure meter were around my neck, and my trusty snake hook in one hand, because I also had a lifelong fascination with reptiles. Perhaps I would see a striped racer, a gopher snake or even a blacktail rattlesnake. I stepped down from the front door of the gallery and walked west along the roadside in the bright morning sun.

It was almost two hundred yards up the paved road and around the bend, where a forest road branches left and south into the trees. It was my chosen direction, but then I saw tracks at the roadside. At first there were only scuff marks in the dry ground, but in a wet patch I looked closer at a nest of tracks I did not recognize. My first thought was that they were

The Forest Road Outside of Mogollon   RickPhoto 1978

javelina tracks because of the hoof-like shapes, but they were larger than those of either javelina or peccary. We had never seen javelina at this altitude. The tracks appeared to me as a split heart shape, but somehow with unusual indents describing a fringe that seemed to surround each individual track. Most of the imprints were too smudged to use for comparison. They were pointing along the path I was taking.

Grass was growing in the center of the forest trail. The pine trees pressed close to the track, and I walked slowly until I came to the foundation of what was probably a house at the turn of the century, only a crumbling concrete pad and scattered rocks remaining.

Scarcely 100 feet further, a rocky hillside presented a jagged granite protrusion, almost too steep to climb. About ten feet up, a rock shelf formed a curious dish-shaped formation. I wondered if there could be basking space for a reptile, and I began searching for a foothold, pulling myself up by grabbing the rock face. I raised myself about three feet when the granite spur crumbled noisily, and I was back on the ground, but suddenly the silence was broken by a rasping sound that seemed identical to a rattlesnake's arousal. Now I had to get up at least to eye level with that shelf, and I struggled to find a way up. When I got a firm purchase, I lifted myself higher until I was at eye level, faced with a surprise. What I thought could be a nest of rattlesnakes turned out to be the residence of a pair of turkey buzzard chicks who imitated rattlesnakes very well indeed.

I could not release my hold on the rocks and take a photo at the same time, so I jumped back to the ground with a grunt and adjusted my camera. Time to walk on. The trees were growing much closer to the road here, and a profusion of young ponderosa pines pressed close, about five feet tall and bristling with greenery. I heard something else, and I stopped, intent on the noise. I thought it might be another buzzard nest back in the trees.

The noise was not more than 10 feet distant in the brush, and I now felt a chill. A buzzing sound was coming from the trees, droning, and varied in pitch. It vibrated in my ears as though a voice was speaking directly to me. As I stood, another sound began as an indecipherable signal on top of radio static. This was no animal. I could see a vague form within the cluster of saplings. It formed what seemed to be words. The buzzing reached my ears, "Iä… Ngah…Iä…" then something unintelligible, and then a repetition of the guttural buzzing words, now getting closer. I also was assaulted by a carrion smell, strong and penetrating, making me wince.

A reaction flooded my mind as a warning from the unconscious, a scream from racial memory as though my soul was in danger. Yet, I did not move, almost as though a throbbing in my head was holding me there. Then a rustling sound told me that the vague shape was approaching through the bushy young trees…"Iä…Ngah…Shub…Ni…" but now I was suddenly alert again, running back down the track, wishing I had my pistol. What would I see if that thing had come out of the trees? I felt a warning coming down to me from a hundred generations, the fear of the demons in the night, of forbidden ceremonies in isolated copses, where circles of standing stones looked up at a hostile night sky.

I didn't stop running until I was back at the main road, and then walking swiftly on the pavement, around the bend and down to the parking area where the white VW bus was standing next to the gallery. A few tourists were walking along Mogollon's only street. My breath was ragged, my heart pounding, my brain recoiling from that hideous buzzing sound.

Just then, a Datsun pickup swung into town with two young men riding, their arms hanging out the open windows. They stopped beside me. "How's it going?"

I shook my head as though emerging from under water, and I rubbed my cheek as if wiping away spider webs. "Uhhh, not bad." When people ask how you are, they don't really want to know. "It's a great day to get out of town."

"Yeah, that's what we thought. How is the road up into the forest?"

"All I can tell you is the road is open. The rest is 'driver beware'."

"Thanks, Man. Want a beer?" I got the idea they had already been drinking this morning. I shook my head. "No thanks."

"Aw, come on. Take one on us. We are going to have a helluva weekend." The bed of their pickup was stuffed with ice chests and bedrolls. There were two rifles in a rack attached to the rear window of the truck.

The Coors beer can was cold in my hand as I waved them away, walking toward the gallery, my heartbeat returning to normal.

When I walked into the gallery, Margo was soldering a seam in a new stained glass panel she was making. She looked up, amused. "I see the hunter was successful."

With a grimace and a phony smile, I went around to put the beer into an ice chest with the sodas. When I walked back to the main room, Margo looked at me a little more closely. "What's wrong, Rick?" I resisted the impulse to say, "Nothing," because that was what women always say when they are asked the question. Instead, I said, "You know I have spent a lot of my life reading and writing about UFOs, and the history of the occult, but I never had any 'sightings' or 'experiences' that should be memorialized. What if I told you I heard a demonic voice?" I pointed as if through the wall.

Margo put down the soldering gun, a wisp of smoke rising from its tip. "Are you sure it wasn't just a reaction from the lights we thought we saw last night?"

"We DID see a strange light last night, and I just heard something up there in the forest track that scared me, and you know I don't scare easily. And there was a sickening smell that turned my stomach." Years before, I had written a magazine article comparing supposed extraterrestrial visitors with the horrific demons of medieval lore. I had always wondered if they were both figments of tortured imagination, but as I explained my experience to Margo, I was no longer certain. I went to the ice chest and brought out a Pepsi before raiding the plastic Tupperware bowl to get a chocolate chip cookie, but I was still fighting a nameless dread, and I wanted the feel and taste of something normal.

She smiled and indulged me, closing the topic by saying, "Could it have been mama buzzard fixing lunch? After what you just said, though, I am certainly not going to walk in that direction any more. I always thought the mine buildings were spooky, and I sometimes think there might be ghosts in the Holland store." She craned her neck and looked out the open front door, directly across the street to the vacant store building, bathed in direct sunlight, while the gallery front was still in shade.

I admitted that I did not know what kind of vocalizations the buzzard was capable of, but I had been face to face with the chicks. "Fear is part of every life, but I'm telling you, even if this was my imagination, it's a different kind of fear. I can smell it on me." I was also thinking about the strange tracks. Whatever I heard, it was not a ghost or a spiritual manifestation. I went to the door of the gallery and looked up the thinly paved road with its rustic and sometimes ramshackle buildings just as Sparky pushed past me into the gallery, tongue lapping; he roughly pushed his nose into my crotch as he did when I wasn't paying attention to his arrival. Breathing enthusiastically, he approached Margo who somehow produced a dog biscuit I did not know she had bought. Sparky plopped on the floor, chewing noisily, and looking up in admiration at his benefactor. I began to wonder if I had magnified some natural phenomenon in the brush, but the only thing I could do is put it behind me, just as I would a road rage incident.

When Sparky bounced out the front door to continue his daily pilgrimage, Margo suggested an early lunch before we went to visit the Brunks. Margo added a comment, "You know, Mattie has really changed since we saw her."

"New glasses?" I was talking with my mouth full.

"No glasses. You will be surprised." Matilda was not a surprising woman, but she was an amiable conversationalist. We finished our sandwiches and, with a lull in tourist visits, we went out the door. I started to walk to my right but Margo grabbed my arm and pulled me to the left. She said she wanted to see the tracks I had described to her.

I hesitated, then went along with her, walking up the road, around the bend, and almost to where the looming forest road disappeared. I took a deep breath and pointed to where I saw the impressions in the damp earth. The strong morning sun had dried the ground, so there was only a disappointing trampled area with little remaining to define the tracks. I pointed down the forest road, "I wonder if I imagined part of it, at least after I jumped down from the vulture nest."

Margo put her hand to her brow, peering to where the forest road turned out of sight "It's just another mystery. I am still worried about that poor woman and her car down on the highway." This deflected my concern as we turned to walk back down the pavement and to the rustic town that always appeared with a suddeness, even to pedestrians.

The so-called ghost town of Mogollon is deceptive in appearance. At first glance it does appear to be abandoned. The rough stonework of the commercial buildings, aside from the stucco on the Holland store, appears neglected and relict. Up the street, there is an illusion of abandonment, the frame buildings and cabins largely unpainted, the walls and porches weathered.

Stovepipes pierce the tin roofs or come out of house walls before an elbow extends a vertical pipe upward, whose finials are classic chimney caps.

Occasional bare places along the street remind me that more than one fire raged through the town, destroying many of the wooden buildings at one time or another. Where the ground was bare, the near-vertical hillsides were penetrated where hard-rock miners searched vainly for "color" in the granite and quartz outcroppings.

Aside from the museum and the theater building, the homes that appeared ramshackle showed more modern doors and windows, occupied by residents or weekend visitors. Farther up, on the left, was a home on the hillside whose porch was supported by a rock wall that raised it several feet above the street, making the house unlikely to be flooded

General Store Movie Set from 1973   RickPhoto 1978

when Silver Creek rampaged down the main thoroughfare. The rustic appearance of the house reveals itself to be an affectation, as a series of signs hang down from the porch roof advertised "Chamber Pot/Antiques/Ice Cream."

One of the cabins on the south side was rented by a counter-culture family, and the week before I had taken photos of the young woman who lived there. She was sitting on a stool, wearing dungarees, her long face and sharp nose photogenic in the way her long hair wrapped around her face and hung down almost to her waist. She was deeply tanned and milking her white goat. The sense of community and pastoral calm characterized Mogollon for me. The girl could have been engaged in the same activity a hundred years earlier.

Up on the hillside north of the family's cabin, tourists see the metal roof of the Mogollon church with its four-foot-tall cross emblem standing on the peak. A sheet of discolored galvanized metal is nailed across the front entrance over its weathered, double doors with their decorative arch designs.

Beyond this, N.M. 78 goes to dirt before disappearing into the forest, and that other worn dirt road winds to the left and up around to the cemetery and on to the Little Fannie mine property.

We stood past the west end of Mogollon, examining the quickly vanishing tracks at our feet, and then walking back around the corner and taking in the canyon vista as people had done for a century. Here was an idyllic frontier town, perfect for a Western movie, and we had photographed its so-called "General Store" framework and the "Saloon" up the street that were both fake fronts for the Henry Fonda movie in 1973. They fit the town perfectly. There were no saloons in Mogollon now, but in its heyday, there were several. Today the town was peaceful, but in the saloon days, there were shootings enough. The Englishes said the "General Store" was one of favorite photo subjects for tourists, though when curiousity seekers go through the front entrance they find only old boards, rocks, and hillside.

Two cars with day trip tourists rolled by and parked on the other side of the museum next to the Brunks' brand new metallic gray Ford 250 crew-cab pickup with Texas plates. We walked two doors down from the gallery. The museum was a sturdy stone building, and its front doors with a shallow arch façade were guarded

Goat Milking, Mogollon   RickPhoto 1978

by a pair of wrought iron gates that the Brunks could padlock when they were not in town. Outside the museum doors was a period iron ore cart on one side and a bench on the other. A circular, red "Coca-Cola" sign stood on an oxidizing street pedestal on the far side of the ore cart. Close to the doors was an antique street lamp the Brunks swore was from the town's early years.

Margo and I entered the museum, and the door tripped a bell that tinkled. By now I had convinced myself that I must have disturbed an angry adult turkey at the side of the forest road and had created the messages in my head. Margo could be right.

With only two front windows, the museum relied upon artificial bulbs to highlight the large historical photos on all of the walls. Lighted showcases and shelves displayed artifacts from the age of Mogollon mining. One display

Mogollon Church on the Hill   RickPhoto 1978

23

included a description of the Apache, Victorio, who massacred dozens of white settlers down the mountain in the settlement of Pleasanton. Just as interesting was a recounting of the late 19th century robberies of the San Vicente-Mogollon stagecoach, most of them by a single individual who was finally caught. In a locked case was a display of period rifles, including a rare Sharps carbine and a Walker Colt percussion revolver.

We had been in the museum less than a minute or two when we heard the sound of heels clicking on the dressed wooden floors. Matilda came from the back of the museum. "Hello, you two!"

Margo smiled and said, 'Where's Art?" while I was momentarily speechless. This was not the Mrs. Brunk I knew from a month before. Margo was right. I was surprised.

"Nice to see you," I said clumsily, avoiding the impulse to call her "Darouse," as though it was a secret she had imparted to me a month before. Her brown hair was longer, tinted auburn, and mascara highlighted eyes no longer depended upon glasses. She was wearing slacks and a bulky sweater in the cool of her exhibit room. She looked at me briefly and then directed her attention to Margo as I nervously looked around at the displays I already knew well, fighting a discomfort in my solar plexus.

"Art said he would be back by now. I think he is trying to talk Akeley out of one of the antique rock boring drills at the mine." Darouse listened while Margo told the story about Ofelia Armendariz and her abandoned Toronado.

Darouse Brunk touched her red lips with a manicured nail. "What do you think, Rick?" She turned her head slowly toward me.

I composed myself quickly, "I saw what Margo saw. When we went to Glenwood and then came back to where she was stranded, we saw no vehicle traffic going in either direction."

Darouse laughed in a conspiratorial way, closing her eyes momentarily. "Strange things happen. Did you know the phones went out last night for about 15 minutes?"

There were only a few telephones in Mogollon, but historically I knew that the first telephone line ran from San Vicente to Mogollon in 1908 to connect the mine with the source of all Mogollon's supplies, and that the Tenney freight wagons constantly ran a 10-horse team on the 78-mile run. By now I was back in the nostalgia of the ghost town, even though I was wondering exactly when the outage occurred and whether the electricity was also affected.

I almost called her "Darouse," but somehow I thought it was a secret. "Uhh, Mattie, when exactly was that last night?"

"Well…" She stretched the word out as she paused, "…it was after 10, because I was asleep…' I was certain she glanced at me before returning her attention to Margo. "Bill and Nikki told me that Nikki was talking to her nephew in Tucson when the phone quit. The lights went out for about five minutes, but everybody up here has kerosene lamps." She slid her hands on her slacks to smooth the front panel.

Margo and I made the connection very quickly. Something unusual had certainly occurred the night before.

Just then, Art Brunk opened the museum door and stumped inside. "Howdy, Folks!"

He was followed by a family of four, who paid the $2.00 admission fee and signed the museum guest book before spreading out to view the displays.

Mattie Brunk gave Art a blank look and then went back to make conversation with Margo, saying something about stopping at our house in San Vicente on their way from El Paso or possibly visiting when Mattie occasionally stayed with her brother in town.

I looked more closely at Brunk. "You got some sun today."

He hesitated, eyes averted and then he looked at me, rubbing his cheeks. "Guess I must have been out too long." The words came out slowly, like drips from an almost-closed faucet. Then he flashed his car dealer smile and recovered. "You know, Old Man Akeley has told me some stories."

"Yeah, but he doesn't talk to most people outside of his mine tour spiel." I wanted to ask him if Akeley talked about the money rumored to be hidden up there.

"Not today. He was showing me the location up by the headframe where Fonda and Hill staged one of the movie scenes." Brunk's face was pink from sunburn. "I'd like to display that antique steam-powered drill, but he won't deal with me." His narrowed eyes darted toward me and then around the room as though he had not seen his own museum for a long time.

"Dar…Matilda…" I stumbled, "…told me about the outage last night. Do you remember it?"

"No…I think I was asleep." Brunk turned and looked out the front window.

Margo came over and pinched my t-shirt sleeve, "Mattie reminded me that Nikki English is hosting a social tonight at their theater. I think we ought to show up." Darouse had gone behind the long counter where the curios and souvenirs were sold, and she was showing the visitors some of the mineral samples.

Now, I do not enjoy socializing, but this was something almost unavoidable, so I acquiesced cheerfully.

I turned again to Brunk, "How are Akeley's tours going? The weekends are usually his busiest times."

Art seemed to ponder, "He closed the gate today—said he didn't feel like doing tours." That seemed strange, because the tours were Akeley's only source of income aside from Social Security, as far as I knew.

When another group entered the museum, Margo nudged me and said we had better tend our own store, so we told the Brunks we would see them at the Englishes' soirée that evening and went back out into the street. Outside, I said that Matilda looked very healthy, "I thought she had major surgery."

Margo rolled her eyes, "You never were too observant," and she spread her hands and held them in front of her chest.

"Huh?" I wrinkled my brow and then lifted my head, "Ohhh. I didn't see it." That sounded awkward.

"Well you never did pay attention to sweaters," Margo laughed as we opened the gallery door and began our afternoon conversations with those who browsed, talked, and occasionally bought stained glass pieces or something from my line of photo postcards. We were

Social at the Mogollon Theater   RickPhoto 1978

occupied enough that I had no time to think about the vulture incident.

As afternoon faded into twilight we ate several more of our steak and chile burritos with Fritos and soft drinks, then cleaned up. I put on one of my silky polyester cowboy shirts while Margo donned an attractive sleeveless top for our impromptu social evening.

Close to 8 p.m. the open area across the street from the Mogollon Theater hosted several vehicles, and inside we were greeted by Bill and Nikki English, whose pleasant demeanor always put guests at ease. They told us that several of the men and couples had driven up from Glenwood and Reserve, but I did not see "Bob" from Glenwood among the chatting assemblage, some of whom were drinking punch and others were holding cans of beer. The long table included chips and salsa as well as other snacks. We tried some of the pink punch, but it had a little too much vodka in it to appeal to me.

As darkness accumulated, I trotted down to the gallery to get my tripod and camera. I set up across the street from the theater and took several time exposures to capture the lights on the porch of the theater with guests lounging in cowboy hats and shirts. Mogollon had come to life again.

The conversations were not audible from across the street, and I was taking my gear back down to the gallery when I heard, faintly in the evening air, a drawn-out moan that made my breath come short. It was almost a thin wail with an echo coming from the mountain north of the theater. Could it be the distant scream of a mountain lion? I thought not, and I felt a chill. It could be animal or even human. The sound was gone.

After my photo shoot, I hurried back to the theater. Margo was talking with the Brunks and the air inside was very warm and noisy with the chatter of 25 or 30 people. Then I saw Darouse Brunk as though for the first time. She was wearing a clinging violet velveteen dress and high heels. Several men were part of the group that centered around her. The dress stretched and accentuated her new breasts.

Margo waved me into the circle and raised her eyebrows with a satisfied grin. I managed an affected look at the ceiling before putting my arm around her. Darouse, for her part stood beside her silent husband and gave only a nod to my arrival as her glance ricocheted from one man to another—like a cat, or a mountain lion.

Frank Triolo, 81st Birthday   RickPhoto 1978

It seemed that most of Mogollon's residents were at the theater that night, including Frank Triolo, who had reached his 81st birthday and who had provided the town's human backbone for most of his life. There was even a special table with a birthday cake for him. Sparky made the rounds of the theater and plopped on his doggie bed at the back of the room after a busy day patrolling the town. Margo and I exchanged pleasantries and passed out our gallery cards to those we had not met before.

Pablo "Brub" McCarty was the loudest party guest, and his raucous laugh rose above the other conversations going on in the increasingly smoky room. I considered McCarty the self-styled "mayor" of Mogollon, a town with no government. He was six-feet tall and over 250 pounds, and his well-liked wife Ouida did her best to keep a leash on his garrulous nature. From 15 feet away, McCarty almost shouted, "Hey, Art, I don't see Akeley. Isn't he showing up tonight?"

Halfway across the room, Brunk looked at the floor and then at where McCarty's belly was like an awning over his rectangular silver belt buckle. "Aw, you know he never comes to these things. He didn't even come to Frank's 80th birthday party."

Akeley belonged in Mogollon. He was in his 70s, his bristling grey beard tobacco-stained above his lips. He was 5'7" but wiry and cantankerous. He never went anywhere on the property without his large German shepherd "Chino" whose attitude was protective and often aggressive when strangers meddled with the frog pond, east of his fenced house, once the residence of the mine manager. At night, Chino roamed through the haunted mine buildings, assuring that intruders would regret their audacity.

McCarty ignored Ouida's elbow in his ribs when he said, "We oughta go up there and bring him down here." Most of the guests were paying no attention.

Frogs Welcome   RickPhoto 1978

Art was now looking directly at the McCartys with narrowed eyes. "I wouldn't do that, Brub. You know how Akeley hates evening visitors." Akeley was well known to keep a 12-gauge shotgun just inside his front door.

I asked McCarty if he had been to the mine in the past week; he nodded and gave me a sidelong glance, lowering his voice a few decibels, "Didn't you know? There's a new company going to open up the Little Fanny again. Call themselves Venture Mines Corporation. They started hauling equipment, did something up along the road, but the honcho—name's Manning—hasn't brought many people in yet. Just did the assay. I don't know how Akeley's involved."

McCarty chortled and then made for the punchbowl. I turned to Margo, but I couldn't resist looking at Darouse Brunk on the way.

Three

Noises in the Night

Margo suggested that it was time to leave because the air was getting smoky. "I wonder if you'll be like Akeley in 40 years," referring to my solitary predilections as a writer and researcher. I gave her a "maybe" nod, and we extended our thanks to Bill and Nikki English before walking out into the refreshing air. As we walked down the thin asphalt paving toward the gallery, the hubbub in the theater faded into silence. In the darkness, I looked back up to where the pavement ended as state road 78 vanished into the Gila Forest. Margo's question was sudden. "Is there something wrong with Art? He's usually so outgoing."

"Yeah, I know what you mean. He is usually the 'Howdy, Pardner' guy day in and day out. Maybe something's bothering him."

"Maybe it's Mattie…" Margo quipped. I didn't respond, but I thought Art was hiding something else. We brushed our teeth, turned out the gallery lights, and went up the outside stairs to the second floor. The quiet was reassuring, and I tried to put away my uneasiness of earlier in the day. I plopped down on the comfortable foam rubber futon, half asleep within a minute or so. I was not aware that Margo had still not readied herself for bed. She put out a snack for the ringtail cat, and I must have dropped off, because the next thing I knew, a half hour had passed, and Margo was standing by the window.

"I hear something." Margo was whispering, and in the light of the table lamp, I figured it was the ringtail cat, but I was sure he wouldn't advance along the rafters until the lamp was switched off. I was feeling the weight of the long day and was ready to go back to sleep.

"Rick, get up and come over here." Margo was insistent, and I knew her well enough to know I was going to get up.

Now, listen…" I switched off the lamp and joined her by the window. There was a sound across the street. It seemed to emanate from the interior of the Holland store. Despite the shadows, it appeared to me that one of the center front doors to the old building had swung inward. I could see no vehicle, but I also knew that Bill and Nikki English had, by the owner's permission, a set of keys to the building.

As we watched, there came a dim steady glow that seemed to be almost green through one of the store windows. Then I heard a crash-thump inside the stone building as though something was stumbling blindly in the dark interior. My breath quickened, and I could feel my heartbeat accelerate as I buttoned my Levi's and pulled on my engineer boots, heading out the door bare-chested, with the loaded .45 in my hand.

I walked slowly down the outside stairs to the corner of our building, peering around the rock wall toward the store. There were three entrances to the building, but the faint green glow was behind the far downstairs window, and one of the double front doors yawned. I looked up the street, but the party had broken up, and there was nobody visible, though the faint orange glow of a lamp emanated from the museum windows, and there was still a light on the marquee of the theater far up the street. All else was in darkness.

My inner voice told me to go back up the stairs to safety, but I was committed. I ran across the road and crouched below the porch, but the railing kept me from getting onto the porch without going to the front of the store. The creek trickled underneath the porch, and the smell was faintly metallic. I crawled toward the opening in the railing and now the eerie illumination within the store had shifted. The downstairs was dark, but a greenish glow was now coming from an upstairs window on the right. I felt the fear seeping into my chest as I crept onto the splintering wood porch. I had never been inside the Holland store, and I did not like the sickly quality of that green glow deep inside.

I got to my feet and edged toward the open door, feeling more alone than I could ever remember. There was no law enforcement in Mogollon, though the State Police occasionally sent a car through the town during the day, and the Catron County Sheriff's office did the same every two or three days, but Mogollon kept its distance from authority because of the winding mountain road. The night was closing in on me as I approached the open door of the Holland Store.

The depth of blackness was intense as I stuck my head in the door and recoiled. An acrid smell was pouring out from the interior. I took a step into the miasma that assailed my nostrils, the .45 pointed to the interior.

Suddenly I felt a stabbing pain in my head. It was not a headache, but a piercing agony combined with the terror of a hissing, buzzing sound that assaulted my hearing. There was something inside the maw of the Holland store, and it was no more than ten feet away. I almost screamed as the buzzing articulated itself, and I heard again the hellish sounds from my morning encounter, "…Iä…Iä…N'gah…Shub…"

THE WHISPERING DARKNESS

It was inhuman gibberish—demonic and threatening. My head was splitting, and through the depths of the vacant store building, a shape was shambling. It was coming toward me as a wave of terror overcame me. I shoved the pistol toward the darkness and fired. The silence of Mogollon was shattered as I pulled the trigger. The pistol bucked in my hand as I fired once, twice, three times, four times, and then emptied the magazine before I fled across the street and up the stairs to some kind of safety.

As I ran, panic-stricken, into the upstairs of the gallery, Margo threw the ceiling light switch. My hands were shaking uncontrollably as I scrambled onto the futon and to the crate where I had a second magazine. I shoved it into the butt of the pistol and pulled back on the slide and heard the comforting sound of a round chambering as the slide slammed shut.

Margo grabbed my shoulders and shook me, "What? What? What did you do?"

I couldn't speak, and I switched off the light again, and stumbling to the window. I was panting with fear as I looked across toward Mogollon's largest building. The door was still open, and there was now no longer a green glow from the interior.

"Rick, what was it? I've never seen you like this."

"Margo, I've never been like this. I can't tell you what I saw, what I smelled." My head was still throbbing, but the pain had lessened. I could tell that Margo was fearing for my sanity. I was still looking down at the vacant store across the street. What if I had again imagined something evil and demonic, throwing my sanity into the balance?

No! There was something in that store, and I had fired a full magazine into a moving shape in the blackness. If it was human, I had killed it, and I shuddered at the consequences when police came up the mountain. The foul odor was still in my nostrils, and I tasted something like sulfur in my throat. I felt Margo's hand on my naked shoulder as I leaned against the wall, looking out into the night. I was not going down there again before the dawn.

I expected the denizens of the town to be out with flashlights and coming down the street, and several porchlights did go on, including the one over the Mogollon Theater. I heard Sparky's unique bark, and perhaps some residents came out of their front doors, but only two doors down, the Brunks did not emerge from their museum building. Of course the multiple shots were so quick, the direction of the gunfire would not have been clear unless that listener had been outside at the time of the shots. When I hastened across the street to mount the stairs to the gallery living quarters, I was sure the light had been extinguished in the museum building. I shuddered and perspired as I drew an empty plastic storage crate over to the window. I sat there looking out, the pistol in my hand. Margo wrapped a blanket around my shoulders as I leaned against the window frame. I could see no movement in the darkness across the street though I did see a wavering flashlight beam pointing from somewhere up the street. I could not go back down there to see what was lurking or dead inside the store building.

A few minutes later, a pickup came slowly down in front of the gallery, headed west, and it turned around just past our building, rolling slowly back up the street. It couldn't be Brub McCarty, as their Winnebago was not more than 100 yards west of the Holland store across Silver Creek where the canyon descended to the north. I could not tell the make of the truck, but I immediately thought of Arthur Brunk.

The terror had exhausted me and though I tried to remain awake until dawn, there was a limit to conversation and to consciousness. When the sky turned grey Sunday morning, I opened bleary eyes and felt the weight of intense fatigue. Dawn washed the Holland store across the street with clear light on the fading off-white stucco. That one center door still stood open. I had not dreamed.

Mogollon residents were coming out onto the street and several people, including Bill and Nikki English walked in our direction, down toward to the west edge of town. Sparky was loping along beside them. I had to go down to meet them, leaving my pistol upstairs, where Margo was now getting dressed and making order of her blond hair.

I joined the five people who were now on the porch of the Holland store, and when they asked if I knew what happened, I openly admitted that it was I who had fired those late-night shots. When I explained that I had fired into the building at something I saw inside through the open door, Bill and Nikki quickly advanced to the door, peering inside. The early sun afforded a glimpse of the interior, and my heart was almost thundering in my chest. Was there a body? The two theater owners were closest to the door, with Brub McCarty looming over them. Art and Darouse Brunk were standing silently in the street. Darouse was dressed in slacks and sweater this morning, looking at the doors of the store, but Art was staring oddly at me. His face was still showing the effects of the sunburn, now with some small red spots on his cheeks.

Bill English turned and addressed us, "Somebody's been in there—that's for sure." Sparky was approaching all of us to get his morning attention, but he seemed to give Art Brunk a wide berth. He shoved his muzzle into my gun hand and left it wet. It was better than his usual greeting. I don't know if anyone else noticed, but Sparky went to the open door and then backed away; perhaps he smelled what I had smelled in the dark.

McCarty asked the obvious question, "How did anybody get in there? The place has been locked up for months."

Nikki English glanced at McCarty, eyes raised. "I'll tell you a little secret about Mogollon that even you don't know. There's a tunnel under the Holland building."

McCarty lifted his cowboy hat and wiped his brow, "Ya don't say!"

So, now I ventured onto the porch, feeling lightheaded and fearful. Looking inside the large interior, I saw the disturbed dust on the floor as though something had swept across the painted boards in a wide swath. I refused to go more than a foot or two inside the building. But I was looking for the first time into the Holland General Store building.

Just inside those double doors was a foyer with doors directly to the right and left. The left hand door was open to what was once a dining room, while the left hand door was still closed. I could see the unsettling tracks in the dust leading along that dining room and to the stairs on the west wall. A table had been shoved roughly to the wall, and two wooden, cane-back chairs were upended and lying on the floor. The clatter had to be what I heard the night before.

In my brief view of the interior, I could see that the foyer dead-ended at a wall with an open door into what, at a glance, appeared to be a broom closet. I could see that there was another door in the back wall of that closet. It stood open to a black, cavernous opening— the hidden entrance to Mogollon's most imposing structure. I would never have guessed it.

THE WHISPERING DARKNESS

The unpleasant, acrid smell lingered faintly in the empty building, and as I mentally considered the direction of my fire, I expected to see where bullets had struck something, but I saw nothing, and I could not see any holes in the back wall. Whoever entered the building must have come through that tunnel and opened the front door before moving into the dining room and up the stairs.

There was no wetness on the floor, and no trace of a body. Perhaps I was the only one standing there who sensed a dark, ominous meaning, but Bill English just checked the door for tampering and checked the spring-loaded antique lock before pulling the door to, the snap of the lock seemed to add finality to the episode. The Englishes' responsibility was only to assure the security of the building for the absent owners.

McCarty's voice almost boomed, "Did ya hit anything, Rick?"

I replied, almost sheepishly, "I guess not. Maybe I didn't see anything after all."

McCarty's braying laugh echoed in the street, "Maybe there are ghosts in town after all." I almost wished that were the case.

The gathering dispersed, each to his own building, but I was certain that I was the only one feeling uncomfortable as though privy to a private delusion. I watched as Darouse Brunk followed her husband back to the museum. Art's walk seemed uncertain, halting as though he had injured a knee, while Darouse walked with an exaggerated sway to her hips that I had never noticed before.

Margo was now coming down the outside stairs, her waved hair neatly primped; she raised her eyebrows quizzically and I responded with a negative shrug, We opened our gallery door to fix breakfast and prepare for the day. My eyes were still hot with fatigue.

The ominous mood of the night dissolved quickly into the normalcy of the day. As vehicles came through town, many pulled in to park, their occupants taking time to walk along the storied street, stopping in the several buildings where there were displays or souvenirs and snacks for sale. I had several black and white prints made during the week that I needed to mount and display. Sparky made his usual rounds, and as afternoon waned, we loaded up the VW bus and headed out of Mogollon for the 78-mile drive to San Vicente. I slowed on the road as we passed the dark pool, now on the car's right side, but I could not understand any possible purpose of the 600-feet square pond unless it was to be a water source for wildlife.

Soon enough I was riding the brakes as we followed the downward convolutions of the road, inching around the acute hairpin turn, very much aware of the wrecked van hundreds of feet below in the ravine. The sheer cliff on my left appeared as though it could crumble with the slightest impact, and boulders were wedged higher on the hill. Now we were through the narrowest constriction and descending rapidly, hundreds of feet. I felt my ears pop. I realized how tired I was with a long drive ahead of me.

Margo had stopped looking down into the ravine, "We're stopping in Glenwood, aren't we?"

I hadn't even thought about it. "Oh, sure. I almost forgot." We were on the final straight stretch that connected with U.S. 180. There was no traffic at the intersection, and we turned left, heading south to Glenwood on the road to San Vicente. The town seemed to be sleeping in the Sunday afternoon light.

We pulled into the service bay of the Texaco station to fill the gas tank. Then I followed Margo into the station where Bob was still on duty. Gas station owners don't get much down time. She asked about Ofelia Armendariz. I had a strange feeling because I noticed a familiar-looking brown Toronado parked unobtrusively at the south side of the station building.

Bob took cash for the 8 gallons of Regular and scratched his head. "Somethin's wrong about that. Officer Coslin stopped in this morning and told me that they had contacted Mrs. Armendariz's family. They've now got her listed as missing. Ol' Cos had me tow the vehicle back here temporarily."

I laughed nervously, "Maybe she was abducted by..." Margo stopped me.

"That's not funny, Rick," Margo just did not like the idea. We had both read Fuller's *The Interrupted Journey*, about a New Engand couple's abduction into a flying saucer.

Bob handed me my change and shut the register, "Oh, I dunno about that. I've seen some strange things and heard some stories from people who stop in here. I've heard a lot of flying saucer talk."

"Oh really? I do a lot of reading about that stuff. Do you have any experiences?" Suddenly I was not tired any more.

A car went by outside the service station window, and Bob peered out momentarily. "Not me, but that road out there has seen everything from Victorio's marauding Apaches to things I didn't want to believe."

"Tell me more." I was thinking about the buzzing sounds and the half-visible thing in the Holland General Store. I wondered where that tunnel might lead deep under the mountain behind the Holland Store.

Bob broke out a Pepsi from the cooler and offered me one, but I declined, and Margo was fidgeting as though we should be on our way. I was not moving. Then he sat down in an antique oak swivel chair with a ratty cushion whose stuffing was falling out.

"It was just last fall. A car pulled in out there..." Bob pointed to the gas pumps. "... the driver slammed on the brakes and two women jumped out of the car and came runnin' in here. It was long about sundown. They said, 'call the cops—call the cops.' Now 'course I jus' said, 'hold on and tell me what's wrong."

Bob paused and looked at us. He had our undivided attention. "Anyhow, these women were almost hysterical—one of 'em was named Sally as I remember. She was really scared, and she said, 'they're going to get us. You have to get help'." He paused as he assembled his memories. "Anyhow, she said they were driving from San Vicente up to Reserve. There was no traffic, just like today. They said they were driving along, mindin' their own business when they saw this thing in the sky outside the driver side window. It was sort of cigar shaped with a row of windows. It was only a couple hundred feet up and it didn't make any noise—none at all. They were scared, and they said the engine began to miss as they tried to speed up."

Bob took a deep breath before continuing, but we were both hanging on his words. "Sally said there were bright bluish lights in the windows of that cigar shape floating along beside their car, keeping pace, almost close enough to touch. Yeah, she said that it 'floated'. There was no other traffic and they started praying to the Blessed Virgin to save them. This thing was at least 100 feet long, and it stayed with them until they pulled into my station. I went outside but didn't see anything. It just vanished. Yeah, I called State Police, and it was

Officer Coslin who showed up and took their report. I don't think he filed it as they described it, but then they calmed down and called their family in Reserve to drive down and accompany them. They refused to go on alone. Coslin told me confidentially that this wasn't the first incident like it that he had investigated."

"They were OK?" Margo's gaze was intense.

"Oh sure—their relatives showed up, and they convoyed on to Reserve. There was no doubt that something scared those poor women—something scared 'em almost to death."

Margo followed up with an edge to her voice, "What about that woman, Ofelia Armendariz? What about her?"

Bob slowly shook his head and grimaced, "I dunno, Ma'am, I just don't know, but something happened. I don't think they're going to find her."

Margo said, "I'm really worried. Can we trade phone numbers?"

Bob found a 5x7 notepad on the counter with the Texaco emblem at the top. He gave a sheet to Margo, and scribbled the station phone number on his sheet.

"If anything happens, you can call us down in San Vicente." Margo wrote our phone number onto the notepaper in her even handwriting and passed it to Bob. She took Bob's information and folded it. I knew she would put it into her day planner folder back home.

I felt Margo take my hand as we thanked Bob for his candor. Driving back and forth from San Vicente would never be quite the same.

Four

Interim in San Vicente

The mundane world of work in San Vicente distracted both Margo and myself from the strange atmosphere that had settled into Silver Creek Canyon and the town of Mogollon. My evenings were devoted to reading about flying saucers, accounts of various alien encounters, such as documented in Coral Lorenzen's book, and of course, the movie, "Close Encounters of the Third Kind" that we had seen a year before in the Gila Theater in downtown San Vicente.

At various times we argued about the upbeat theme of the movie. Margo was adamant that any beings from other worlds would be very much like humans but with more advanced technologies and a benevolent attitude toward struggling humanity on Earth.

While I wanted to believe it, I was more likely to see the possibility of alien visits to be more like Harold Hawks' 1951 movie, "The Thing From Another World" as I had seen it when I was a kid.

Yet there was more to my thinking. In my library were such old books as *Wonders of the Invisible World* by 17th Century divine Cotton Mather, and I had read Sinistrari's 17th Century *Demoniality*, the manuscript of which was not published until 1875.

More disturbing to me was reading the Puritan writings about demons and the Black Man of devil worship. It is described in these early American books how people walking in the woods were sometimes assailed by noisome voices luring them to come sign the Devil's black book of souls. The god-fearing Puritan would flee these voices in terror and never see the form behind the insidious voices. Had I not heard a demonic voice coming from the trees? No, it had to be a misidentified mother buzzard worrying a carcass outside my range of vision.

We then were victims of our Zeitgeist, from the witch paradigm of the *Malleus Maleficarum* to the modern E.T. myth of Steven Spielberg. Were alien visitors more real than supernatural demons? When I read H.P. Lovecraft and Arthur Machen, I could see little that separates these phenomena. Perhaps the limitations of our structured minds kept us from perceiving the reality behind appearances. Maybe Margo was right and visitors from the stars would be not much different than the diverse races of Earth, even passing for human if they now walked among us.

Yet, I was also a student of teratology and knew that even on Earth we have found monstrosities and creatures dangerous to humans, though none so dangerous as evil humans.

Many people had seen ghosts, and though I hadn't seen one, it did not mean there was no such praeternatural form in the night. I had not seen a flying saucer, but I was convinced that there were such things in the skies of New Mexico and elsewhere. We had even heard rumors of actual flying saucer crashes somewhere near Roswell and close to Aztec, N.M., but I had not seen the evidence as yet. Yet, what if alien visitors or demonic creatures could invade the human personality, physically, mentally, sexually and steal a victim's humanity? The medieval peasant found an incubus in her bed chamber, and the modern abductee is spirited from her bed to suffer hideous invasions and even impregnation by alien creatures in UFOs. The only difference is the terminology of the times.

Perhaps it was ancestral memory, but I had now tasted the fear of an alien contact, be it illusion, invasion, or supernatural inquisitor. As I sat in my living room, I could still taste the sulfurous air of the Holland store entrance, and I felt a surge of righteous anger wash over me for each shot I fired into the darkness on Saturday night.

Lying in bed or talking with Margo during the day, I went back more often to the witch times and the presence of evil beings in the woods who spoke in a droning voice to the unwary. And in the dark of night, there was the appearance of a hideous visage at the lattice windows or a rattling of the catch on the front door as the light from the fire faded. Perhaps I had not encountered a physical being after all. Could it have been a demonic energy or a ghostly presence such as described by the Puritan preacher Cotton Mather?

Wednesday I returned from work later than usual to find Margo chatting energetically on the phone. When she hung up, she said, "That was Mattie down in El Paso. They are going to Mogollon early this week and want to stop by Thursday to pick up these stained-glass sun catchers. Mattie has offered to display them in their museum." In a petty thought, I caught myself before correcting Margo on the use of Mrs. Brunk's first name.

Some say that spring is the ideal time for people to purchase real estate, and Margo found herself booked up every day, inevitably pushing into the weekend. It looked as though she would not be able to go with me on the coming weekend.

Thursday afternoon at 4:30, Margo was home as planned to give Darouse a carton with a half dozen small stained glass designs representing New Mexico Zia symbols, abstract roadrunners, box turtles, and sunflowers. I pulled up behind the gleaming grey Ford 250 with Texas plates as Darouse and Margo emerged from the front door of our house, chatting , and I noticed that Art Brunk did not look back; he was sitting in the driver's seat of the Ford pickup staring straight ahead as Margo walked Darouse to the truck. I just said hello and hung back on the sidewalk toward the house. I don't know why I was uncomfortable.

By Friday morning, Margo threw up her hands and said, "I can't do it. I have three appointments this afternoon, one of them after five, and then I have a showing late Saturday morning. Can you go up and tend the gallery?" She kissed me before I could protest.

I nodded and we talked about weekend provisions for one person—and Sparky. Friday afternoon, Margo helped me load the bus at 4:30 and I kissed her good-bye. It would be awkward without her, but I enjoyed solitary drives, even with the mystery of the woman who disappeared on U.S. 180 the week before.

The washing machine roar of the four-cylinder VW air-cooled engine joined the tinnitus in my ears as I listened to the Blaupunkt AM radio until I could no longer find a station in range. As I passed the Texaco station in Glenwood, I noticed that the brown Oldsmobile Toronado was no longer parked beside the station. Either Mrs. Armendariz had suddenly appeared or the car was towed to an impound lot, possibly in Reserve. Perhaps I would ask Bob—no last name—when I came down from the mountain and through Glenwood Sunday.

Five

Horror and a Fall From Grace

Driving a VW bus is a physical experience. As I shoved the long floor shift into third gear to meet the steep climb of N.M. 78 to Mogollon, I was aware that my right leg was pushing the accelerator pedal hard against the floor as my arms stiffened, shoving the steering wheel forward to milk the entire 40 horsepower out of the straining engine. When I came to the great hairpin turn in second gear, I hit the brakes. Just around the bend I met a pile of rocks that had cascaded down from the steep hillside and onto the cliff side of the road. Carefully, I edged toward the chasm, looking directly down into the ravine, my left arm on the doorsill as I inched forward. The hillside collapse was minor, and I was able to drive over the gravel and rocks because my vehicle had almost a 16-inch clearance—enough to get over the pile.

As I picked up speed again, I thought back almost a century to the time when the Tenney 10-and 12-horse freight wagons made the regular trek from As I picked up speed again, I thought back almost a century to the time when the Tenney 10-and 12-horse freight wagons made the regular trek from San Vicente to Mogollon. I wondered how they maneuvered the wagons with their tons of supplies and negotiated this turn, which would have been only dirt and

Mogollon Street Vista, Looking East, c. 1914   Courtesy Silver City Museum

Mogollon Street Vista   RickPhoto 1978

gravel in those days and was no doubt washed out whenever a hard rain pummeled the mountains. History recorded that in 1912, Tenney once hooked up 24 horses to his freight wagon to haul a six-ton flywheel on the precarious trip up the mountain, destined for one of the engines at the Little Fanny mine. I tried to imagine 12 paired draft horses wending their way up a thousand feet and down again to their goal.

At the high point, I began to make the long descent into town, finally passing the dark, fenced-off pond off in the trees and promising myself to ask somebody about its function. In the early evening light, the town was a post card image, and I tried to imagine the depth and extent of the tunnel behind the Holland General Store. I rolled into town and parked beside the gallery. When I climbed down from the driver's seat I surveyed the street, somehow comforted by the few people still walking along the roadside where normalcy seemed to rule. I looked across the street at the Holland store and the four locked front doors; I visualized the hidden door to that secret tunnel. No, I did not like what might be lurking inside the dark catacomb, be it a wraith or something worse. It seemed I was the only resident who sensed anything abnormal.

Several cars and trucks were driving along the street as I opened up the gallery and realized that setting up was more difficult than usual without Margo's energy. Two or three visitors came in to browse the photos and stained glass pieces on the walls and on the display table against the east wall. Evening was settling on the town when Darouse Brunk came into the gallery with a covered dish. She said she thought Margo was not going to be here, and she lifted the cover to show a savory green chile stew with flour tortillas wrapped in foil at the side.

I asked Darouse about Art, and she averted her eyes. "He's OK…well, he's kinda withdrawn. I think he is still obsessed with the mine. He says that Old Man Akeley is not well and needs some help up there. It's almost a mile up there, but Art usually walks. Don't know the reason. I've got all I can do keeping the museum going." I noticed her blue eyeshadow and enhanced lashes, and after I thanked her for the stew that had my stomach growling, she wished me a successful weekend. My eyes could not help following her as she left the gallery.

Later, as I walked up the outside stairs to the second floor, I snapped the spring latch shut on the front door and thought that it was the same style lock as found on the building across the street. Sleep evaded me, and several times I went to the window to look across the street to the Holland store. It seemed quiet. Visitors to Mogollon often commented that they found the town "creepy," but it never struck me that way until my encounter the week before. When I did fall asleep, I was suddenly awakened with a flash of terror. There was a scratching noise.

The flashlight was in my hand, pointed to the door. Nothing. Then I heard paws scrambling along the rafter, and my light reflected in the quizzical eyes of the ringtail cat looking at me, his luxurious striped tail with a small crook at the tip hanging down. He communicated silently, reminding me that I had forgotten something. I put on my shoes, went back downstairs and tore a remaining flour tortilla into small morsels, bringing them up and depositing them on the towel Margo had placed at the back of the upstairs floor. Guilt assuaged, I left the irresistible little creature to his bedtime snack and this time fell asleep in the spacious and unfinished room, not waking until morning.

Cookies for breakfast began a typical Saturday, with gallery visitors passing through, occasionally taking something with them, but never enough to foster an illusion of profit.

Halfway through the morning, Sparky made his belated entrance. Instead of jamming his muzzle into my midsection, he came in carrying a piece of plastic—at least it seemed to be plastic at first glance.

Sparky wagged his tail as I took the irregular piece from his mouth. Then I noticed that there were blotches of blood on his chest with what appeared to be three separate wounds. When I took the plastic-like fragment I told him, "Here! Don't chew on that. You don't know where it's been." But, maybe he did know. "I guess the question is: where have you been?"

When I took the object from Sparky's mouth, I hesitated before throwing it into the trash because I could tell from the feel that it wasn't plastic. The object was approximately the size of a saucer approximately eight inches wide, with a smooth arc to one edge, and the other side jagged as though torn from a larger piece. It was dry and slick to the touch, and as best I could describe, the color was a light brown hue with elusive light orange highlights when held to the light a certain way. Though thin, it was remarkably hard, and the reverse of the fragment was a greyish-white spongey material that reminded me of moist styrofoam. I suddenly wanted to get it out my hands as though it were contaminated somehow. There was something disquieting about the strange fragment, and I immediately scrubbed my hands while Sparky stood there, tail wagging.

"Oh yeah, I almost forgot. Here's your tithe." I found the dog biscuits and gave him one. "Now, when you're done, we'll go see Bill and Nikki so they can check you for injuries." My own opinion was that Sparky could hold his own with almost any creature in the forest. Where had he found that fragment? I thought it possible that somebody had brought king crab up the hill for a seafood feast and that Sparky had retrieved a portion of the shell from the garbage. I discarded the idea. I considered whether the fragment had come from the frog pond or the mine property, but it was unlikely because Akeley's dog Chino disliked Sparky, thus keeping the Akita down on the main street of Mogollon.

We walked up the street to the theater, and Nikki gave Sparky the "bad dog" routine before examining the blood spots on his coat as he licked her face. She turned to look up at me, "These are nasty little wounds. I can't tell what caused them." Her finger spread the fur, and I could see what appeared to be two inflamed punctures that had now stopped bleeding and one that had just barely penetrated the skin. I commiserated but did not mention the piece of material Sparky brought to me.

Nikki patted her dog. "Oh, I should tell you, Bill and I are going to a family gathering in Scottsdale next week. We'll be gone from Tuesday through Sunday. I think we'll take Sparky to the vet over there just to be safe."

"Good idea. Margo and I will both be here next weekend, so if there's anything…"

Nikki stood up and brushed her hands on her slacks and interrupted me, "Thanks, but I think it will work out just fine. I'm sure Brub McCarty will rise to the occasion and supervise

Entrance to the Fanny Mine Tour   RickPhoto 1978

the town. You probably don't know, but the Chandlers are away in Tucson, maybe not making it back until after next weekend—death in the family. They wanted to keep it hush-hush."

I left Sparky and went back to the gallery, entertaining occasional visitors and listening for the intermittent noise of vehicles as they passed through town. It was early afternoon when I heard the distinctive thrum of the three-wheel red Honda belonging to Brub Mc-Carty. He stopped in front of the open gallery door and revved the engine as the big man riding the machine beckoned to me.

When I stepped down into the street, Brub almost shouted over the engine noise, "Let's go up to the mine. I went up there this morning but didn't see Akeley or his dog. You might bring your gun." So, I went in and grabbed the .45 from under the counter, jammed it into my Levi's pocket and locked the gallery door before climbing on the vehicle behind Mc-Carty. Not much room there.

We sped up the street and swung left at the fork, up the hill behind the church, stirring up a cloud of dust. We were now headed west again, past the cemetery and a pond with Akeley's "Privet Property" warning sign against trespassers. We continued along the dirt road above the town until we reached the misspelled sign reading: "Inter for Tour," McCarty went the remaining distance and braked in front of Akeley's sagging front porch and the rock wall foundation with the stairs leading up to the porch. Akeley's blue 1970 Chevrolet Blazer sat in the yard beside his house, the paint on the hood and roof having faded from harsh high-altitude sun.

We dismounted from the Honda and walked up to the porch. I noticed that paint was peeling from the white windowsills flanking the door. McCarty's fist was thumping on the door frame, and the interior door opened, leaving the screen door as a filter. The screen itself had darkened with oxidation, turning the mesh a rust color at the corners.

The screen kept the interior of the house in darkness, but the face at the door was not Akeley. It was Arthur Brunk who stood in shadow behind the screen door. There were no lights burning in the front room of the Akeley house.

"Yes?" Brunk seemed withdrawn, disconnected as he looked through the screen. I was certain that his cheeks were freckled from a sunburn that had a toxic effect on him.

"Hey, Art, we need to talk to Hiram." McCarty was sporting his usual sunny smile, his voice insistent.

"He is not well…right now. You will have to return…later." Brunk's voice was halting and it seemed worse than out of character to my ears.

"C'mon, Art, we just wanted to check on him. My wife wanted to send some cookies up to him."

Brunk did not move; his eyes were shaded by one hand as he looked through the screen as though outward toward the town. He paused and then repeated, "He…isn't able…"

Then I heard a chilling whisper from inside the house, a voice rasping and almost in-audible but unmistakably that of Akeley. I edged up close to the screen, peering into the darkness as Art Brunk took a step backward, his face in shadow. I could see a figure sitting in a vintage deep leather chair, his hands like claws on the plump chair arms. I could not see his face.

McCarty reached for the screen door handle, but Art Brunk advanced. "I said…he is not well. I…am…here." Brub glanced at me and released the handle.

Then came the whispering voice from the darkened room, and the words seemed omi-nous to me. "They took Chino…" a long pause, and "They took 'im, up there…" Then I could hear stertorous breathing and my breath caught. I heard Akeley's whispering, "They's up there. I saw 'em…ngahhhhhhhh," as his voice trailed off. The smell of stale cigarettes seemed to flow through the screen as I stepped back, my hand unconsciously resting on the butt of the .45.

Brunk raised both hands behind the screen, "Go now. I will see you both…later." It was Art Brunk, but his voice was disturbingly different. As we turned to leave, there was a noise within the house, beyond the front room. Akeley was still whispering, but Brunk turned as something fell from a shelf, or else someone else was in the house. I knew it was not Darouse, because her museum door was open when McCarty and I roared past only minutes before.

McCarty looked at me, "Want to go up to the mine?" he was unusually hesitant.

I shook my head, "Not today, Brub." So we climbed on the Honda and turned around to get back to town. I wondered if something had really happened to Akeley's dog or if

Akeley was just suffering from a cold or flu.

At the museum I climbed off the Honda, and McCarty said he wanted to talk and would grab a couple of beers from his RV and meet me at the gallery. For myself, I stopped in at the museum to be greeted by Darouse Brunk.

"Did you know Art is up there at the mine?" I asked her as she crossed her arms and leaned forward on a glass display case. She tilted her head slightly, but I was not looking at her face.

"Rick, I think he is obsessed with Akeley. He said something yesterday about getting involved in that Venture Mining Company business before the start up." Darouse looked at me as though sizing me up for a confidence. "You know, he had this problem with his face and now he is kinda different. He even seems indifferent to his own son."

"How about you?" I wondered how Art was responding to the new Darouse, and I wondered if she would introduce herself to those who knew her as Mattie. Even under her sweater, I recognized a different woman than I had known before.

"Oh, you know. Business cuts into the personal life." She was smiling.

"OK, gotta go. Brub McCarty wants to talk to me." I was not sure if I wanted to go or stay.

"Then I'll see you later." She waved at me as I looked back from the door of the museum.

Ten minutes later, McCarty walked into the gallery with a pair of Coors beers in a paper sack. We sat down on two folding chairs, and I got a lesson in gold mining from the informal mayor of Mogollon. He began, "I don't know what's goin' on up there, but there's something more than wrong." We popped the key tabs on the beers and I realized my throat was dry. I was very thirsty.

Akeley had set up his tour with posts and cords so that a person could pay for the tour and then proceed unaccompanied if Akeley did not want to conduct the tour in person. Apparently, Art Brunk had done tour guide work for Akeley on many occasions. All that made sense to me.

"Those Venture folks are bringing a new ore crusher up the hill this summer, so I guess that the ore must assay at least four ounces per ton." That seemed to be sparse pickings to me, but McCarty said it could be very profitable. McCarty was one of those founts of technical knowledge that he reveled in expounding at great length.

Mogollon building owners did not own the ground under their structures. All of the mineral rights were apportioned to other owners, and the mine was no exception. The Venture group had purchased the mineral parcels going deep into the mountain.

McCarty took a deep swallow of his beer and gave me a tutorial on gold mining. The new miners were gambling on the cyanide leaching methods of extracting gold from ore. I knew that gold could only be dissolved using aqua regia, the mixture of hydrochloric and nitric acids, but I did not know that dissolved sodium cyanide poured through gold-bearing ore would leach the gold from the crushed ore.

McCarty held up his finger, "The gamble here is that if there is copper in the ore, the process can be wasted because copper dilutes the power of the cyanide." He went on to tell me that the dissolved gold still had to be refined and smelted, something done in Mogollon's heyday.

At the turn of the century, the wagon teams bringing supplies to the mountains returned to San Vicente loaded with heavy ingots of gold and silver. The story is that these ingots were stacked on the sidewalk in front of the Palace Hotel in that town without any concern of them being stolen.

"So, that pond just up the road is…?" I pointed to the west.

"Yeah, that's not water. It's that damned cyanide solution. Drink and you die." McCarty chortled.

As he talked, I was dwelling on the increasingly bizarre behavior of car salesman Arthur Brunk and the whisperer in the chair. I would not tell McCarty, but I was relieved to get off Akeley's porch, and the absence of Akeley's ever-present dog companion seemed unsettling. As for the mine buildings, they were always eerie, and because they were constructed of heavy lumber and corrugated sheet iron, they made strange noises, especially when a strong wind coursed through the town and into those artificial metal caverns on the mountain. Suddenly, I thought about the deep tunnel disappearing from behind the Holland store. Did anybody know where it ended, brooding in total blackness under the mine? I shuddered inwardly.

After McCarty's visit, the afternoon waned pleasantly, with a few visitors and even fewer sales. I had taken no new photos today, but the gallery exhibits were pleasing to me, and I reminded myself that this venture was a pleasant diversion from weekday life. Traffic was dwindling, and I was ready to eat and do some reading in the gallery before bedtime. I realized that since the week before, I had joined those who said that Mogollon seemed a haunted place after dark. If I had first driven into this town after sundown and seen the dark buildings looming over the street, I would have known the fear of the unseen lurking in the canyon of Silver Creek.

Now and then I went to the front window to look across at the Holland store, feeling relieved when it appeared dark and abandoned as it should be. I had brought books by Donald Keyhoe and Coral Lorenzen. The latter's book UFO Occupants again confirmed my theory that conflated stories of evil spirits and demon visitors with anecdotal accounts of flying saucer occupants. I had even discovered a used copy of the famous book from 1950 documenting a flying saucer landing and recovery. Frank Scully's Behind the Flying Saucers was sensational in its day, describing dead saucer occupants discovered near Aztec, N.M.

It was difficult to verify other authors, and quackery was rife in flying saucer literature, including wild stories of authors being transported through the universe in "ether ships." The work of responsible authors, however, suggested a dark truth behind the accounts, something that could not be dispelled by a movie such as "Close Encounters of the Third Kind." Lorenzen published detailed and verified information about an abduction in Arizona in which a man was taken by a flying saucer and returned, disoriented and dehydrated five days later in the same area.

In some cases the alien visitors were described as humanoid, but a few others were described as beings that could only be described as monstrous. The case of the Sutton monster in 1952 West Virginia was laughed at in popular media, but responsible writers had done the research and found that the residents of Flatwoods, W. Va., had encountered a 12-ft. monster or machine related to a flying saucer that landed for a short time on an isolated hilltop. How would our distant ancestors describe a horrible alien visitor? Probably that visitor would be seen as a spirit or a demon. The question would be whether these things intervened in human existence, abducting humans or worse. This was reading guaranteed to breed anxiety, even with the most stolid reader, such as me.

I was startled from my concentration by a tapping on the glass of the front door. I sprang to my feet and saw somebody waiting in the growing darkness. I tripped the latch and opened the door to find Darouse smiling at me. "Mind if I come in?"

"Of course not. Can I get you anything?" She made no move to sit down, but she looked around the gallery as I noticed that she had changed her sweater for a tight-fitting blouse. I swallowed.

She was not smiling now. "Art hasn't come back from the mine, and I'm starting to worry."

I assured her that he seemed all right when I saw him in the afternoon. I exaggerated the "all right" part, but Darouse's knitted brow suggested true concern. She said that he had never stayed up there so late.

"Would you check in at the museum in the next hour or so? It would ease my mind." She moved toward the door.

"Oh, sure. Let me wash that dish and bring it back to you." Now she smiled strangely and looked directly at me before leaving. It left me feeling uncomfortable again. As I went back to reading, I was looking at my watch every few minutes.

I spent the next half hour thinking about what I saw in the Holland store seven nights earlier, and what I thought I heard on the forest path that same morning. In the Mogollon night, I was more and more certain that I had experienced something nobody else in town seemed to recognize. I also felt a different kind of fear than I had ever known. It was fear of something beyond description or my understanding.

It was two minutes' work to clean the casserole dish, its cover, and the plate underneath before I went out into the darkened street. I stopped. It would be better if I waited until the morning to return the dish; because I felt lustful stirrings. I could do some reading and go upstairs early to sleep; however, I could not stop thinking about Darouse and wondering if she was offering something beyond friendly conversation. I didn't want to go see her, but the compulsion was irresistible. I did wait for another half hour, though.

Then I was walking out the door, looking very carefully to see if anybody was on the street, but even the lights illuminating the theater front up the street were turned out. I walked swiftly two doors up and found the front door of the museum ajar. I saw the back end of the new pickup truck, with Texas plates sticking out from the side of the building. I eased the door open and found the interior dimly lit from the low-wattage bulbs inside display cases. "Darouse?" I felt my pulse quicken, my breath shortened.

"Hello, Rick. He still isn't back." She emerged from the door of their living quarters beyond a partition at the rear of the museum, and I stopped breathing for a long moment, my solar plexus churning. I was frozen as she walked slowly toward me, her heels clicking on the board floor, a faint smile on her red lips. I just stood there with the dishes in my hands.

Darouse was wearing a floor-length turquoise and brocade kimono and it was hanging open. She took the dishes from my hands and placed them on the display case before turning to me, the shimmering kimono opening as she raised her arms. I was immersed in a haze of perfume as she stepped into my arms, her lips on mine, her tongue pushing into my mouth. She was naked under the kimono.

Time stood still, and I should have recoiled in righteous indignation, but I was only a man, and I was swept away in a fog of fierce arousal. This was not the Mattie who chatted with Margo on Thursday, and my arms went inside the kimono, pulling her warm body tight against me, her enlarged breasts pushing against my chest.

"Latch the door, Darling. He's not going to be back tonight." The words made no sense, but I went to the door and dumbly pushed the button and heard the spring latch seek its socket before I followed Darouse to the back of the museum, into a dimly lit bedroom, hearing her heels clicking on the wood floor. She pushed the door shut, and the only light was a 15-watt bedside lamp, the shade covered with a multi-colored transparent scarf.

Our kisses were hungry, then frenzied as she struggled with my clothes. Then we were coupling as she took me with an astounding hunger, and as we exploded, I fell back in stunned silence with an ache in my abdomen that did not feel like desire. She kept me there for more than an hour, and I had no thoughts of resistance. Her whimpers and moans drove me to take her again. Or did she take me? We had almost nothing to say, except when I dressed and struggled to my feet.

"If you come back early in the morning and the door is unlatched, I'll be waiting," she softly whispered as she kissed me at the door. I again heard her heels clicking as she returned to the damp sheets of her bed, and I stumbled into the street, looking left and right in profound guilt, hoping nobody was watching. I was determined not go back there.

My head was throbbing, and the smell of Darouse on my body now made me want to wash in hopes of erasing an indelible stain. A waxing crescent-moon was hanging over the mountains at the east side of town. This was something that should never have happened, and my mind desperately sought Margo's image. She seemed farther away than the 78 miles to San Vicente.

I washed myself and sat for a few minutes, head down as I tried to understand my own failings. Some people say only children are unaware of consequences for their actions, but my actions stood in the face of inevitable destructive consequences. Suddenly Mogollon was not an exotic Old West town with secrets, but an oubliette from which there might be no escape.

The stairs to our sleeping quarters were steep tonight, and the cool mountain air did not comfort my fevered headache. Sleep would be impossible as I found myself in that endless loop of agonizing worry that had no beginning and no end. I remembered to put food out for the rafter crawler and his plumed tail, but the darkness gave no respite. I lay there, staring at the faint silhouette of the rafters above me in the accusing silence.

Dressed only in my briefs, I climbed to my feet and went to the window, looking out at the brooding town. Somehow, the faint lights from windows up the street did not belong with that tableau. My failures brought back all the stupidity and bungling of my personal life throughout the years, all leading up to a compulsion I could not resist.

Wait! In the air up the street—what was it? The deep sky was tempered by the cresent moon as I pushed my face close to the cold glass. Yes—I could see something in the air above the storefront buildings and the metal-roofed cabins. It was slowly gliding, following the meander of the street, its dark shape difficult to discern against the looming mountains bordering the canyon. I could not measure the distance. Perhaps it was a Great Horned Owl, and as I strained my eyes, I saw outspread narrow wings sweeping vigorously, supporting a bulbous body as it glided eastward until my view was blocked. There was something strange about the shape that I could not place, and my imagination made me shudder. It was gone, and I returned to my self-loathing and self-recrimination. I was determined not to see her again.

Then I did doze off, and when I suddenly woke up, it was still dark. The hands of my watch read 5:00, and a powerful need to urinate sent me down the stairs to the outhouse, emotions from the night before still churning in my abdomen. Perhaps breakfast would settle my stomach, and I walked around to the front of the gallery. I pulled the door key from my pocket and then paused. I remembered the words of Darouse Brunk, but I refused to consider going to the museum.

I stood at the gallery door, looked to my left and felt the heat of irrational arousal suddenly welling up in my solar plexus as my eyes found the silent façade of the museum. I had to know whether the door was unlocked. The smell of Darouse was still in my nostrils, and my excitement overcame my revulsion. Slowly I walked two doors down, my eyes carefully searching the street for anybody else abroad in the pre-dawn. Art Brunk would certainly be back by now, and that would be the end of it.

When I reached the museum door, a vertical stripe of black separated the door from the jamb, and my limbs began to shake with anticipation. I paused once again, looked up the street, and pushed the door open, quickly entering and then closed the door. The dim light from the rear painted a pale splash onto the dark museum floor, and I heard Darouse's voice turned sultry. "Make sure the door is locked, Darling. I need you." As I pressed the latch, I locked myself in.

I entered the small bed chamber and fixated on the table lamp as light radiated through the multi-colored silk scarf. Darouse was lying there in the open kimono, still wearing her shoes, and it was the first time I heard her unique throaty laugh as we repeated the frenzied embraces of the night before. I should have been thinking of Margo and Art Brunk, but I was besotted with the erotic woman wrapped around me. What if Brunk were to come to the door? It did not matter at that moment.

Exhausted, we parted. I dressed again, now left with emptiness in the pit of my stomach. Darouse caressed her breasts, sat on the edge of the bed with legs crossed and picked up her lipstick tube as I got up. Her eyes were on me, knowing I could not help wanting to be inside her, but now I wanted to flee and could not imagine how I could remain in the same town. "Rick, sometimes I visit my brother in San Vicente during the week." She gave me the street address, and I knew I could not forget it.

THE WHISPERING DARKNESS

As I cowered outside the museum, pulling the door closed behind me, I slunk back to the gallery, keeping close to the building walls. I should have questioned why Art Brunk would spend a whole night at the mine, but I was too busy feeling the curse of betrayal.

As Sunday dawned, food had no taste, and I set up the gallery, every five minutes expecting a violent Arthur Brunk to burst through the door, but he did not come. I did not think Darouse would hide the new aspects of her personality from him.

I tried to stay inside the gallery as much as possible, my mood swinging wildly from wanting to close early and flee Mogollon, to wanting to hide here for fear of what home in San Vicente might be like in the wake of my actions the night before. Once I went into the street to exchange greetings with Brub McCarty; he thought we should go up to the mine, but I made excuses before retreating back into the gallery. As I backpedaled, I saw Darouse Brunk talking with visitors at the door of the museum. She was wearing her trademark sweater and slacks. She did not look in my direction.

Back inside, I wondered what kind of family life Arthur Brunk would have after his disturbing retreat into Old Man Akeley's mouldering house and his wife's transformation. Thinking about this kept me from dwelling upon my own devastation.

As the day progressed, a substantial number of visitors passed through town, many stopping to visit the open buildings and to photograph the picturesque cabins and storefronts. I saw Brub McCarty's red three-wheeler go past at least twice.

Sparky was late in his daily visit, and he bounced into the gallery, going immediately to my aluminum trash can filled with discarded pieces of stained glass, spoiled photo prints and trim from mounting cardboard. When he put his paws up on the edge of the three-foot tall bin, I realized what he was looking for. I patted his head and pulled him away so that he could settle for a dog biscuit instead of that peculiar fragment buried under other trash. I noticed that the dog's wounds were liberally daubed with ointment. Then Sparky was off to make his usual rounds.

It was almost noon when McCarty filled the doorway, a toothpick in his mouth, hands in his pockets, cowboy hat pushed back. "Hey, Rick, you wanta take a ride up to the mine? Mattie Brunk just told me that Art was up there again this morning."

My mouth went dry. I almost told him that Brunk never came back last night, but stopped myself. My bowels felt watery. "I don't think so. Yesterday was strange enough for me."

"You're probably right." Brub leaned against the door frame. "You believe in the Devil?" The question was sudden.

Even though I certainly did accept the existence of evil principles and powers, I was cautious in admitting it. "I guess so. If there's a God, there is a Devil."

"Exactly my thought. You know the Petroskis? They live in the big cabin up the street."

I knew the house with a new metal roof, but I had never met the couple. They were at the social in the theater a week ago. "No, I've seen them but never spoke to them."

"After 25 years in the copper business, Vic—Victor—and Sarah's kids grew up, and they wanted to get away, so they bought this house…" Brub threw his thumb over his left shoulder, "…and live here year-round."

I wasn't sure how that was linked to philosophy, but Brub shifted the toothpick and

Fanny Mine Buildings and Head Frame   RickPhoto 1978

continued, "Anyhow, I was talkin' to 'em this morning, and Sarah told me the Devil talked to her last night." He chortled and looked down.

I felt cold hands on my back as I thought of Cotton Mather and the New England witch times. "Did Mr. Petroski hear the voice?"

"Ha! Vic is deaf as a post when his hearing aid is turned off. Sarah said…well, why not meet them and talk to her. Vic says she's gone mental, but they argue all the time. When he's tired of arguing, he switches off the hearing aid."

Now it was my turn to laugh. "Sounds interesting. I'm ready when you are." For Brub it seemed to be a peculiar affectation of Sarah Petroski, but for me there was a connection that would be unsettling if I had no other problems inside my head.

I put the "back in 15 minutes" sign on the door, and we jumped onto McCarty's three-wheeler, roaring up the street to park at the right hand side of the road. A sturdy wooden foot bridge crossed over the trickling Silver Creek, and we walked up steps to the Petroskis' front porch.

McCarty introduced me to the spare, clean-shaven Vic, whose iron grey hair receded at the temples. He was wearing denim coveralls and work boots. Sarah was wearing a flower print dress, her very black hair wound into a bun.

After pleasantries and declining the offer of coffee or tea, Brub asked Sarah to tell me what she heard. Her husband smiled and shook his head. "I didn't hear nothin'. I think my bride is hearing crickets."

Sarah opened her mouth to chide him but turned back to us as we sat down on a very new sofa and love seat set. I thought about the delivery truck's long trek to bring the furniture to Mogollon.

Mrs. Petroski seemed eager to tell her story. "Now, I'm Catholic, even if we don't go to church any more, but I swear I was scared to death last night." She primped her hair and sighed heavily.

Brub's voice seemed overly loud in the tasteful living room of what appeared to be a rustic cabin from the outside. "Strange things goin' on in town, Sarah. What did you hear?"

Vic Petroski gave his wife a dismissive wave as she gathered her thoughts. "Well, we were listening to records on the stereo and went to bed kind of late. I didn't go to sleep right away, but he…" She pointed at her husband, who rolled his eyes, "…dropped off like a rock. Anyhow, I was lying there while he started to snore, and I heard a scratching on the roof."

Sarah paused, and I thought about raccoons and ringtail cats "You never heard anything like it before?" I looked at the wall where a crucifix overlooked the living room.

"Some things I just know. I came from Europe to marry Victor where we know about these things going back hundreds of years." Here was a woman who heard tales of demon voices seeking to accost walkers on lonely paths in the forest.

Sarah continued, "My heart started beating a mile a minute, and then I heard the Devil's voice."

Now I was eager, "What did it say, Mrs. Petroski? My curiosity emerged

She closed her eyes pensively and then her dark eyes fixed on mine. "I felt almost hyp-notized. The voice was a buzzing sound, changing its pitch and talking directly to me from outside the bedroom window. I can't tell you how hideous the sound was to me."

The woman did not have to tell me how hideous it was. "Did your husband hear it?"

"HA! He doesn't hear anything at night!" She glared at Victor.

Vic Petroski pointed to his head, grinning, "She's got bats up here—bats!"

Sarah raised her chin, held out her fist let it spring open, fingers splayed, "That's what he has for brains." Their sparring was good-humored. "Gentlemen, the noise was as clear as our voices in this room, but I could not make out the words. My mind told me that I should know the words, but it was a jumble of whispers, buzzing, hissing, and yet I knew it wanted me to come to the window."

I wanted to push her for more details, "You went to the window?"

Shaking her head emphatically, Sarah said, "Not for all the gold that came out of the Little Fanny mine. I picked up my crucifix and prayed out loud to St. Michael for protection. I was so afraid."

As I imagined demons rising from the depths of the earth, pouring out through deep mine tunnels to attack the residents of the ghost town, reaching out to compel a signature— to get my name—in the black book of the damned. "It must have been very scary." I was understating.

"You bet it was. I woke up Rip Van Winkle over there, and tried to get him to go outside, but he just went and looked out the window. Said he didn't see anything."

Vic shrugged, "Didn't see a damned thing, and there was just enough moon rising to prove it." He gave his wife a stage grin.

McCarty stepped in, voice booming, "If it's OK, we'll take a look outside."

Sarah was staring at her husband, "That's a great idea. My husband should have thought about doing that." We all went out onto the porch and Sarah pointed around to the rear of the house. We picked our way through the rock-strewn yard and went to the bedroom window, hoping to see animal tracks at the very least. We were disappointed because of the rocky soil, although there was a sign that strands of grass seemed to be pressed down.

We reported our non-findings and took our leave of the Petroskis, but as our boots sounded hollowly on the footbridge across the creek, I had my own suspicions that the others were not aware of, and I began to see Mogollon as a source of lurking horror whose roots were beyond my understanding.

As we started to cross the street, a Jeep with Texas license plates slowed, and a young couple leaned in our direction. The female passenger in oversized sunglasses said, "Hey, we heard that you could take a tour of the old mine up here."

Brub answered in his mayor's voice, "You heard right. Just make a u-turn, turn left at the end of town and you go up around to the gate. The sign is misspelled. Can't miss it." For once, that was true.

The driver shook his head, "We just came from there. There was a barrier with a 'Road Closed' and 'No trespassing' signs."

I chipped in, "The signs weren't there yesterday. I'm not sure what's going on. Sorry about that."

The Jeep rolled on down to the center of town, pulling in to park in the broad lot beside the museum, while McCarty and I wondered aloud about the unheard-of barrier around the bend to our left.

McCarty said, "We better go talk to Akeley." He had lost his toothpick somewhere in the past half hour.

"Not right now. I'd better get back to the gallery." The gallery was the least of my objections for returning to that aging house at the entrance to the mine, with the whisperer sitting in his darkened front room. A possible confrontation with Arthur Brunk also left me with a tightness in my chest.

I could have walked back to the gallery, but McCarty fired up the Honda, and I climbed on for a quick ride to the west side of town. Back in the gallery I was hearing Sarah Petroski's story in my head, and linking it to a looming dark shape under a waning moon in the Mogollon night.

Gallery visitors kept me occupied for the remainder of the afternoon, but my mind was whirling with thoughts of secret tunnels, hellish voices on a forest path, the raspy whisper of Hiram Akeley in a darkened room, shots fired in the night, naked Darouse, betrayed Margo, and a missing woman on the highway below the mountains.

Too soon I was putting the sales money into a bank bag, loading the VW bus with the detritus of a weekend, then double-checking the door locks as I prepared for the return to San Vicente. In the warm sun of afternoon, the town of Mogollon seemed a normal New Mexico tourist stop. I was thinking about the witch times and the bedeviled residents of Salem. Had I been witness to paranormal entities? If that was true, how did the shape inside the Holland store come through the tunnel warrens? How did a ghost or spirit unlatch the front door of that iconic place.

Trash went into garbage bags to be hauled back to San Vicente. I separated Sparky's disquieting fragment from the rest of the trash, bundled it in plastic wrap, and sealed it in an additional freezer bag. The edges of the strange shell-like object were turning greenish-brown, and a faint, disgusting odor emanated from its spongey reverse. In Mogollon, if you carried it in, you carried it out. There was no garbage pickup.

Just as I was preparing to get into my vehicle, I saw a figure walking down the street. I felt a wave of fear. It was Arthur Brunk. I was transfixed as I saw him approaching his museum. He acknowledged no one, looking straight ahead. Though he was 45 yards distant from me, I was shocked at his appearance. His clothes were rumpled, no hat on his head. But his face— his face seemed to be covered with red spots that appeared to be freckles at first glance. No, they were more than freckles. The sunburn of the week before must have become infected, and the appearance of mark on his face reminded me of measles spots, which was unlikely.

I had a twinge of protective emotion. Was his wife in any danger from hostility or infection? Brunk's gait was halting and uncertain, his arms hanging loose at his sides. Without a glance of recognition in my direction, he entered the museum and was gone. There was something very strange going on up at that house on the mine property, and I pictured Hiram Akeley sitting there in his darkened living room, his rasping whisper still clear in my mind.

Before I was ready to leave, I heard the rumble of a V-8 engine, and watched from the gallery door as the grey Ford 250 pickup truck headed out, its driver leaning toward the windshield. I could see Darouse in the passenger seat, but neither looked in my direction as they began their long drive through San Vicente and on south to El Paso.

Twenty minutes later, after checking the upstairs door lock, the back-door lock, and the front-door gallery locks for the third time, I was ready to leave. With the VW engine running, I started up into the forest and out of Mogollon as weekend visitors commonly did. I did not want to think about home in San Vicente, and even less about the week that would follow.

Six

An Ominous Week in San Vicente

I went through the wooded area, rolling past the fenced-in pond, noticing now small metal "Danger" signs that warned of the cyanide hiding in its shallow depths. Then I finally reached the summit and wound down to State Road 78's serpentine descent to the main highway far below. I slowed to a crawl at the great hairpin turn and was pleased to see that a Catron County road crew had cleared the debris from the partial collapse of the cliff bank that looms over the road.

When I reached Highway 180, I turned south toward Glenwood. Despite my problems, I felt that a burden of uneasiness was lifting with my distance from the mountain ghost town. When I slowed down through the picturesque village of Glenwood, the Texaco station was closed, but I had more than enough gasoline for the 78 miles to San Vicente. When I passed the well-remembered spot where we first saw the Armendariz woman standing beside her car, I wondered again whether her relatives in Reserve or in San Vicente had heard from her.

When I drove over the final hill and down to San Vicente in its valley, I was thinking more of the Mogollon mystery than I was about my guilt, and when I parked in the driveway and went inside carrying material from the weekend, I was unusually happy to see Margo as she started telling me about her whirlwind weekend. She had dinner waiting, and I realized that I had eaten very little during the weekend.

Margo was bubbling about her successful showings, laughing in our shared amusement at how local people added a vowel to her profession—real-a-tor—and then it was my turn to describe the visit to Akeley's house and how Mrs. Petroski had heard something so similar to what I had heard the week before

At this point, Margo had settled on what we called the "buzzard solution," but I was certain that something outré had come to Mogollon. She was correct that nothing had really happened, although I had fired several shots into the Holland Store, and Arthur Brunk seemed to have contracted some kind of skin disease.

Margo stood beside me at the kitchen sink while I took my turn at doing dishes. "Do you think Art and Mattie are OK?"

I felt a stab inside my stomach but responded immediately, "No, there is something really wrong with Art. He is nothing like the guy we have known for months." I didn't say that he spent the entire night Saturday with Akeley at the mine.

"Is Mattie worried about him?"

"I haven't really talked to her about it. I think she's be more likely to talk to you." It wasn't exactly lying, but dissembling was not something to be proud of. I went on to describe Brunk's bizarre behavior, but most of the details could have had a multiplicity of explanations.

"Do you think there is anything dangerous going on up there? Maybe something toxic in the mine? That would really ruin the charm of the place."

She knew that I was set on a paranormal explanation, something she was highly skeptical about, and because we had a substantial investment in the gallery, even as a weekend operation, it would be best to ignore the praeternatural. "Well, you have to admit that a ghost in the Holland Store would be a great tourist draw." The clink of flatware in the dish drainer was the sound of sanity and normalcy, and we could turn to putting the gallery accessories and account books into the appropriate cabinet.

"What's this?" Margo's voice next to me was demanding.

My heart skipped in blind panic, but then I relaxed. She was holding the double wrapped fragment. "Oh, that was a gift from Sparky. Really peculiar."

Margo held it up to the track lights over the sink. "Are you sure it isn't a crab shell?" Her brow was furrowed, lips pursed. She turned it over, "It doesn't look like plastic, either."

I explained that I had rejected that possibility, but there was nothing in Mogollon, or in nature as I knew it, that matched the flat, semi-convex chunk of chitinous material.

Margo put the plastic-wrapped piece on the counter and moved to stick her hands under the faucet stream, as though she found the fragment repulsive even through the wrapping. Her face reflected the reaction.

The rest of the evening passed uneventfully, and we watched the latest episode of "Battlestar Galactica" on television. I was feeling awkward at bedtime, but as soon as we turned out the lights, the telephone rang. I stiffened as Margo picked up the receiver. Something was wrong.

Margo was more distraught than I had ever seen her as she sat on the edge of the bed, the phone pressed to her ear, tears tracking her cheeks. For a moment I had a psychotic thought that Darouse was calling, but then ascribed the thought to paranoia as Margo asked me to get pen and paper.

I got the material began to write as she pointed toward me, "Washington…University… Medical Center…area code 3-1-4…" I immediately thought of her brother and his family in St. Louis. I wrote down the phone number she was repeating and listened as Margo demanded more details.

As the hour grew late, the bedroom light was on, and Margo called the hospital, then talked to her sister-in-law again. As the story unfolded from Margo, I found that shortly before midnight in St. Louis, a pair of thugs in hoodies had battered down her brother's front door, intent on home invasion. It was fortunate that her brother had a gun in the house. He shot the first assailant in the chest, killing him. He shot the second robber, but not before the thug's handgun landed a bullet.

Margo's brother was in surgery, but his wound was not fatal. Apparently, the other invader was apprehended after collapsing from lack of blood in a downtown Emergency Room. Needless to say, we didn't sleep much that Sunday night, and the ensuing week was cramped by work and contact with Margo's family. The Mogollon mystery seemed diminished by more immediate concerns.

We were having dinner Wednesday when Margo blurted out, "You know, if there are space aliens, I know they are good guys. I mean, to have the ability to travel from the stars, they wouldn't have crime or war or violence. They would be nice to us."

I did not agree, but I just said, "If they are extraterrestrial, I hope you and Spielberg are right." After Von Daniken's book *Chariots of the Gods* it seemed that ancient astronauts were replacing God as the guides for humanity. Somehow it seemed to me too simple an explanation.

"Don't you have a book by that guy who said he had met the space guys and he called them space brothers?" Margo was trying very hard not to worry about her brother as he convalesced in the St. Louis hospital. Margo had learned that her brother was not charged in the death of the career criminals who had staged their last home invasion.

"Yeah, but he has been soundly discredited. He claimed to be a professor of astronomy, but he just operated a concession stand at the entrance to a popular observatory."

Margo's essential goodness affected her world view, and I envied her for that. "Well, if humans evolve to be space travelers, we will have live together in harmony first. I am sure if there are any advanced space beings out there, they will want to help us if they come here." She was one of those who agreed that ancient space visitors could have seeded human civilization.

I wished I could agree with her, but I had never reconciled the lore of space aliens with the ancient grimoires and the cavalcade of demonic entities that have bedeviled men and women since the beginning. Great Asmodeus, Belial, and a hideous host of misshapen demons, assaulting their human victims, whispering to them on lonely forest paths, intruding into bed chambers to seduce wives and the retiring women of the cloister—sometimes yielding horrific offspring spoken of by classic chroniclers of demonology. Did these demons lurking in the night have their counterparts in the vastness of the cosmos? Many things that cannot exist become frightening reality and are yet not believed by those who have never been outside in the night when they accidentally became witnesses to primordial blood rites at Walpurgis.

We debated whether we should open the gallery on the weekend, but as we considered the absence of two major families, it was obvious that the town of Mogollon would have fewer attractions without our presence. I was thinking about the museum and whether the Brunks would be making their weekly journey from El Paso. Though harboring guilt, I still found I could not rid myself of the carnal thoughts I had for Darouse Brunk.

As I held Margo to comfort her that night, she vacillated between wanting to fly to St. Louis and her commitment to her job, to the gallery and our mutual creative projects. I persuaded her that her brother's wound was not life threatening, even though a .25-caliber bullet had bruised one of his ribs.

Finally, Margo nodded with a shudder and agreed that we should drive to Mogollon on Friday as we usually did. The strangeness I had experienced had not proved dangerous, although I was not sanguine about Arthur Brunk and his changes in behavior and appearance.

Thursday had us both up early and off to work without so much as a piece of toast for breakfast. That's what cookies were made for.

I arrived home before Margo that afternoon, retrieved the rolled-up copy of the *San Vicente Daily Enterprise* from the front sidewalk, and I went inside for something cold to drink, removing the rubber band and leaving the newspaper on the sofa in the front room. Then I went to my darkroom area to mix chemicals for making black and white prints as I did every Thursday evening. When I heard the front door close, I knew Margo had arrived.

She always went right to the newspaper to check that her real estate ad listings were all in order and properly displayed. We exchanged greetings from room to room, and there were minutes of silence.

"Rick! Rick, come out here and see this!" Something had caught her eye. I rinsed my hands and wiped them dry on a dish towel that was sporting holes from errant splashes of fixer. I went to the front room. Margo shoved the paper at me, pointing to a front-page article below the fold:

Misssing SV Woman Now Returned to Her Family

A woman reported missing two weeks ago in the Glenwood area was found and returned to her family in San Vicente, according to N.M. State Police Wednesday.

Ofelia Armendariz, 43, of San Vicente, was reported as missing after she failed to arrive in Reserve where she was planning to visit her extended family the weekend of May 5.

State Police reported her car abandoned on Highway 180 south of Glenwood.

A search of the apparently abandoned car led Police to file a missing person's report.

Investigations in the area over several days did not locate Armendariz, and Police gave no details as to when Armendariz was returned.

Armendariz is currently recuperating in San Vicente Hospital where she was admitted and suffering from exposure and minor injuries.

THE WHISPERING DARKNESS

Now I was more than puzzled. How could Mrs. Armendariz have wandered off so quickly with no traffic on the road? Much as I hated the idea, I felt compelled to contact the Armendariz family, and Margo agreed. Of course, I suggested she was far better at making cold calls than I was. Besides, we had been the last to see Ofelia Armendariz before her disappearance.

Margo grimaced but smiled as she agreed to check the directory, which thankfully listed only three with that surname in the county. Seven dialed numbers put Margo in touch with a man who said he was Ofelia's husband. She put her hand over the mouthpiece and mouthed a whisper, "husband…" Margo explained how we had encountered the man's wife and how we had thought about her for days afterward.

Of course, Margo asked how Ofelia was faring in the hospital, and I watched her face as she listened to a long answer. Margo smiled and nodded as she thanked the man. I was forced to wait until the phone call was over before my curiosity could be satisfied.

Now she sat with her knees together, forming a platform for her elbows. "OK, Manuel—that's her husband's name—said that doctors were sure Ofelia would be just fine, but she has no memory of what happened during the days she was gone. The doctors say she had bruises, several cuts, and abrasions, particularly to her face. The cops are wondering if there was an assault but there is no evidence of that."

We sat on the sofa together, thinking separate thoughts. I could not help but be reminded of the Travis Walton case published in Coral Lorenzen's *APRO Bulletin*. He too disappeared for several days and suffered temporary amnesia. The story was a tabloid sensation in 1975, but the fact-based Lorenzen periodical concluded that it was an abduction case similar in most ways to the abduction of Betty and Barney Hill in New England years earlier. In neither case was there a Black Man presenting the Devil's book for signing. That left only one possibility in my mind.

Margo was pensive, eyes straight ahead, but I think she drew the same conclusions. "Well, at least she is going to be OK."

"I wonder." If her trauma was deep and dark, Ofelia Armendariz might never return to being the woman we met along the highway that Friday afternoon.

As always before a Mogollon trip, we had to prepare everything on Thursday night to make our Friday afternoon departure as early as possible.

That evening I found myself reading again the famous 1950 Frank Scully best seller *Behind the Flying Saucers*. This was the first book to document a flying saucer crash and recovery by the U.S. military. My correspondents were currently excited about the findings from a nuclear scientist named Stanton Friedman who had penetrated the cover-up to another flying saucer crash and recovery northwest of Roswell, N.M. in July, 1947, which was billed by the government as a weather balloon. A book was supposedly coming that would prove the interplanetary case.

Growing up in New Mexico, I had always believed there was some kind of alien presence in the state, but I had only second-hand accounts. I was reading the Scully book that I had not even known about when I was a kid in 1950. A government disinformation campaign had effectively destroyed Scully's story about the recovery of a flying saucer near

Aztec, N.M., in 1948. That story helped confirm Margo's belief that otherworldly creatures would be similar to humans in form, although the dead creatures recovered inside the 100-foot diameter Aztec saucer were the size of children.

As we talked about Scully's book that Thursday evening, Margo was more certain than ever about the benign motives of any visitors from the stars. We argued briefly, but it was so theoretical that we could never imagine the frightening reality of such an encounter, even with benign aliens. I knew from my Mogollon encounter that there is something different from any other human experience—the screaming fear that comes with meeting an entity beyond human comprehension. It mattered not whether the being was from outer space or from the black acherontic river of supernatural evil. The evil within must be mirrored in the evil from outside.

After we put things away and got ready for bed, I went to the bathroom door where Margo was brushing her teeth with a vengeance. "Let me ask you something I just thought about."

She turned on the faucet, washed out her mouth and made a kiss in the mirror, "About flying saucers and aliens?"

"Yeah, I think it is. Tell me, if these space creatures are really good guys and want only the best for mankind, why has the U. S. Government, and most other governments, done everything they can to deny the existence of flying saucers? Why has the U.S. military threatened witnesses and sworn them to secrecy? What does the government know that they don't want us to know?"

Margo patted my cheek. "Heck, I don't know. Maybe they don't want us to make friends with them."

Maybe she was right, and maybe I had seen too many movies about monsters from outer space and evil demons from beyond. My imagination could be working against me. In bed I also asked Margo if she thought a visit to Ofelia Armendariz might shed some light on her experience; if her story was even a little like that of abducted Travis Walton, it would be an article I would want to write. The ominous events in Mogollon seemed very distant as we turned out the lights. With all that was happening, I also realized that my brief affair with Darouse Brunk was making it almost impossible for me to be intimate with my wife. I had not anticipated that the stain of guilt would drive a stake into my domestic life.

The thoughts about Mrs. Armendariz consumed me at work, and I used my noon hour to visit the hospital, hoping that my story of how we met would get me into her hospital room. It was unusually assertive of me.

The San Vicente Hospital sits just west of Highway 180 at the intersection where Highway 90 branches off and heads south. The three-storey building backs up against a hill, the parking lot looking down on the highway as it descends toward the town center. I had been to the hospital several times over the years when family members were patients.

A row of barely comfortable chairs with chrome-plated arms were underneath the windows looking out to the parking lot. Five members of a family were grouped together, talking with animation as though waiting for a patient to be released, and at the other end of the row, a man in a suit was sitting, legs crossed, his face hidden behind an open edition of *The El Paso Times*.

THE WHISPERING DARKNESS

At the reception desk, the lady behind the counter was moving from one end to the other, barking pleasant orders to her staff. She had frizzy iron grey hair and her swift movements made me think of an energetic wire-haired terrier, especially since she could not have been taller than 5'4" as she scribbled notes on a clipboard, appearing to have command of the hospital in her starched white tunic. A blue plastic name tag identified her as "Diaz," and behind her was a bank of grim Steelcase file racks stuffed with the fates of thousands of patients, past and present.

I approached the counter, "Excuse me—can you tell me which room Ofelia Armendariz is in?"

Diaz looked me up and down in the manner of a Sergeant inspecting an enlisted man. "Family?"

"Uh, no, but I know her." I didn't get a chance to explain my interest.

Diaz went to the patient registry, put on her glasses, and snorted. "Sorry, but patient Armendariz is allowed no visitors. What's your name?" I blurted out my name, and she wrote it down, then tapped her lip with the top of the pen.

"Name's familiar. Your wife in real estate?" I nodded. "She sold us our home out on Swan Street. Really nice lady. Hold on just a minute." Diaz went to the phone and dialed. I wondered if Mrs. Armendariz had her family with her as I fidgeted with my left hand in my pocket, fingering my key ring.

Diaz was listening on the phone, face impassive. Then she hung up the phone and shook her head almost imperceptibly. "If you'll wait here, somebody's coming down. Yes, your wife is so nice, and we really love our home."

"What about Mrs. Armendariz? I just wanted to talk to her again since she came back home."

Diaz looked at me, and her face softened, "There is a note in the file with the word 'quarantine' at the top. Let me tell you confidentially that the poor lady must have had a terrible time. She was dehydrated, clothes torn…some bruises, strange cuts on her body. I was on duty when they brought her in." She paused.

"But she's OK now?"

"No, she's not OK. She has no memory of what happened to her. None at all. But the worst part is her face."

The way Diaz said it was alarming to me. "Well, she is a very attractive woman, so I hope there isn't anything serious."

"That's just it. Never seen this before. You know what measles and chicken pox looks like?"

I had to grin. "Sure do. I had those and mumps when I was in the 4th grade."

"Then you have the picture. Almost like she fell face first into a cactus. Know what I mean?"

When I bunched my shoulders in sympathetic pain, Diaz smirked.

"Her face is covered with tiny, infected punctures…"

Now I leaned forward, intent on the nurse's description. When I thought of Ofelia Armendariz, I was seeing another face behind a screen door in Mogollon the weekend before.

63

Diaz was just about to continue when the elevator door opened 30 feet to my right. Suddenly she stopped as a man stepped out of the car and walked briskly in our direction. The nurse seemed to forget that I was there as she looked at the approaching figure, so all I could do was follow her eyes. The man was looking at me, smart suit jacket unbuttoned, a grey fedora in his right hand.

I heard a rustle of paper behind me, and my eyes darted toward the row of chairs. The man who had been sitting in the waiting area now abandoned the newspaper and stood up. I hadn't noticed before, but there was a charcoal grey fedora on the chair beside where he had been sitting. He stood apart, buttoning his own suit jacket.

"Can I have a word with you, Sir?" The voice was cool and impersonal, brooking no refusal.

"Yeah, I guess so." Nurse Diaz went to the other end of the station as I acquiesced, sizing up the man confronting me. He was my height, with the confident posture of a man in peak physical condition, He was wearing a silk and wool blend tailored charcoal suit, with a dark blue silk tie that complemented his suntanned complexion. I noticed immediately that his black shoes exhibited a perfect shine, and his short haircut was fresh.

Because of his appearance, I was surprised when he said, "I'm with the State Department of Public Health. I'd like to ask you a couple of questions concerning Mrs. Armendariz." My mind was in confusion. I was rejecting the idea that he was with public health, and I knew instinctively that he was not from New Mexico. Only lawyers and insurance salesmen wore suits, and while local men wore baseball caps and cowboy hats, nobody in San Vicente today wore New York hats, as we called them. It was obvious that the man standing just outside my peripheral vision was part of the team. When he asked for my name and address, I was immediately on the defensive, determined to tell him as little as possible.

"We need to know how you met Mrs. Armendariz." His eyes flicked momentarily to his partner standing off to the side. "We just want to make certain there is no possibility of any disease transmission."

Of course he couldn't be FBI, as they were required to identify themselves, but this clean-shaven guy in his 30s acted like a cop, and I suddenly felt perspiration condensing in my armpits. Was I a suspect? If Margo and I were the last to see the woman before she disappeared, we could be implicated as agents of her disappearance because she had no memory of what happened to her.

Reluctantly, I explained only that we were driving that Friday and encountered the disabled Armendariz vehicle, left her with the car when we drove to Glenwood and then returned, followed by a wrecker and a state cop. My story stopped with finding the vehicle abandoned.

The second man advanced a few steps while my interrogator made some notes. "You say it was Friday May 5?" He didn't say "fifth." He paused, then asked, "And it was maybe 1800 to 1900 Hours?"

"Yeah, yeah, about then. I don't remember looking at my watch." Though we were guiltless, I knew that trying to help people was often dangerous. Margo and I would be the perfect suspects if Ofelia's memory did not return, and I was feeling queasy. I had not eaten anything since breakfast. I jerked my thumb over my shoulder, "You guys have names?" I said it pleasantly.

The suit in front of me straightened his shoulders and gave me a narrow look. "I'm Roberts, and that's Pluman. Department of Public Health."

"Got it."

"So, what were you doing out there on May 5?" He knew it was none of his business without credentials.

"We were on a long drive, and we stopped to talk to our friend Bob in Glenwood."

Roberts moved his tongue as though searching for a piece of food in his cheek. He wrote it down.

"So, could I talk to Mrs. Armendariz?" I tilted my head.

He set his jaw. "Not possible. She is not having visitors." Roberts didn't mention that he was the exception to the rule. "We are making sure she is not contagious."

I didn't tell him that the best place to catch a disease was in a hospital. The two well-dressed men made me uncomfortable, but I shrugged and admitted defeat. I stuck my hand out and waved it at the friendly but prim nurse, "Thank you, Nurse Diaz," and I bid farewell to the men in the reception area, walking out into the parking lot as though I were escaping.

The noonday sun was brilliant and hot, despite high, broken clouds on the western horizon. I walked out onto the paved lot that was 50 percent full. Instead of going directly to the VW bus, I walked down a line of cars, looking for a New Mexico Government license plate. At the far end of the lot, I found a government license plate, but it was a U.S. Government plate, attached to a medium blue four-door Chevrolet Caprice, probably 1977 model. There was no logo on the door.

All afternoon I wondered if we would ever know the whole story of Mrs. Armendariz and whether we would be interviewed by police in connection with her strange disappearance. It was a relief to know that she somehow survived an inexplicable ordeal. I was reminded of an article I once read in a men's magazine years before, the author of which claimed that thousands of people go missing each year in the United States and never heard from again. I took the article with a grain of salt at the time.

After work, I gassed up the VW bus on the way home, listening to a reprise of news sponsored by Community Public Service on KSIL-AM. Yesterday's newspaper item was repeated in broadcast-speak, and I now knew there was more to the Armendariz hospitalization than the story revealed. Two men in suits had confirmed that.

It was not unusual, but Margo was a little late getting back from her office. I couldn't wait to tell her about my hospital adventure. She listened carefully, then picked up the phone, her voice animated, "Hello, Mom? Let me speak to Dad." There was a pause as she waited.

It then dawned on me that the call was about the men I encountered. Margo's father was a retired Air Force Lt. Colonel. I knew he did one tour at the Pentagon years ago. Margo had a quick mind, and when her father got on the line, Margo recounted my story almost word for word. Then she leaned over, into the phone as she listened, only saying,

"Really…you think so…you don't mean…I can't believe it…" After several minutes of listening, she finally said, "Ok, Dad. I appreciate it. We are off to Mogollon. Tell mom I love her. Bye!"

She scooted back on the couch and turned toward me as I sat beside her. "OK, Dad says…" She put up her finger and grinned, "…Dad says he knows who these guys probably are."

"You're kidding of course."

"Nope. My dad knows stuff. From the description of the car, and the guys you saw, you were interviewed by the AFOSI. Ever heard of them?" Her expression was winsome.

"It's all alphabet soup to me, but I think I've heard the term before."

Margo said it slowly, "It stands for Air Force Office of Special Investigations."

I felt my brow furrow, "That's really bizarre! What the hey would the Air Force be doing in San Vicente?" It didn't make sense because the USAF did not investigate domestic problems 150 miles away from the nearest Air Force base, much less masquerading as health department officials.

"I don't know, Rick, but Dad was very definite. He says they probably gave you false names and never did show you their ID. Is that right?"

"Come to think of it, they didn't, but they sure got my name and address, and it was obvious they weren't from around here."

"Maybe we can find out why they were visiting poor Ofelia Armendariz. I'm so glad she is back home."

It seemed we had just solved one mystery, only to be faced with another.

Seven

The Mogollon Horror

As it turned out, we did not leave San Vicente until a little after 6 p.m., and it would be twilight by the time we got to Mogollon. As the miles rolled by, I listened to the sound of the engine and tried to sit on the cavalcade of emotions stirring inside me. I tried to think about Margo and suppress intrusive mental images of Darouse Brunk. Our intermittent conversation in the car got me up to date on houses for sale in San Vicente, and we talked about our gallery plans for the long Memorial Day weekend, deferring any talk of UFOs and the paranormal.

Traffic was moderate and not unusual for the beginning of a New Mexico weekend. As we finally approached Glenwood, Margo jostled my arm. "Let's stop and talk to Bob. Maybe he knows about Ofelia."

Figuring that I might as well top up the gas tank, I downshifted as we entered the village limits and veered left to roll up beside the chrome-trimmed gas pumps. Bob was walking out of the station center as we approached. He was one of the last of the true service station attendants who still pumped gasoline for his customers. When I killed the engine, Margo and I unbuckled our seat belts and got out of the vehicle.

"You two headed up the hill?" Access to the tank was on Margo's side, and she nodded. We waited until he had pumped 4.7 gallons, and we followed him into the station office to make change from a $5 bill. We didn't even have to broach the subject of Ofelia Armendariz because Bob seemed eager to pick up where we had left off two weeks before. He stood behind the counter, made change, and leaned on the scratched Formica counter top.

"You missed all the excitement. Officer Coslin was the one who found that woman—the one with the Toronado. Most excitement we've had this year…or last three years for that matter." Bob smoothed back his thinning hair.

Margo jumped in, "We saw a newspaper story when Mrs. Armendariz got back home."

"Once our state cop found her, all hell broke loose. EMTs from Reserve, Catron County Sheriff, other State Police, and they were interviewing everybody in town. Nobody had any answers—still don't."

I was now more curious, "So, where did the officer find her?"

"You know, she was found close to the river, but about nine miles up toward Reserve."

I was visualizing the San Francisco river that ran south through Glenwood and as well through the forest. Silver Creek in Mogollon eventually drained into this small river. Even an experienced hiker would have a challenge going across country north past the Mogollon road and on toward Reserve. It seemed unlikely that the woman could have survived unless she had been kidnapped, and we knew there was no such opportunity the day we met her.

Margo was still pressing him, "So, do they think there was a crime?"

"Don't really know. Instead of taking her to Reserve, they came down here—lots of flashing lights, and officers talking. But, you know the funniest part came a few days ago." Bob shook his head.

"You mean funny, ha-ha?" I goaded him.

His head shake was definite, "Nope, it was funny strange. The two guys who came in—and they sure weren't from 'round here—seemed to know that her car was parked here for a couple days." Margo and I looked at each other. "They spent an hour questioning me and Officer Coslin. I couldn't figure what they wanted."

I didn't mention my encounter, but I asked Bob what he thought about them.

"Something' about their nice suits and haircuts. Thought they could be FBI, but they never identified themselves. I'll tell ya, they made me real nervous." Bob stabbed his left palm with his right index finger."

Margo sympathized, "I think you're right. Maybe we'll know more in a week or two."

It was obvious to me that we would not know more in a week, two weeks, or twenty years. We said good-bye to Bob and wished him a good weekend.

Bob came to the door as we went back to the bus. "One more thing—somebody told me it might rain tomorrow."

I threw an answer over my shoulder, "Bob, you know better than to bet on rain in New Mexico." Margo laughed, Bob waved dismissively, and we were on our way to Mogollon.

As the loaded little bus strained up the road in the fading minutes of the day, the vista of the valley and the forested mountains to the north was almost otherworldly. As we slowed for the great hairpin turn, we could see that the bank on our right was still crumbling but not obstructing the way forward. It seemed we always looked over the precipice and commented about the deep canyon below, where a line of tiny telephone poles gradually climbed the slope as they must have done since their installation in 1908. Margo also mentioned that she had taken the plastic-wrapped piece of shell and put it into the garbage can under the sink. "It was sitting on the counter for almost a week, and it looks to me like something dead." I agreed. It probably would have sat there, ignored, for weeks without Margo's practical decision.

We reached the highest altitude, now passing through the ponderosa pines growing close to the road, then down the twisting serpent road into Mogollon that always seemed longer than it actually was.

I saw the town as though for the first time, gloomy in the fading light, its buildings brooding as though fortified against the coming night. With little effort one could see shuffling ghosts of long-dead miners meandering up the street, going in and out of buildings. In the silence, it was almost possible to hear the raucous laughter of men stumbling out of the saloons in this canyon where there was little to life but the mine itself. This was a romance of the ghost town, now kept alive by a handful of residents and those who maintained the buildings as weekend getaways. Because there were no overnight accommodations in town, visitors either drove on into the forest to camp or back to the main highway. The absence of mainstays such as the Englishes and the Chandlers produced the aura of abandonment.

As we got out of the VW, I looked up the street. Not even the usual pair of lights above the overhang of the theater marquee greeted us, though a porchlight above the museum front door caused my stomach to jump. We carried our goods and supplies into the gallery, putting things into the small bar refrigerator in the kitchen area. As we put things away, I bumped into Margo. On impulse, I put my arms around her, "I love you, Margo."

Her smile was infectious. "What brought that on?"

"It's not the first time I've said it." As I held her, I felt the tug of real emotion while still feeling that duality that made me also desperately want to be in bed with Darouse Brunk. I could not reconcile the paradox then—or now.

When we finished organizing for the Saturday opening, we walked out into the darkening street. West of us in the leveled area south of the road, the McCarty Winnebago was hulking, a light glowing from a side window. "You know, I never thought about it, but it must have been a chore to get that monster up the road and around the turn."

Margo put her hand to her brow, "Well, they don't come up every weekend, but Ouida said, because they're retired, they sometimes stay up here for a couple of weeks at a time."

"I guess somebody's got to run the town." The modernity of the recreation vehicle was in stark contrast to the old buildings stretched along the canyon sides pressing against the main road. Then we looked up the road toward the town, and I saw the back end of the Brunks' Ford 250 pickup protruding from the far side of the museum. It seemed to me that the truck was in the same place as I remembered it from the week before, but it seemed unlikely that they would have left their son alone in El Paso for an entire week.

Margo took my arm, "Let's go up and say hello. It's still early."

I pulled back. "Oh, you go ahead. I think I left something in the bus. Let me know how they are doing."

"OK," she said brightly, as she walked up the road toward the museum. I stood there in shadow with queasiness in my stomach. Then I went to look inside the empty vehicle and to putter inside the gallery, waiting for Margo to return.

She seemed pensive when she came back to the gallery 15 minutes later, and I was relieved when she gave me the update. "Mattie is really worried about Art. I think she's actually afraid of him. She says Art never threatened her until recently. She says he is up at the mine all the time, and he took a leave of absence from the dealership in El Paso."

"Is there something wrong with Art?" I was thinking about looking at Arthur Brunk through the filter of a screen door up at the mine.

Margo squinted and put her hands up to her hair as she shook her head. "Mattie says that there is something wrong with his face…"

I took a sharp breath as though suddenly smelling something putrid.

"…Mattie says that he has small open sores all over his face—sort of like smallpox—but when she wanted to take him to a doctor, he shoved her against the wall and walked out to go back to the mine. It's kind of creepy, don't you think?"

…like falling face first into a cactus. My thoughts ricocheted as Margo recounted her conversation. "But if they were in El Paso, it would be easy to get him to an emergency room." My protest was feeble.

"That's just the thing! From what Mattie says, they've been up here since last week. If I didn't know her so well, I would say she is scared. She even says she's heard strange noises and the museum door rattling in the middle of the night."

Of course Margo did not really know Darouse; she only knew Mattie. I was ashamed, but I did not want to say anything that might scare her, especially since I was more confused than ever about the darkness settling over the town, in more ways than one. I thought we would find this weekend that the strange phenomena had a reasonable explanation no more arcane than a poltergeist or some erratic haunting event, with the rest being a product of what was possibly collective imagination. Now immersed again in the Mogollon atmosphere, I knew none of that thinking was true.

"Later I'm going to take her some of our food. I don't think Mattie has much in the way of supplies right now." Everything Margo said enhanced my guilt.

Margo continued, "It seems so lonely here tonight. We should at least go up to Brub and Ouida's RV. They must be bored to death."

It was still twilight when we walked up the entrance road, and across the rocks, gravel and brush to the graded track that led to the bulldozer leveled space where the luxurious McCarty home on wheels was sitting, with Brub's red three-wheel Honda parked behind the RV. Ouida answered our knock and invited us in. "Come in, come in. We missed you last week, Margo." The very small number of residents in the ghost town meant that there was a normal interaction among most of them on a daily basis—old man Akeley excepted.

Ouida ushered us into the compact living room, and we sat on their comfortable couch. Brub had not moved from his recliner, which he filled with his considerable six feet. Leaning back, he raised his eyebrows and lifted his head along with them, "So, Rick, you want to visit the mine again this weekend?" His hands were clasped on his stomach. "Far as I know, the new mining company won't be moving in their ore crusher until after Memorial Day."

I snorted. "Don't know about that, Brub. They didn't make us feel welcome last week."

"You know, I drove up there during the week, and the barriers are still up, so I didn't try to stop in. Akeley doesn't want visitors, Brunk is up there all the time. Doesn't make sense."

Margo interjected, "Doesn't make sense?"

Brub grinned at her, "Hell, I mean he even spends the night at the mine, while his wife is looking better every day."

Ouida turned from the kitchen area with cups of coffee for us, her sparkling eyes fixed on her husband, "Brub! You're worse than any gossip from here to San Vicente." She was the perfect foil for her husband's leonine expansiveness.

I took the cup of coffee and noticed a paperback book wedged in the corner of the couch. I recognized it: the 1967 book by Coral and Jim Lorenzen UFO Occupants. I wanted to change the subject. "Brub, I didn't know you had an interest in flying saucers." It was a question.

"Nah, not me," he jerked his thumb toward his wife, "my bride of 26 years is always reading about stuff like that. I just let her educate me. Right, Dear?"

"Somebody has to do it." Ouida edged past him, squeezing his leg before sinking into her soft chair with the flower print cushions.

Margo leaned forward toward Ouida, "You know that Rick has always been interested in stuff like that. I think he has that book you're reading. I believe there are ordinary reasons for most of the strange stories."

Brub chuckled. "Sweet Cheeks, it doesn't matter what you believe—stuff happens, even here in this place."

Margo smiled indulgently, "There may be strange things here in Mogollon, but I'm sure they can be explained. Rick talks a lot about flying saucers and strange events, but I think he is looking for a fantastic explanation. As for aliens, I'll bet they are like the movie 'E.T.' rather than scary things."

Ouida was shaking her head. "Well, Margo, you've heard about that Travis Walton abduction three years ago just over the border in Arizona. Whatever did that was not a nice, friendly visitor, and I think Betty and Barney Hill in New England were taken aboard a big flying saucer too—that was in the '60s."

"Oh, I should tell you that I was wondering about that missing woman, Ofelia Armendariz, but she turned up after all." Margo was her charming self.

Ouida scrunched her lips. "Wouldn't be too quick to write that off."

I interjected, "What do you mean? Did you know about that case? We were the last to see her before she wandered off."

Brub's wife settled in her chair and leaned back against the puffy head cushion, careful not to mess up her hair, "There you go with the 'wandered off' explanation. I read the newspaper story, but just because we are used to normal events doesn't mean that strange things can't happen. More coffee?"

We both declined as Brub injected his opinion, "I don't agree with my wife most of the time, but I know there are events that are just…well, out of place. Something happened to that woman."

"I have to agree with you," I said, putting the coffee cup on an end table. "I keep wanting to make things fit with what I have experienced in my life, but I know when something doesn't fit."

Ouida introduced the name Ivan T. Sanderson to the conversation, and I knew of his work as a biologist, cryptozoologist, and UFO writer who died five years before. "Most people know about the Braxton County monster, and he went to West Virginia only days after that happened."

I had vaguely heard about the 1952 case but it was discounted by the U.S. Military as a large owl in a tree rather than a monstrous being. "What did Sanderson find?"

"He interviewed the witnesses and reported that they all saw a monstrous being, possible in some kind of metal suit, and that it had come out of a large craft that landed on a hill. But that wasn't the strange part. Even if we pooh-pooh flying saucers, we have made flying saucer beings part of our culture—E.T. and all that stuff."

Margo leaned forward, "And, so?"

"OK, so Sanderson followed the locals' directions and found more than one site where something heavy landed and left again." Ouida's eyes glinted as she got into her story.

Brub was looking at me and challenging me with his grin. "She'll get to the strange part, don't you worry."

"I always remember what he said he found. He was an educated biologist, and he found what appeared to be a landing site on a saddle between two hills. There were three deep impressions, like landing pod traces, and a large circular space where the grass was flattened. He and his companion saw a small pile of white, curled up fragments that looked like plastic. Sanderson suspected they were organic and took them away for testing."

"Were they identified?" She had my attention.

"Not really. Sanderson said they looked like scraps from reptile eggs, except when soaked in water, one of the fragments stretched out to six-and-a-half inches—too big for any reptile egg on this continent."

Margo wrinkled her nose, "Reptiles piloting UFOs? That sounds so…"

"Strange." I finished her sentence.

"Yes, like Rick himself," Margo smirked, and I accepted the compliment with a nod.

"That's what I am thinking about here in Mogollon. When you experience something that doesn't fit, you have to explain it or pretend it never happened." Ouida was voicing so many things that were racing around in my mind since the first sounds I heard on the forest path.

I put my hand on Margo's knee, "You guys know that I never saw a flying saucer or a ghost, so it has been academic up to now. But I have to say that I saw something in the Holland Store two weeks ago."

McCarty's laugh was braying, "Yeah, and you shot up the place! Wait'll the absentee owners come back from wherever the hell they are."

My smile must have been sheepish. "There was something in there," I protested, "and don't forget what Sarah Petroski heard outside her bedroom window."

McCarty nodded vigorously, "Like I said, stuff happens, and we can't always make sense out of it."

THE WHISPERING DARKNESS

Now I was remembering an experience I had in the Organ Mountains east of Las Cruces, N.M., when hiking in those rugged slopes in the years right after college. There was a dammed-up area that served as an occasional stock pond to catch summer rains. It was in a declivity between two rocky slopes. It only held water once or twice a year, and I had never seen anything unusual except larva, a few toads, and an occasional garter snake. One summer day, though, I made my way over the rocks to the usually dry bed, only to find it brimming with rainwater. And that was not all.

I saw a mass of grotesque undulating little creatures I had never seen before. I describe them now, as I did then, as looking just like miniature trilobites from the Triassic period. There were hundreds of them, wriggling in the shallow water, multiple legs paddling, snouts moving in the muck. They were alien to my experience, and I even tried to compare them to tiny horseshoe crabs as I tried vainly to categorize them. There was something ugly about their flat bodies that stimulated caution as well as curiosity.

Back at the university, I went to the Biology Department, and one of the young professors suggested that they were hellgrammites. Years later I ran across a reference that illustrated the hellgrammite as a larval form of the Dobson's Fly. Its long body looked nothing like the tiny horrors I saw in that pond, and three weeks later, when I climbed to the same spot, there was no trace of the creatures. I never saw them again. In a microcosm, this was the unexplained.

Ouida continued, "It's a good thing that only a few people experience such strange things. Travis Walton and the Hills never will have the comfort of the ordinary world. Something is out there, and I pity those who are targets of those things."

The tendrils of dread were returning, wrapping around my stomach, "I don't care how much education we have or how fearless we are, I know that we are all frightened when we experience the unbelievable. If there are ghosts, they produce terror in ordinary humans, and if we were to meet the Devil on a lonely path, we would be cold with fear. Maybe there are friendly space aliens, but I think that to actually be confronted by a being from outer space would reduce us to panic."

Brub raised his arm, index finger pointing, "Or make us empty our guns." He looked at me under lowered brows. I grimaced.

Margo effected a stage shudder, "Rick knows I have never had interest in horror stories, but I always carried a camera just in case I saw a UFO. It has never happened. The closest I get is with Rick's occult and flying saucer talk."

"Guilty as charged! But, I have written an article for Fate magazine." I was now hoping my next article would be "The Mundane Mogollon Manifestations."

Margo snickered and brought out her best argument against alien meddling with the human environment—one I had difficulty disputing. "Rick here, and that guy Von Daniken, talk about UFO visitors, but if these cute little guys have the ability to fly among the stars, they surely would have resources far beyond what we have here on Earth."

I started to blurt out a defense, but Ouida beat me to it. "Oh, Margo, you absolutely have to read this book, even though it is ten years old. There are absolutely credible stories of people watching strange craft floating on small lakes and putting hoses into the water.

Others have observed strange creatures carrying what looks like minerals and plants. Then we could talk about many cases reported where these things attacked humans or grabbed them and took them into their craft."

Margo's shudder wasn't artificial this time. "Mmmm, I don't want to hear about that. I don't like to think that people really get abducted."

I just put on an exaggerated grin as Margo ignored me, her knee moving over to knock against mine. I turned to Brub, "We're not solving anything. We could all be wrong. Anyhow, you and I could take a ride up to the cemetery and the mine tomorrow afternoon, if you want to pick me up on your three-wheeler."

Ouida seconded the motion. "Yes, you boys go up there, because I am more than worried about Mattie and what is happening with her husband. I don't know what kind of business Art is concerned with up there at the Akeley house." We all sat silently, thinking about the discomfiting change that seemed to have come over Arthur Brunk, even to some kind of physical decline.

We stood up and, thanking the McCartys for their hospitality, we stepped down out of the RV and walked back to the gallery under the waxing moon. The sky was black velvet with diamond stars undamped by the light pollution of towns and cities. As I looked up, I remembered one of my early memories as a pre-school child, wondering what was beyond the last star. Even this night, the vastness of the universe was spread out before us, challenging the boundaries of our knowledge as it has done from the beginning of human life.

For some reason I thought of Akeley the recluse, and I remembered the inhuman wail I had heard that night across the street from the Mogollon Theater. We stood together momentarily, looking up Mogollon's main street. The faint yellowish light from the museum window reminded me of the woman inside. Was she thinking about me? Mercilessly, I pushed the thought from my mind as though it was a demon voice calling to me.

The street was vacant, and Margo leaned close to me, her fragrant blond hair on my shoulder. "Rick, do you hear that? I thought Brub said the new mining people weren't going to start anything for at least another couple of weeks."

"Hear what?" Margo had particularly sensitive ears, and besides, women hear high frequencies better than men, I rationalized.

"Just listen."

I closed my eyes and concentrated. Then I heard it, almost a whisper of a noise in the night, like the muffled sound of strange machinery somewhere beyond the range of perception, reflecting off of the near-vertical mountains forming Silver Creek Canyon. Could the sounds be the whine of a generator? Perhaps the whistling rush of air stirred by the rapid the movie sets from the 1960s fit the period. As vehicles started coming into town, we opened the gallery early and were engaged in business and conversation for the most of the morning. More than one family asked us about the barriers that kept them from touring the old mine, and neither Margo nor I had convincing explanations.

About 11 a.m., there was a lull, and we walked out into the street only to see Darouse Brunk standing outside the front door of the museum. Margo walked up the street to talk with her, but I hung back, feeling apprehensive. They talked briefly and then Darouse ushered Margo inside the museum. As she followed my wife inside, she turned briefly and looked at me as though knowing I wanted her. My balance was upset, and I cursed my own weakness.

Back in the gallery, I agonized as I imagined the conversation between Margo and Darouse. It seemed that Margo was there for a half hour, but it must have been far less. She came back and said that Mattie could use some of our spare food items. She reported that Art was now staying full time at the mine, and she hadn't seen her husband for days.

As Margo talked, I imagined impossible things—Arthur Brunk signing the Devil's own book, or Arthur Brunk becoming a soulless agent of some unspeakable horror lurking invisibly in the town of Mogollon, crawling through hidden underground mineshafts or walking abroad in the night. I was ambivalent, but now I wanted to confront Arthur Brunk and to interview Akeley to see that he was not being held hostage by Brunk, or any other hidden individual we had not identified.

Margo delivered some groceries to Darouse Brunk and, once again, I made excuses not to walk down to the museum with her. I knew that if Darouse did not hint what had happened between us, Margo's keen intuition would sooner or later suspect the encounters.

Fortunately for me, the next two hours were hectic as visitors were in and out of the gallery. One young man in a cowboy hat and boots, who had obviously brought beer on his trip into the forest was intent on purchasing a stained-glass roadrunner suncatcher, but Margo had sold the only one she had. She promised that she would complete a second one if he was willing to come back in about 90 minutes. He agreed, and Margo worked under intense pressure to cut the glass pieces, grind the edges, wrap the edges with adhesive copper foil, and then assemble the design and solder the pieces together until the colorful glass bird panel was ready to fly.

I assisted in the grinding and foil application, so when the man returned, the 8" bird was ready for display, and the young cowboy from Arizona said he was pleased. It was just after noon when the traffic dwindled, and I walked out into the street, feeling the waves of heat from the overhead sun as it radiated from the dark pavement. Margo was inside working on a stained- glass panel she hoped would be displayed in the gallery window during the Memorial Day weekend.

As I stood in my jeans and t-shirt, I looked up the street, half-hoping to see Darouse Brunk come to the door of the museum, but instead I found myself watching a 1972 Ford Pinto with a light green paint job now fading to grey on the hood surface. It was moving unusually fast, and the driver looked at me in passing and then cranked his steering wheel as his two-door car slid into the parking area alongside our VW bus.

A young couple came out of the vehicle in a burst of energy, walking swiftly up to me, and I greeted them, suddenly becoming aware that they were agitated. The man was in his late 20s, dark hair already thinning while his wife had enough massive curls for two people. "Is something wrong?" I asked, unnecessarily.

The girl was almost hyperventilating as she blurted out, "Do you have any cops here?"

I opened my arms and made a sweeping gesture, "No government, no police—just your regular ghost town here. They even closed the post office in 1947.

The man put his arm around the girl as she caught her breath and continued, "There's a maniac up there."

"Up where?" I followed her pointing finger up the street, but somehow I knew what she was talking about. "Maybe we can help."

Taking turns talking, the way married couples sometimes do, they described how they had driven up to the cemetery and then saw the tour sign for the mine but their curiosity was stronger than the "Keep Out" signs.

The young man did not make eye contact, but his gaze shifted right, left, and up the street as though expecting a pursuer. He took on the narrative. "OK, we didn't mean any harm, and the sign says, 'Tour.' We were on the dirt road and walkin' past this old house when a crazy man—or a drunk—a guy on drugs, came staggering out of that house, pointing at us."

The wife cowered against her husband. "He was horrible—horrible." She was shuddering.

I stepped closer. "What do you mean? His language?" Again, my words were absurd as I imagined what she was going to say next.

"He was cursing us and using words I never heard. He stumbled off the front porch and came at us. His face was all bloody and dripping. My God!" She buried her face in her husband's chest, as I thought that God had nothing to do with what was up there at the mine.

Mogollon Fanny Mine   RickPhoto 1978

"What did he say? Do you remember?"

The man looked full into my face, "I'll never forget that face with its bleeding sores. He had foam on his mouth. He pointed like he was casting lightning bolts and saying, "No trespassing. Go away. Then he said something like 'eeeya.' The guy has to be looney."

Margo had come to the door of the gallery, and I shot her a glance. "Did he have a weapon?"

The girl looked at me and shook her head vigorously, her curls flying. "He didn't need a weapon. His face was horrible—evil. He held out his arms and his hands pointed at us, vibrating-like and looking like claws."

I ventured, "Was he a really old guy with a bushy beard?"

The young man didn't hesitate. "Uh-uh. He looked clean-shaved except that his face was covered…" He screwed up his mouth in bitter distaste.

I scratched my chin and looked up. "Did he actually charge at you?" I knew who it was and hated the realization.

The girl touched her husband's cheek, still in the protection of his sheltering arm. "No, no, he was staggering, walking like a drunk, dragging his feet. I am still scared. We're getting out of here."

I looked over at Margo, who was staring in disbelief, as I framed a meaningless response. "I think we know who that is, and he is a local character. I'm glad he didn't attack you, and I think his family will be taking him for evaluation."

Margo approached, "Can we get you anything?" The young woman sighed, her face relaxing as she asked for a glass of cold water, something we had plenty of from the well. Margo took the pair inside while I stood in the street, visualizing the descent of Arthur Brunk into something worse than madness. While I stood there, three older people emerged from the museum two doors down, and Darouse Brunk followed them outside as they all talked cheerfully. When the visitors walked past the Brunks' grey pickup, Darouse was still standing there shading her face with a hand over her brow; then she turned and gave me a languid gaze. She was wearing a tight-fitting burgundy blouse, and she slowly put her hands under her breasts, not saying anything as she turned and went back inside. Someone once suggested that men desire women for what they appear to be, and women desire men for what men can do for them. I had no idea what Arthur Brunk's wife really wanted.

My heart was pounding, and the horrifying implication lurking in the ghost town was suddenly forgotten for a moment, as were other things that should be important to me. I called it my "brainstorm," and it was my nemesis.

As the young couple came out of the gallery, I looked upward to the western sky and saw an unexpected sight for a May afternoon. A wall of dark cumulo-nimbus clouds was looming but not yet masking the penetrating heat of the sun.

Margo bade the couple good-bye, promising to report the incident when we came down from the mountains at the end of the weekend. As they went to their two-door Pinto, Margo talked to me, though her eyes were on the departing tourists. "It's Art Brunk. Poor Mattie. We've got to do something. He might hurt her."

"Margo, I don't think he's crazy. It's worse than that. If she's smart, Da…Mattie…

Fanny Mine Bath house and Head Frame   RickPhoto 1978

should pack up, get into that truck and get out of here."

"Do you think Art is dangerous?"

"Yeah, I think he is." I jerked my thumb toward the McCarty Winnebago 100 yards away. "He and I are going to ride up there in a little while."

"Well you better get going in case it rains."

I dismissed her concern, "Rain? First, it's Bob down in Glenwood—now you. Never bet on rain in New Mexico."

Margo compressed her lips as though about to laugh, but she was courteous enough to let me persist as she decided to go encourage Mattie Brunk to consider leaving for safety's sake. Again, I found an excuse for not accompanying my wife as she headed for the museum.

I stepped up into the gallery to await additional visitors. I surveyed the photos and stained glass pieces on display and several 8x10 Agfa Brovira black and white prints on the work table awaiting the mounting process. One of my prints showed Sparky the dog sitting at the door of the gallery looking in. Flash fill enhanced the details on his face, but I was now thinking about a chunk of shell-like substance that he had brought me. Something was not right in the rustic ghost town.

It seemed to me that Margo was at the museum for a long time, and I could not help agonizing in case Darouse decided to tell my wife what had happened the week before, and when Margo broke my photo concentration with her entrance, I was relieved at her pleasant demeanor.

"Well, Mattie says she's really worried about her husband, but she doesn't want to leave without him. She hasn't seen him all weekend, and I think she probably doesn't want him around her. I hope she'll be OK down there." Margo held up a plastic grocery bag. "She made some egg salad sandwiches—enough for you and me. Let's have lunch."

As we took time to eat, I glanced out the front windows and noticed that the bright sunlight had dimmed as though clouds were advancing over Mogollon. Margo found a dab of Miracle Whip in her sandwich and used her index finger to reach out and put it onto my nose. "Maybe rain, huh?" She was enjoying the moment.

"Yeah, yeah. Don't rub it in." I wasn't talking about the cream on my nose.

A half hour later, the sun was totally occluded, and it corresponded with a decline in traffic. It was possible that rain was falling on the west side of the peaks, and when I went back outside, I could sense an increase in humidity but no raindrops. The trickle of Silver Creek wandered under the broad porch of the Holland store as it had for a century, presenting me with a ghost town idyll always worth photographing. The sky was now completely overcast, and my concentration was broken by the sound of McCarty's Honda three-wheeler rolling down from his RV site and headed for me.

Interior, Mogollon Gallery   RickPhoto 1978

He came to a stop beside me and shouted over the engine noise, "Ready to go?"

I drew my finger across in front of my throat, and he killed the engine. I explained the encounter with the distraught couple before lunch, and Brub nodded, shifting the toothpick from one side of his mouth to the other, his face shaded by the beige cowboy hat. That was when I noticed that he had added a shiny and compact black pistol holster onto his belt. The walnut grip of the pistol carried the metal signet with the "S&W" logo.

McCarty said, "I'm ready. Are you?" I had to admit the cowboy hat gave him a rakish look.

"Hang on." I looked at the sky, made a quick judgment and then hurried up the stairs of the gallery to retrieve my .45 and a couple of spare magazines, shoving them into my pockets. It was warm enough that I did not consider changing to a denim shirt. As I trotted back down the outside stairs, my steel-toed engineer boots made a racket that brought Margo to the gallery door.

McCarty nodded to Margo. "If you get a few minutes, you might go talk to my wife. With the Chandlers and the Englishes gone, she hasn't had many people to talk to."

"Rick, do you really need that gun?" Margo always did hope I would outgrow the habit.

"Maybe not, but it's better to have it and not need it, than need it and not have it."

Margo rolled her eyes. "Well, you boys have fun. See if you can talk to Art Brunk. I think he needs some serious help."

I climbed onto the Honda and waved back as we jolted up the street. We passed the museum, the theater, the Hollywood movie store front, and I noticed small dark spots on the street before I felt droplets hitting my shoulder and my face. A light sprinkle was beginning, and I wished I had thought to wear a cap.

The Mogollon Church   RickPhoto 1978

THE WHISPERING DARKNESS

We passed the closed church, looming above us with the corrugated metal sheet nailed to its doors, and McCarty made the left turn up the hill toward the cemetery and around toward the mine.

Another half mile of dirt road led to the mine where he pulled in and stopped. As we climbed off the Honda, I breathed the intoxicating rain smell but it was not so comforting as it usually is in the desert Southwest.

Stretching across the dirt road beside the metal sign advertising "Inter (sic) for tour," were the sawhorses and hastily hand-lettered signs on white painted plywood. One read: "Mine Closed," and another still-wet panel sitting on the ground and leaning against the barrier, read: "No Trespassing."

I looked at McCarty, "Well, Mr. Mayor, let's go."

McCarty gave me his raised chin, and we walked around the end of the barrier and proceeded toward the Akeley house under the light sprinkle. The faded blue Chevrolet Blazer was still sitting beside the house, but this time with the hood raised. I walked up onto the hollow-sounding porch and started to knock on the ancient screen door, but I noticed that the interior door was closed. I heard no sounds from the interior.

McCarty was motioning to me, "Come on, I saw somebody." He said it quietly, and I came off the porch as silently as possible. We started walking along the gravel path lined with dry tumbleweeds.

Towering above was the girdered headframe with its silent pulleys and dangling severed cables. The mill was a complex of metal-and lumber frame buildings with galvanized roofs that had weathered the decades. The light rain under a leaden sky set up a staccato rhythm on the metal roof sheets, sounding like salt poured on a sheet of aluminum foil. There were metal posts linked by sagging ropes to guide the tours. The first building was identified with a two-piece wooden sign nailed to its corner by the door that read "Bath House," and we looked through the wood-framed portal into the blackness.

Suddenly there was a clash of collapsing sheet metal in one of the buildings along the path, and we picked up the pace, pushing aside a hanging panel and entered a cavernous mill building. The sound of rain on the building roof was punctuated with water now dripping through separation in the roof panels. The few windows no longer had glass and an acrid chemical smell assaulted our nostrils as a dirty cloud of dust from whatever had collapsed now engulfed us. Grey light diffused through the dust as I tasted something bitter on my palate. "What's going on in here?" I muttered.

McCarty said the obvious, "Damned if I know."

The mill building was built along the incline of the hill, and at one side was the framework of a conveyor system whose heavy belts had long since separated and drooped on the bearings. A decrepit wooden ramp followed the conveyor system up into the semi-darkness with spaced 2"x2" pieces of wood in the stead of a stairway.

"Listen!" I put my hand on McCarty's sleeve.

The sudden high-pitched whine Margo had heard the night before was now piercing my temples and it felt like a supersonic dentist's drill inside my skull. McCarty had his hands to his ears. He looked at me, eyes squinting, teeth gritting, "There's no power in here now. The

Head Frame and Fanny Mine Buildings   RickPhoto 1978

Venture guys haven't got anything hooked up yet."

We were here, and my growing fear was overcome by my need to appear competent to another male. Without saying anything, we dared each other to ascend the ramp toward that high pitched whine with the drumming on the leaking roof, the acidic taste in our mouths and the dust sticking to our skin. As we walked upward on the worn and splintering ramp, the last window frame was below and behind us now, and there was a dark, level place at the top of the conveyer.

Yet, it was not dark. There was a dim, reddish-orange nimbus in the cavernous enclosure, as though emanating from a bonfire but with no flickering, no wavering of the unseen flame. The whine began to soften, decline, until it disappeared, but my temples were still throbbing, my throat burning from the acid dust. Dirty water was dripping from the gaps in the roof, and my mouth was gritty. I knew from past experience that the mine underneath the mountain was layered in galleries connected by a rabbit warren of tunnels.

We were almost to the upper level from where the red-orange glow emanated. Suddenly it did not matter if the Devil and his minions were supernatural or otherworldly. The unique sense of fear would be the same. Were we about to see something indescribable? Even Brub McCarty, as earthy a man as I had ever met, was silent and staring into the semi-darkness. The thrumming of rain on the roof mocked any normalcy that should have existed.

Something was moving at the top of the incline, coming from the direction of that sickly illumination. McCarty stuck out his arm to stop us as a shape lurched, shambling in our direction. An image flashed into my mind of a grinning demon approaching with the Devil's black book in which to sign away our eternal souls, but the reality was perhaps even more disturbing. I did not like the way the approaching shape began to reveal itself.

We were still on the ramp and not yet at eye level as the figure came at us, almost stiff-legged. McCarty intoned, "Damned if it's not Art Brunk," but he was too generous in his description. Thankfully, the grey light was limited, and the disused milling machines created hulking silhouettes and dark shadows from which Arthur Brunk was becoming visible.

THE WHISPERING DARKNESS

His disheveled clothing hung upon him like burlap, and his arms were at his sides. Emblazoned in my mind was the hellish manner in which his forearms and clawed hands were twisting, ever-moving, as though he were opening the handles of invisible faucets.

Thank God for the dimness, as it partially masked the hideous appearance of Brunk's face. The small sores that began as a sunburn, then pock marks, had become swollen, suppurating sores, infected and dripping, his eyes sunken, lips squirming. The sepulchral voice was hollow and menacing. At first, it was jumbled muttering, almost a whisper, but it became more articulate as he approached.

Neither McCarty nor myself thought to draw our guns, because this, after all, was the Arthur Brunk who drove a new truck, had an attractive wife, and who sold cars in El Paso, Texas. Still, we began to back away down the ramp as he approached.

The menace in the voice chilled me as though a curse from an evil, supernatural entity of which Brunk was but its sleepwalking agent. The ever-twisting hands reached outward as the two of us backed slowly down the wooden ramp.

"This place…Iä…is the gate…Shub Niggurath…You will…come…will come to us…ftagn." The thing that was Arthur Brunk shuddered, lifting its head as though listening to something—and I heard it too.

It was like the modulated buzzing of a giant insect, not a vulture. It was the voice I had heard on the forest path. Brunk was also listening as its unintelligible drone whispered and then grew in volume as though in some unknown tongue, ending with those hellish syllables, "Iä…Shub Niggurath."

From my place on the ramp, still below the upper level, Brunk seemed to loom above us, blocking vision of what lay beyond, but I could see more—I saw a bulbous shape rising in the unhealthy glow, filtered by the dust stirred up by water dripping in a dirty stream through gaps in the root panels. I saw it—a thing—rising up, spreading bat-like black wings. It was a frightening vision such as must have assaulted those who saw devils and demons in medieval times. In my mind I could see hideous creatures deep inside the earth, pursuing an alien mission for purposes we could not even guess.

My mind was whirling as I remembered horror fiction I had read in my youth from a writer considered mad by some as he wrote of a seething chaos he named Azathoth at the center of the universe, and eldritch tales of hideous visitors to Earth—ah, the black goat of the woods with a thousand young. These things were not after all fiction, but the ravings of one who had stripped away the mask of the ordinary world to reveal a horror that made humans cower in their dwellings, fearful of what lurked in the darkness of the world, and what might lie beyond in the unimaginable reaches of empty space.

Brunk came toward us, haltingly, and we backed down, even though my impulse was to turn and flee as I had never wanted to run before. Was Brunk following us? We reached the lower level at the base of the conveyor belt system, and we then broke into a run, coming out into the slow rain still drumming on the roof of that terrible, hulking mill building. I looked back into the darkness but saw no sign that Brunk was following. Driven close to panic, we were fast-walking under the low-hanging clouds; desperate to get away, our clothes beginning to get wet, even though I had no thought for the steady, slow rain. I noticed that

McCarty had lost his hat, his wet hair plastered to his forehead.

"How about Akeley?" I asked as we approached the old frame house where Akeley lived.

McCarty was firm, "We need to get him out of there. I don't understand what I just saw with these eyes." His two forked fingers pointed to his face.

"You saw it too?"

"Damn right, and I'm never going to tell Ouida what we saw in there."

As we hastened along the dampened dirt track, I was still numb from the unthinkable things I had just witnessed and which tied together all that I had experienced and tried to deny in the previous two weeks. Behind us loomed the giant metal headframe with its dangling cables, and I thought of the warren of mine tunnels underneath the mountains, and wondered how one of those branches might emerge into the black tunnel at the back of the Holland store building. What if these hellish creatures were swarming under the earth, ready to vomit out onto an unsuspecting town?

Rainwater was dripping in thin streams from the metal roof of the Akeley porch. I pulled open the ancient screen door that still had the 18-inch-long coiled spring attached to the jamb to allow it to close automatically. I knocked urgently, my anxiety obvious in the force of my knuckles. There was no reply from the inside. McCarty and I looked at each other before he jostled me and grabbed the worn elliptical iron doorknob with its floral pattern and worn coat of paint. The door was unlocked and McCarty gave it a push as we were rewarded with a gust of stale air whose odor was a mix of common as well as indefinable smells.

There were no lights on inside the house, but an old console radio was humming with static as it stood against a far wall. I recalled that Akeley had a 20-foot tall wooden mast attached to the outer wall of his house to support a radio antenna. The radio against the wall was not tuned to any station. A ragged leather sofa was against the south wall with a low coffee table in front of it. A tarnished 19th Century brass surveyor's transit sat atop a wood and brass tripod by the west window, beside a set of shelves lined with mineral samples. Straight through from the front door was the entrance to what must be the kitchen or a dining room, but the door was closed. Two other closed doors may have led to bedrooms. There was no shotgun leaning against the wall by the front door, despite Mogollon rumors. The varnished pine flooring was covered by a grimy 9x12-foot area rug.

A rasping whisper from the darkest part of the room told me we were not alone. "Did you bring him back?" Old Man Akeley was slumped in an overstuffed leather chair whose arm coverings were torn. A floor lamp stood in the corner behind Akeley's chair, and his slippered feet were stretched onto a dilapidated leather footstool. He was wrapped in a terrycloth robe that had seen much better days, his desiccated hands poking out of the sleeves and gripping the chair arms. "I want Chino back here. They took him," Akeley's whisper seemed unsettling in the darkness of the afternoon with rain drumming on the roof.

I could not help but notice a large cushioned dog bed against the wall behind the chair. Around the chair, the floor was littered with the remains of plastic frozen dinner trays, empty glasses and two cups half full of cold, milky brown coffee. An overflowing ashtray on the floor supplied the stink that combined with other unidentified smells to make the aura of Akeley's house.

Only his mouth seemed to move, and his bushy hair and stained white beard covered much of his face, but I could see cruel penetrations on his sunken cheeks. I remembered the wailing night sound I heard when I was standing outside Mogollon Theater two Saturdays ago. Could this have been Akeley? What was this terrible syndrome that afflicted Arthur Brunk, and now Hiram Akeley? Was it some loathsome and unknown disease?

Akeley's rasping breath joined the muted static from the radio and the sound of the rain on the roof. We stood staring at the wreck of a man, his body almost a part of the deep chair, his head slumped forward on his chest. His voice chilled me as though it came as from a distant place, "I saw it…saw the ship…up to the mine…" his breath wheezed as from a toneless accordion. "…the light blinded me 'n' Chino. Ah, Gawd, when the light faded, they come outa the ship. They was comin' right through the wall. I feared fer me and fer Chino…" He did not look up, but both McCarty and me were riveted to his narrative.

"That ship. It's up there t' the mine, like a giant aluminum egg. That's what it is. But when ya look at it sideways, ya can see inside it…orange light…and they come outa it… Gawd knows what they want. They got Chino, and now…they got me." His last sentence ended with a deep cough.

Suddenly a tremor passed through Akeley's body as he seemed to be answering an inner call, "Yes…they…Iä…"

What was that? A word, that sound, chilled me as I stared at the figure in the chair. He was not speaking to us, if he even knew we were in his house. I squinted and looked more closely at the mineral display, and could see that there were 18 sample vials in a three-tiered display rack, each at least half full of gold dust and so labeled, and one vial with small gold nuggets lay on the shelf, its cap removed and the tiny irregular nuggets scattered on the shelf. One nugget was the size of a peanut—a considerable find, even in Mogollon. Was this what had drawn Arthur Brunk into Akeley's domain? Was the story of Akeley's treasure more than idle gossip?

McCarty approached Akeley, "He's in a bad way. Looks like Art was taking care of him."

"Doesn't make sense."

"Nothing going on up here makes sense, Rick. I don't mind admitting that I'm scared."

"Maybe we could get him onto your Honda or take him out to his car, if it will start."

The decision was made for us. A clatter erupted beyond the kitchen door. It was the metallic creak of a screen door opening in the back of the house, and of hard footsteps stumbling into a pile of kitchenware, spilling pans or dishes onto the floor in the room beyond.

"Art Brunk coming in the back door?" My first guess was wiped away as a powerful odor seeped into the room from beneath the kitchen door.

McCarty screwed up his mouth and blurted, "Jesus, what's that?"

I was already at the door, because the odor was something I knew well. I yanked the door open, and McCarty rushed out ahead of me. In seconds, I had pulled the door closed behind me, just as the kitchen door was opening. We were off the porch, down the steps, and sprinting toward the barriers. I let the soft fresh smell of rain cleanse my nostrils. The precipitation was now light but steady; the three-wheeler was wet and glistening. As McCarty started the engine, I sat down and felt the cold and damp soaking my backside.

McCarty shouted over the engine noise, "What the hell was he talking about—a ship?" I shouted back, "I sure don't want to go back to find out."

We rocketed back along the mine road, bouncing and skidding as we made the loop down the hill onto the pavement, mud spraying from the tires. We found a town that gave the illusion of being almost abandoned. There was no traffic, and I was sure we spent more time at the mine than I thought. Our pants were wet and muddy below the knees.

Under the snarl of the motor, I found myself thinking of an old Appalachian ballad "In the Pines," but I was changing the mournful lyrics and hearing myself singing under my breath, "In the mines, in the mines, where the sun never shines, and you shiver when the cold wind blows." On the right side of the road, trickling Silver Creek was swelling.

The Honda came to an abrupt stop in front of the gallery, and I swung off. McCarty looked at me; I thought he was naked without his lost hat, "Somebody needs to talk with Mattie. You want to do it?"

"Maybe…but let me talk to Margo first." I wanted to avoid being close to Darouse Brunk. "We should all think about getting out of here," I shouted over the revving motor. He gave me a brief wave and headed toward his RV site. The street was almost empty except for the rear end of the Brunk pickup visible near the east wall of the museum.

At the door of the gallery I saw a piece of paper affixed to the window pane with the large magic marker message "Back in 15 Minutes" and a smiley face. I entered the gallery, still feeling anxiety in my stomach along with the lurking undercurrent of dread. The ceiling lights flickered as I walked through the gallery to look behind the kitchen partition. Where was she? A sense of urgency was rising in my chest. Then I thought she might be at the museum with Darouse Brunk, and that also added to my discomfort.

I went to the back of the gallery, and several minutes later I jumped when the front door opened. I hastened to the entrance and found Margo collapsing an umbrella. "Where did you get that?"

Margo shook the umbrella, "I brought it to the gallery months ago, and you look like a wet puppy, tracking mud on our clean floor."

"Gee, thanks. Where did you go in the rain after we went up to the mine…?"

"I walked up to the RV and visited with Ouida McCarty when I saw that no cars were coming into town." Margo's good cheer seemed out of place to me as I stood with mud-spattered jeans and my shirt plastered to my body.

Margo looked quizzical but obviously not fully convinced. "The loudest noise down here was that noisy three-wheeler as you two vigilantes went up to the mine. One of the last visitors told me that it was raining harder on the other side of the mountain."

"Margo, I'm telling you that Art Brunk has turned into something horrible. And there was something not human at the mine." The lights flickered again.

Margo hugged me. "I know something is strange, but most people in town haven't seen anything. I don't know what to believe. Do you really think we have to leave after all we do to organize these weekends?"

I breathed heavily. "Yeah, I really think so. Maybe we should warn people."

"I don't think that's for us to do. Besides, most of the other permanent residents have phones. I know the Brunks have a phone in the museum. Help isn't that far away. Ouida told me that actually Frank Triolo is also gone this weekend—he has an appointment with the VA Hospital in El Paso."

As we were talking, the lights went out in the gallery, and I was sure the town was totally without power if the transmission line from Arizona failed. In the late afternoon greyness, the town seemed even darker. The light from the windows was not sufficient, and we went to the kitchen area where the kerosene lamps were kept. There was also a lamp upstairs in the living quarters that we had never had occasion to light.

Two lamps with clean chimneys added a warm 19th Century ambience to the gallery. "OK, Margo, I know that Akeley is in bad shape, and I'm telling you that Art Brunk tried to attack us up there. What if he comes down from the mine and attacks his wife? Maybe somebody should call the Catron County Sheriff or the State Police."

Margo was pensive. "He probably needs medical help. I'm sure Mattie would call somebody if she were worried."

"You are always so reasonable, but I can't tell you how scared I was—and still am. It is beyond anything I have ever encountered. You have to agree that I don't scare easily." I tried and failed to describe the visceral panic washing over me when I was confronted by something from the outside—it was the true Satan, a blasphemous vision from the Pit. It did not matter whether it was supernatural or extraterrestrial. As I thought about it, I felt the hair on the back of my neck rising.

We argued briefly, and my mention of real alien visitors brought Margo's adamant response. She was so definite about what was possible, and I understood how most humans coped with the unexplained, be it paranormal or extraterrestrial. It is comforting to think that we understand the nature of the universe, regardless of the evidence of the indescribable. Margo again closed the argument with her reasonable question of why would anyone bother to visit Earth. She rejected my argument that alien motives and desires must not only be unthinkable but their reasons for being here must be unimaginable to us.

Then Margo relented, "Rick, you saw Art, and I didn't. If you think he is a threat, then you should go down to the museum and tell Mattie to get somebody up here. She wouldn't believe me"

I shook my head, feeling a different kind of fear. "You might be more persuasive…"

Now I saw a hint of suspicion in her eyes. "You were up at the mine, not me."

"Let's get everything together and get out of here. It's all real. There's something that has come to town, and it has done horrible things to Old Man Akeley, and to Art Brunk."

Margo pondered for a few moments. "Maybe, just maybe, something is happening, but there are a bunch of people who live here…" She stopped momentarily, "OK, I will go upstairs and start getting things together—if you will go down there to the museum right now and call the police."

Scared and backed into a corner, I agreed and went out the door, feeling cold rain drops of rain on my face, my heart beating faster. As I pushed open the door to the museum, I saw Darouse at the counter with one of three oil lamps. She was lighting the tapers on a five-branch antique candelabra as I came in. She was wearing a satin blouse, and she was smiling.

"Rick, I was wondering when you would come to see me." She came closer and the subtle arrogance of her perfume was exciting. Her jutting breasts were almost touching me when I spoke, "You know I can't do this. Your husband has gone crazy up at the mine. We have to get somebody up here. The phone should still be working."

Darouse slowly closed her eyes, "I didn't want to think that, but Art started behaving strangely two weeks ago—and that infection on his face—I'm almost frightened by him now. Go ahead and call." She pushed against me briefly and then went to the counter to pull out the thin multi-community Bell Telephone directory that covered all of southwestern New Mexico, with the emergency phone numbers in the first four pages.

I got a tone and dialed the State Police. The connection was not good, but I explained that we had a person who was a danger to the Mogollon community, giving Matilda Brunk as the contact. The voice on the other end said that a unit would be dispatched when available. After hanging up, I put my hand on her shoulder and told her we would be leaving town shortly but that help was on the way. I suggested that she close the museum, get into the

Enchanted Light Gallery at Night　　　　　　　　　　　　　　　RickPhoto 1978

truck and head for El Paso before her husband came down from the mine.

Darouse's smile was enigmatic. "I'll be waiting for you, Rick."

I hastened from the museum, seeking emotional refuge at my gallery. Silver Creek was running stronger as it flowed beneath the broad porch of the Holland Store across the street. Somehow in the time after our experience at the mine, the hours had fled, and the overcast sky was part of a wet darkness as night came early to Mogollon. I knew we would be much safer tonight if we could just get on the road back to San Vicente. The dim glow of the kerosene lamps cast slightly wavering shadows on the gallery walls as I went outside to climb the stairs, leaving the door ajar.

Margo had everything ready as I entered the upstairs quarters. "Rick, you can take this box down to the car. Let's wait a few minutes until the police arrive. You need to talk to them anyway."

"I don't know. There hasn't been a vehicle on the street since Brub and I got back from the mine. I think we need to go."

"OK, but first, get the scissors and help me cut a sheet of plastic from the roll over there that we can put over the mattress, just in case our little friend in the rafters drops bombs on the bed."

That made sense, and we made sure that our possessions were safe for at least another week. As we were finishing, I heard noises through the floor. "What the heck is that?" We stopped and could definitely hear somebody downstairs.

"A visitor this late? Did you leave the door open?"

"I think I did. I'll go down and see if it is a very late tourist."

Replete with muddy jeans and scuffed boots, I went outside and back down the stairs to the gallery. The drizzle was tapering off, but the creek was running full with a harsh, threatening sound. I rounded the corner and approached the front door that was indeed standing open, but then I glanced across the street and saw the center doors of the Holland store yawning and wide open. A shock of fear pierced me as I stepped up into the gallery.

Then I saw It. The moment seared my retinas, and I could not understand what I was seeing inside my own building with its mundane art objects. I was frozen in the doorway. The guttering lamps now created ghastly shapes, and I could not move. The lamps cast a monstrous shadow on the rear partition leading to the kitchen area. A bulbous form glistened dully in the dimness, and my ears were assailed by a hideous buzzing sound.

The .45 was still in the right-hand pocket of my Levi's, and, with fumbling fingers, I desperately yanked it out and pulled back the slide. The thing was 10 feet away, and I crouched and took a two-hand stance as I fired, the explosions deafening in the enclosed space. Once, twice, three times, four times, five times! The sound of the 230 grain copper jacketed slugs striking the thing was like the THWACK of bullets striking the dense wood of a bowling pin. The bullets struck between the leathery demon wings affixed near the top of what could only be called a carapace. The arthropod form seemed to shudder.

And then, haltingly, jerkily…it turned around to face me.

It was a horror that should not exist anywhere in the cosmos—it was the bubbling heart of chaos from the beginnings of form, and now it was lunging toward me. The body was a bulging lozenge shape close to five feet tall, its rugose ventral side was segmented in horizontal bands, the extensions that must have been feet were cloven, and the entire body was fringed with stiff, hairlike spines. Protruding from the body were two pairs of extensions that were parodies of arms, each three feet long and approximately three inches in diameter, the segments constantly moving like wriggling ropes that terminated in cruel, three-pronged nippers of the same dull brownish horn that formed the body and feet of the horror. The nippers seemed to click in concert with the modulated buzzing noise coming from…

Dear God, it was a winged demon such as that which climbed out of the Pit, illustrated in woodcut engravings of the demonographers or was incubated in the crucible at the beginnings of a mindless universe. While it could have come from the vastness of space, it also could have broken into the world from the depths of the mine, wet and soiled from nitre-encrusted rock walls and hideous, dripping ceilings, down, down within those black tunnels deep inside the mountain. The monstrous thing had no head. Atop the chitinous hulk of a body as it lurched toward me was a domed protuberance perhaps 10 inches high and 6 inches wide.

I cannot describe my terror as I stared at a swollen excrescence that was not a face at all. From the flat surface of that faceless hump extended a mass of squirming, wormlike cilia, each the diameter of an earthworm, ending in a tiny black hole. These had to be sensory organs designed in a hell that even the mad artist Hieronymous Bosch could not conceive. Somewhere within that seething mass of tiny tentacles was an opening that made the buzzing words. "Iä…ftagn…Iä…"

I was overcome by the noisome stench, and I could see an oily black substance dripping onto the gallery floor, excreted from the bottom fringe of the lumbering body. My vision blurred, and I fired the last round into the chest of the horror as it lunged forward. The bullet staggered the thing, but its momentum carried it forward.

I yelled and threw up my left arm as those loathsome glistening, squirming worm things leaned into me. The writhing limbs struck me, and I felt a savage pinch on my side from the thorny jointed nippers. For a moment, the room disappeared as I fell backward to the floor under the gallery window. When I regained my senses, the thing had gone out the door into the night. My breath was ragged and choked. I struggled to my feet, my head throbbing as I pulled a full magazine from my back pocket to replace the empty one in the pistol, pressing the side lever on the .45 with my thumb to chamber a fresh round.

It must have been another full minute that my head reeled, while fragmentary hallucinations stormed my consciousness. In the vertigo, I saw things that could not be, and a sulfurous taste in my throat attended sounds and images that were meaningless to me. No drug-induced vision could be so horrific as what was filling my mind as I fought to gain control. I felt a mild stinging sensation on my left forearm where venom-laden tinctures from those hideous worms had touched me.

I tried to move my feet, and I looked down, certain that I saw cloven hooves as vertigo again assailed me, slamming me against the gallery wall, the alien stench clogging my nostrils. I looked down again and this time I could see my boots.

I shook my head and tried to rub away the blur to my vision. Just outside the door I could hear the punctuated buzzing of the horror creatures. Slowly, the film over my eyes began to dissipate, and I regained control of my body. I had to exorcise the images of cosmic terror injected into me and which had shown me things beyond my ability to understand. I had to get to Margo and keep her from being attacked by some alien horror whose existence she could not accept. She must have heard the gunfire, and I prayed she would stay upstairs until I got to her. I shook off the fog of that revolting touch, and I heard Margo calling my name.

I stumbled out the door, shouting, "Stay up there. Don't move. Shut the door." I heard the upstairs door close with a "thunk." Across the street I saw the monstrous arthropod wobbling as it mounted the porch of the Holland Store and disappeared into its maw, no doubt seeking the black tunnel that led to the mine and god knows where else.

When I turned to look up the street, I was faced with a tableau reminiscent of Dante's Inferno. Where was that State Police car? At the limit of my vision in the post-twilight I saw a bulbous figure gliding over the rustic houses and cabins, black wings spread, while clustering in the road were at least seven or eight of the faceless horrors. What were they seeking? Or were they sowing their loathsome seed in some manner yet unknown to us. Poor Akeley, poor Brunt, poor Chino. In a halting, shambling gait, the cloven-hoofed monsters were advancing. Could we escape before they reached this end of the road?

A shaft of light came from the direction of the McCarty Winnebago, and I saw Brub's figure, casting a long shadow onto the wet ground. At least his vehicle had a self-contained generator. I shouted in his direction, "Keep your gun handy and button up that RV!"

Maybe he saw what I was seeing, maybe not, but he waved briefly before slamming the side door of his dwelling on wheels.

Taking advantage of the time remaining, I ran up the outside stairs and knocked before entering our upstairs apartment. I was suddenly aware of the insanity of packing and loading the VW. To escape with our lives was the best we could ask for, unless we chose to barricade ourselves inside the building.

When Margo opened the door, I pushed inside and told her to grab her tote bag while I picked up my camera bag. By now she knew that we were in some kind of danger, even though she had thankfully not been face to face with the dark shapes advancing down the street.

"Get down the stairs and get into the car. I'll blow out the lamps in the gallery and lock the door. Whatever you do, don't look up the street!"

She no longer questioned what I had been saying all along, and I heard the metallic sound of the VW passenger side door open and close.

The tide of horror was creeping toward us on the paved street, and I went inside the gallery to snuff out the two kerosene lamps before hitting the latch switch, running out the door with the keys clutched in my left hand, the .45 in my right.

I opened the driver's side door and the dome light seemed very bright in the darkness. Margo was staring at me in stark horror, "Rick, you have to warn Mattie! The Police aren't here yet.'"

My impulse was to ignore her, but her eyes were serious and pleading. So, pistol in hand,

I took a deep breath. I went in a second time to make sure the lamps were extinguished and sprinted toward the museum. I still do not remember if I bothered to close the gallery door. I sprinted down two doors in the face of advancing shambling horrors, whose whispering buzz was resonating in my ears, almost as though I could understand what the sounds, "Iä… ftagn…shub niggurath" meant, and if I once understood the words, I would be lost to the world I knew.

The Brunks' truck had not moved, but the museum door was open, and the kerosene lamps were casting their shadows on the museum walls. I burst through the opening, calling, "Darouse, you have to get out now, or come with us…"

I stifled a yell as I saw her standing near the counter where I had last spoken with her. She was not alone.

Frozen by the hellish image before me, I wished I could erase what I was seeing. Arthur Brunk was standing silently close to his wife, staring in her direction, his suppurating face hideous with its running sores, his eyes blank, his arms at his sides, rotating, hands clutching as he made buzzing sounds in his throat. The words! The words were the same barbarous incantations that I heard on the forest path and within the sanctum of the gallery.

If Arthur Brunk were the only obstacle, I could save her, but my stomach was already lurching as I saw what stood between Brunk and his wife. And what I saw will never leave me—the blasphemous vision is seared into my brain that not even prayer can expunge.

Between Brunk and his wife was a loathsome horror whose body vibrated with buzzing as its rope-like tentacles wrapped around Darouse Brunk, its hellish protuberance pressed against her face, the wormlike cilia feasting upon her as she limply submitted to the embrace. It was the infernal kiss no less horrific than the kiss of the witches sabbat wherein the initiate kissed the filthy fundament of the Goat of Mendes—that image of Satanic adoration.

God help me, but I knew that the horror from beyond the solar system was feasting on the life force of Darouse, expressing a hellish ecstasy while Arthur Brunk stood in approval of the alien mission being accomplished.

The .45 was in my hand, but I was unable to move. I could not shoot the thing as it wrapped around the woman of the museum. As Arthur Brunk turned toward me, I saw a distorted look of triumph on his mangled face, and I bolted from the museum, running back to the vehicle that was our only hope of escaping from the horror of Mogollon.

I ran to the VW bus, grabbed the chrome door handle and vaulted into the driver's seat, slamming the door, throwing the pistol into the well between the seats and transferring the keys to my right hand in the span of a single second.

Margo seemed terrified. "What is it? Is she all right?"

My head was shaking, "No, she is not all right. Her husband is with her, Margo. I can't tell you…" And I couldn't.

With the clutch depressed, I turned the key, fearful that the engine might not start, but it caught instantly as I plunged the gear lever down and pulled it toward me. I let out the clutch and backed into the street, engine screaming.

Margo turned and looked out the window as the van careered onto the pavement. It was the first time I had ever heard her scream. "Those things, Rick, those things. What are they?"

It was more a demand than a question.

How could I tell her what I knew? As I rammed the shift lever into 1st gear, I mumbled something about "aliens" or "demons;" I can't remember which. What was now horrifying me was the noise inside my head—vibrating in the cells of my body. I was hearing the meaningless barbarous syllables in the punctuated droning whisper of those arthropodal horrors. I did not like that I could almost decipher their meaning, and I did not want to hear that insidious buzzing that seemed to be inside my head.

The four cylinders were winding to peak revolutions as the bus picked up momentum, the sealed beam headlights illuminating the wet pavement, with the trees shrouding the sides of the road.

Now into second gear, we picked up speed for the ascent. Both of us were on the edge of panic in the dim glow of the instrument panel, as though we were being chased by a ghastly throng of monstrous beings. We passed the cyanide pond, almost invisible at the right side of the road but for the colors of the "danger" signs on its perimeter. The rain had tapered off to a spackling of drops on the windshield. The trees rushed by like ghostly sentinels as we wound toward the summit. The road was littered with gravel and small tree limbs.

I gripped the wheel tightly, still imagining winged horrors following us. It seemed an hour of climbing with the engine laboring, but to reach the top and start down the western slope brought a sense of blessed relief, even though the night and the overcast hid the breathtaking view from us. Then I gasped as I saw the condition of the road.

As we started downward, the furious extent of the rain on the west side of the mountains revealed itself in the mud and detritus on the pavement. Water was still flooding the road and tumbling into the canyon on our right-hand side. We were forced slow the VW to a crawl, driving over ridges of mud and rocks where streams of water still coursed over the road.

Ahead, the bank had crumbled, and I had to drive over a ridge and hear the rocks scrape on the belly of the bus as I steered it near the edge of the drop off. Twenty-five yards later I steered hard against the bank because the pavement had caved into the ravine leaving barely enough room to allow our vehicle to pass.

With my hands clenching the steering wheel, I negotiated the treacherous pavement until we suddenly came to the hairpin turn and I slammed on the brakes, stopping just barely in time. The steep bank had partially collapsed, making the road appear impassible. In the blackness, we could not see the forlorn vehicle hulk at the bottom of the canyon, but I imagined our own white bus tumbling into oblivion. As we surveyed the collapsed bank, we saw a crumbled pile of rock at the inside of the pavement, blocking the road. At the extreme right margin of the pavement was a lone conglomerate boulder shaped like a ragged pear about three feet high. A ridge of mud ran across the highway, and water was cascading from the towering bank and pouring into the chasm on the right. Now we could see why Mogollon was out of reach for the authorities this night.

"Rick, what are we going to do?" I could tell that we were both feeling the return of desperate fear. "We can't walk, can we?" I appreciated Margo's gallows humor. The idea of walking through the storm-wracked darkness more than six miles to Alma or Glenwood was unthinkable. What if those things could fly over the mountains.

I put my face in my hands, trying to think. The engine was idling as I looked at the impassable obstacle in front of me. "There's only one way out…"

Margo grabbed my shoulder, "NO! That's crazy."

She knew what I was thinking. The only hope seemed to drive back into Mogollon and drive through the hell of alien creatures and to take the long, rough "travel at your own risk" road east into the forest and eventually winding northward to emerge onto the central plains of the state near Datil.

We could not stay here, alone and trapped, in case those flying hell creatures were to follow and find us with our backs against a crumbling wall on one side and hundreds of feet down into the canyon on the right.

In the faint glow of the instrument panel we talked about going back to Mogollon and barreling through town on the pavement and escaping into the forest on the eastern side. At least it was a chance, so I inched backward into the bank, cranked the wheel, turning and backing for a foot at a time, again and again, until the bus was pointed back up the road. We were grimly headed back toward the nest of horror.

Once more at the summit and winding down through the tree-lined road, my pulse was pounding, my pistol now in my lap as I held the wheel, white-knuckled, with both hands. We swung down the final curve and into Silver Creek Canyon, the pale bulk of the Holland Store on the left, our blacked-out gallery on the right. The headlights on high beam lanced out along the pavement.

The monstrous arthropods were there, waiting, even though the bus was hurtling at close to 40mph on the street of Mogollon. Two creatures with gesticulating tentacles stood by the open doors of the Holland store building, and the museum door was also wide open but no light was visible inside. Above the windshield, a dark, winged form was descending toward us from the dark sky above. At least a half dozen more alien things stood along the sides of the street as we barreled down along the pavement. Margo covered her eyes, unable to accept the monstrous nature of these indescribable beings that seemed too ghastly to be alive, yet they had somehow entered this world from the pitiless cosmos or from Hell itself.

On the left was the dark façade of the Mogollon Theater, and then on the right, the general store movie set. We hurtled onward toward where the road branched and went upward toward the cemetery and the entrance to the mine. By going straight ahead another hundred yards, we would be past the pavement and into the forest!

Then, to my horror, I saw in front of me the image that made me slam on the brakes. The bus slid on the wet pavement. Margo's eyes were now wide as she grabbed the handhold above the glove box. The road was blocked!

In the glare of the headlights was a new grey Ford crewcab pickup truck setting up a road block. My headlights shone into the truck interior, and there was nobody inside—just an empty truck parked crosswise on the only escape route from Mogollon.

Fear crystallized into panic, and desperation turned the steering wheel for us. We could not sit still with a host of faceless entities closing in, so a u-turn had us rolling back up the street and not sure why. I watched the lurching entities as they clustered at the edge of the pavement, their bodies reflecting the peripheral glow from the high beams. As we passed three of them, I saw flailing sets of arm-like appendages reaching out, the horny nippers striking the sides of the bus with hollow banging sounds.

One of them faced us in the center of the street as we approached, and I yanked the wheel, sending the bus into a parking area just east of the museum, then regaining the pavement. Yes, we could barricade ourselves upstairs in the gallery, but I was desperate to escape from the hellish forms and the doom that had come to Mogollon.

We passed the museum, whose door stood open, visualizing momentarily the loathsome tryst I had witnessed inside was still burning in my brain. My stomach lurched as I pushed the accelerator. Darouse Brunk was at the mercy of the alien horror and of her husband who was now their agent.

No other doors were open, and there were no other lights, not even inside the silent Winnebago at the west end of town.

As I downshifted to meet the incline and the turn leading out of the canyon, the rain picked up again. We were climbing, the engine straining as Mogollon disappeared behind the taillights. While the blocked road lay ahead of us, there was a temporary relief at our narrow escape from the nest of alien creatures. An involuntary image came to my mind of the mine chambers under the mountain, tunnels that even led into the Holland General Store. I could imagine a huddling mass of alien beings underground, perfectly attuned to darkness as they pursued the hellish mission that brought them to this world.

The road straightened out, and then the bus shook as something landed on top of us, sending shock waves through us with the sound as of a baseball bat striking the roof. When I saw a black, leathery wing tip wetly sticking to my side mirror, I acted instinctively.

I jammed the brake pedal as the bus slid forward. Margo grunted as inertia threw her forward against the restraint of her safety belt. She had not yet gathered the composure to scream as the bus came to a stop and the engine died.

As the vehicle lost its momentum, I heard a sliding sound catapulting a winged horror off the roof and tumbling onto the road in the glare of the headlights. Panicked and gasping in terror, I grabbed the .45 and threw open the driver's side door. Perhaps they couldn't die. Earlier, my bullets seemed to have very little effect, and I somehow knew they did not have human organs inside those hideous exoskeletons.

I could see no alternative, and the thing used its four horn-tipped tentacles to push it to its loathsome feet, black wings spreading, its body almost vibrating with angry, modulated, buzzing that was rising to the level of a droning noise.

There was no other sound in the forest except the soughing of raindrops coming down through the pine branches. The engine had died. The thing was advancing toward me from ten feet away as I stood behind the door of the vehicle. In my peripheral vision I could see Margo's pale face reflected from the headlights as she stared at an abnormality that should not exist.

Driven by desperation, I fired. The first shot was into the center of the segmented ventral scutes of the creature, but it was still advancing. The next shot went wild but seemed to strike the leading edge of the looming black wing on the right side. The wormlike cilia of the top protugerance were squirming wildly as my next two shots went directly into the writhing mass of what would be a head in a sane universe.

A moment later the thing launched itself into the air, the sound now indescribably hideous as I prepared for it to collide with me. Inexplicably, it did not happen. The bulbous shape rose upward out of the glare of the headlights, but instead of attacking me, it seemed to veer off to the right side of the road, and I ran to the rear of the bus. The black shape, with its beating wings careered past a young ponderosa pine and then plummeted. The next thing I heard was a loud splash followed by a sound I shall never forget. The buzzing, droning accelerated until it morphed into an inhuman scream from unthinkable organs deep within the misshapen hulk. Thankfully, the buzzing shriek was short-lived as it changed again into a wet, bubbling sound.

Of course! It had fallen into the cyanide pond, and I prayed it was drowning, dying in the deadly water. There had to be more of them, but I was now even more desperate to escape. I pulled the door shut with a boom, and twisted the key. The starter cranked the engine, and it sounded as though it could be flooded, but I kept trying until the motor caught, sputtered, and then came to life. With no time to waste, we were headed back toward the blocked section of road, not certain what we could do. In the worst case, we could take our chances, abandon the bus and flee on foot down the mountain road to Alma or Glenwood. It would be an extreme gamble.

I think Margo was too stunned to cry or talk as we made our way to the heights, and broke through the trees to begin the descent. The road was still littered with mud, rocks, and gravel as we wound downward toward the great hairpin turn where the road was blocked.

We drove over mud ridges and felt the vehicle jostled by rocks as we descended, following our earlier tracks. Too soon came the blocking point. The bank had collapsed, with water still running across the pavement, carrying gravel and rocks that disappeared over the canyon edge, down into the blackness. Right in front of us was the boulder—too large to move with our hands. It was like a squat ice cream cone with cruel edges, a narrow base swollen, then tapering to a jagged upwardly pointing tip. It sat almost in the center of the road in front of the mud and gravel pile beyond it.

I got out of the bus and walked to the ridge of mud, rock, and gravel that extended halfway across the pavement perhaps 12-15 inches high. At the canyon edge, pavement had collapsed, making for us a challenge I would gladly retreat from if there was a choice.

Back in the driver's seat, I told Margo to unbuckle her seat belt as I backed up the hill, determined to risk a catastrophic plunge into the canyon.

I told Margo to climb back and crouch directly behind the driver's seat. When she was settled, I put the transmission in low and pressed the accelerator pedal. The bus jumped forward, the engine racing. We came down the hill, closer, closer, as the boulder seemed to grow in front of my eyes. Seconds later the Volkswagen bus slammed into the boulder just right of vehicle center with a resounding crunch as the front panel partially caved inward. The accelerator was still on the floor and though the bus seemed to falter, it was moving ahead, and the boulder was teetering toward the edge of the canyon. We had overcome the inertia of the massive rock and momentum was pushing it toward the lip of the canyon. I did not think the boulder was a random event, but there was no time to ponder causes. I felt the rear wheels starting to slip, but I was still moving.

Suddenly the slowly moving boulder tipped over the edge and I could hear it crash out of sight where the pavement had crumbled. Even with the engine noise I could hear the boulder careening down the canyon slope into the abyss. I had no time to be grateful that the air-cooled engine was in the rear of the VW.

I let up on the accelerator and the engine dropped to idle speed. We listened to the boulder tumbling in the dark, destined for the bottom of the canyon. Margo leaned over the seat and I warned her to stay where she was, because we still had another challenge a few yards ahead. I got out of the bus and looked at the damage, with the steel bumper severely dented and the flat front of the bus appearing as though a semi-truck had backed into the right side. The right headlight was casting a skewed beam, but it was still functioning. Now began the hard part.

A mud and gravel berm ahead extended to the middle of the pavement, tapering from a height of at least two feet close to the bank and tapering toward the edge of the pavement. As I approached in low gear, the left side of the bus began to rise and I felt the left front wheel rolling into soft mud. The right front was at the pavement edge.

I urged the bus ahead very slowly. Now it was inclined at almost a 30-degree angle. A hollow rasping sound told me that the compacted mud and rocks were scraping the belly of the bus. The skewed headlight was pointing into the canyon. I could faintly see the white carcass of that van that had plummeted to the bottom long before we bought the gallery.

"Margo! Lean against the bulkhead." I wanted her to add counterbalance as I felt the bus grow unsteady, as though it could tip over and take us tumbling over the edge. We inched ahead, and the rear wheels kept driving us forward. Then I heard the rear wheels slip on some gravel, and I thought we might high center, but the wheels gained traction again.

Now faced with a steep ridge of mud, I thought we were not going to make it, but then the rear wheels bit into a patch of pavement, and the scraping underneath eased. We were still moving, though leaning at a more precarious angle. I could look out the passenger door window and see the abyss waiting for us.

The rear wheels pushed the bus even higher onto the berm. We were tipping!

Suddenly the wheels slipped and I felt the rear end of the bus sliding toward the edge. I pressed the accelerator! We jolted forward, into a trough, and I now heard Margo scream for the first time. I knew without asking that she was looking across out of the side windows down into the canyon. The bus jumped, almost out of control as we came down heavily on the other side of the collapsed bank. We were through!

We were now on the lee side of the hairpin, and a shock knifed through me. I turned the wheel violently toward the bank as the bus picked up momentum because a crater suddenly yawned where solid pavement existed on Friday.

With the bus almost out of control, I felt the left bumper collide with the bank but we were blessed with enough road and momentum to get us past the sink hole. We would not join the forlorn wreck at the bottom of the canyon.

Ahead, the pavement appeared solid though littered with vegetation and rocks fallen from the hillsides as a result of the heavy rain. We stopped and got out of the bus to survey the damage. The vehicle was battered and smeared, but it was still running. Before we got back inside, I pointed out the deep scratches on the white body of the bus that were just below the side windows. No rocks or trees had made those cruel gouges. I would have shuddered had I not been exhausted from a trauma such as I had never known.

Finally, we approached the intersection with U.S. 180, and life seemed to make sense again. The rain had brought out kangaroo rats and spadefoot toads. I wished I could be following my naturalist bent, but now I just wanted to get as far away from Mogollon as fast as we could. There was no traffic on the road south through Glenwood, and nothing was open there. Only a night light was visible inside the service station. There was a pay phone booth outside the station, and I wanted to call the police again, but what would I tell them? They certainly knew the road was out, but the rest of the story would make no sense to them aside from the report of a disturbed man up at the mine.

The rest of the drive back to San Vicente was almost without memory as we fought fatigue and adrenaline, along with the lurking fear of winged monstrosities that could be abroad anywhere in the night. Had we seen a police vehicle anywhere on the road, we would have stopped them, but there was almost no traffic, and it was close to midnight when we came down the hill into San Vicente.

We did not unload the car, but instead, we jumped out of the VW with whatever we could carry, slammed the doors, and rushed to get into the house as as though the Devil was indeed behind us. Now Margo cried for the first time in a long time. My arm was around her, my heart still pounding in my chest. "We have to notify somebody…anybody." Margo nodded as I went to find the directory we kept underneath the telephone on the end table next to the sofa. I found the numbers for the Catron County Sheriff and the State Police station.

The sheriff's office was noncommittal but acknowledged that there was a road closure on N.M. 78, and one call for assistance they were unable to service. With Margo looking at me, I just said, "There's a crazy man loose in Mogollon."

The person serving as dispatcher said a unit would go up from Reserve when the road could be cleared. With that, we succumbed to our fear and exhaustion, sleeping until late Sunday morning. It was not until afternoon that we carried in the items we had brought home with us, including my cameras. Our conversation revolved around the previous night, and I spent time inspecting the damage to the bus, but in wondering how the vehicle could be restored, I could not help seeing the bus as a metaphor for how our lives could be reassembled and knowing it might never be the same. In my head, the inchoate alien images boiling in my brain would be part of me for the rest of my life, gradually becoming familiar but never to be understood or brought to mind without fear.

Margo was agonizing over the fate of the residents who remained Saturday night, and she discovered that the phone line to Mogollon was down. We could only hope for news when the road was repaired.

Despite the crisis that brought us together over the previous days, I sensed an awkwardness in our relationship that was created by my own guilt. It was almost a relief to end the day. Yet, I underestimated the intuition of my wife, and she approached me with such subtlety when she asked if I had spent any time alone with Mattie Brunk. My dismissive response ended by sounding like a confession. It was only the horror of the ghost town that distracted her from the obvious. Desperately I thought of the controversial comedian Lenny Bruce's routine when he advised his male audience, brashly, from the stage, "Deny it, deny it—if they got pictures, deny it." Now I learned that there is no such thing as having to prove guilt when it comes to human relationships. That night we slept together, but separate.

Eight

Aftermath and Omens

It is again that Monday night following the invasion of our home by the degenerate form that Arthur Brunk had become. I did not know how he got to San Vicente or where he went when he left our living room. If my VW bus could find a way down the mountainous road, the Brunks' brand new Ford pickup could jump the gap as well. Was he taking his alien contagion to El Paso? Was Darouse with him? I only know that I feared him because he was able to subdue me without touching me, then leaving me unconscious while he destroyed my typed narrative and apparently went through the house searching for something. Why would he want to silence me? As it is, nobody would believe what happened to us, I thought.

After thoroughly cleaning the .45 and reloading the magazines, I spent the next hour sitting at the typewriter, but I seemed unable to recover the words I had typed just before being confronted by the shadowy invader who destroyed my manuscript. When the words would not come, I took time to close the neck on the plastic garbage bag lining the bin under the kitchen sink. I took it out the back door and slammed it into the metal garbage can at the back gate, then clamped the lid on it. I recognized the cosmic rule: it is always the responsibility of the man to take out the garbage

Then Margo came through the door, her face in shock, "Rick, what have you done?" I was not sure which transgression to which she was referring, but I tried to tell her about the events of an hour before. She no longer seemed skeptical of the outré turn our ordinary life had taken. The smell of fear was still in the room. We tried to put the house back in order, and the darkroom area was perhaps the most seriously vandalized, one of the Nikon cameras was without its back and undeveloped film was ripped from a cassette and coiled on the tile floor. If he was looking for proof of what we had endured in Mogollon, it was a waste of time. I was certain that we had nothing that would prove our wild tale.

"Margo, tomorrow I think we have to call Glenwood. The cops are no help, but maybe our friend Bob at the Texaco can tell us what is going on."

"Oh, Golly, I wonder if I saved the number. I'll look for it in the morning."

"I know you have never lost a phone number. I'll bet it is in your day planner."

"Probably." With that, we finished straightening the furniture and putting strewn clothes in the laundry. Margo checked the phone messages, because I seldom listened to them, and she retrieved a voice mail from Brub McCarty simply asking us to call them. It cut through our disarray and scattered thoughts, reminding us that we needed to discover the fate of our ghost town neighbors. At least we knew the McCartys were back in San Vicente. Because we had to get up early on Tuesday, we put off the call.

In the morning we were both of to our jobs, and the house still smelled of spilled photo chemicals, particularly the indicator stop bath with its glacial acetic acid base. My thoughts flashed to Darouse and the embrace of horror she endured. I wondered where she was as my mind conjured the twisted, suppurating face of Arthur Brunk. I could not reconcile the effect he had upon me, and I connected my reaction to the passing touch of an evil entity in the dim light of the gallery Saturday night.

When Margo got home shortly after me, she had the Glenwood phone number in her day planner, which was easier than rummaging through the directory. She also had the Armendariz phone number, and she said she wanted to confirm that Ofelia Armendariz had recovered. I said, "You call first."

The snick-whirr of the dial kept my attention, and then Margo's amiable voice as she spoke to someone, reminding them who she was. Then she listened, and her eyes focused on the living room wall, her mouth firm. When she hung up, she sighed deeply. "This is not good. Mr. Armendariz says that some government people came with an ambulance to take Ofelia to Hospitals of Providence in El Paso. They said something about a contagious disease. Awful. It doesn't sound normal."

"It's not normal. You saw what I saw. Let me call Bob in Glenwood."

Margo passed the phone to me, and I dialed the 539 exchange that would be long distance from San Vicente. The phone rang five times before Bob himself answered. "Hey, Bob, this is Rick and Margo. Remember us? There was some excitement in Mogollon this past weekend. Have you heard anything?"

"Well, you kids must have missed all the fun. I told ya it was goin' to rain. The road washed out, but you musta got out before the bank crumbled on top of the hairpin. They said it would take a four-wheel drive to get down the mountain after that soaking."

…or a new Ford 250 Crew Cab, I thought.

"Anyhow, ol' Cos came by in his unit and said that he couldn't answer a call to

Mogollon, but yesterday there was more activity than the opening of hunting season. There must have been half a dozen vehicles parked at the Blue Front Bar across the street on Monday. I was gassing up vehicles all day.

"Ya know, those nice, frosty fellows in suits came by to talk to me again too. Asked me a ton of questions about who was in and out during the weekend. They told me a state crew was fixin' the road to Mogollon, but it would be closed for several days.

"Got curious, and I took a quick run up 78. I sure saw some heavy trucks, but they weren't the regular orange State Highway Department. This stuff was all painted grey with no names painted on the doors. Guys in hard hats stopped me a couple of miles in, and they told me that the road was closed. Ya know, they didn't look like road crew. Strange. One of the Allred family came by the station this morning and said the same thing.

"When those two guys in suits visited, they kept telling me that everything was under control—nothin' ta worry about. They musta repeated it a half dozen times, joking in between the questions, but making notes of everything I said."

"Bob, did they say anything about the woman in the Toronado?"

"Yeah, they did say something about the 'woman who took sick,' but they didn't answer my questions—just kept repeating…"

I interrupted him, "…that everything was under control, right? You can either trust the government or your lyin' eyes."

Bob burst out laughing. "That's about it. Just let me tell you two that there is no use trying to get up to Mogollon for a while. I'd be glad to phone you when they open it up again. I don't know why the government is doing road repairs. I wonder if there's something goin' on up there. Maybe a disaster at the mine?"

I thought about that fatal pool of cyanide and the buzzing horror splashing in it, "I think that may be an understatement." Then I thanked him, and we said good-bye. I filled Margo in on the latest and agreed to go pick up a pizza at the local Pizza Hut instead of flipping a coin to see who was going to cook. Margo gave me her keys, and I was happy to make the pizza run.

After dinner, Margo wanted to watch the new show "Dallas" that she had saved on the video cassette recorder. Margo had added HBO to our cable subscription, and they offered the movie "Halloween" that neither of us were inclined to watch. Horror was too real. I had pre-recorded episodes of "Adam-12," but neither of us got the chance to play our programs.

Given my experience Monday night, the knock on the door startled and frightened me. Standing on the porch in the twilight were the two men I knew as Roberts and Pluman. They invited themselves in, greeting both of us by name. They used the same names when they entered.

Roberts was the talker and Pluman was the watcher. "I believe I have spoken to your husband already." He did not say he was with the department of Public Health this time. We ushered them to the sofa and sat separately on chairs.

"We understand you were in the town of Mogollon (he pronounced it Moe-gollun) during the toxic mine spill this past weekend." Roberts' eyes were narrowed, and Pluman was playing poker in his blank gaze. He had a poised pen and a notepad.

I retorted, "There was no toxic spill, and you must know…"

Roberts cut me off, and Margo looked at each of us in turn. "Ma'am, I understand your father is retired Air Force. Is that correct?" She nodded, looking as though her privacy was being violated. I wondered how they knew so much about us.

Because I had met the two agents at the San Vicente Hospital, where they claimed to be health department officials, I let myself test the interrogators. "You know we have an investment up there in Mogollon. We have to get back up there as soon as possible." They could not know that we had no intention of going back.

"I'm afraid that will be impossible for some time to come. It could require several weeks to clean up the spill, and the roads will not be open to the public for at least two weeks." Roberts was using his official government tone.

The man who called himself Pluman leaned forward, "Whenever there is a toxic event, we have to take whatever measures necessary to see that the public is protected."

"Wait a minute—" I was also feeling under duress now. "What about the Armendariz woman? She wasn't up in Mogollon."

Roberts snapped, "We do not answer questions. We ask them. Mrs. Armendariz has the best possible care." Pluman was again scribbling on the notepad.

Even though I was only wearing a t-shirt, the room seemed stuffy to me. "So, what do we have to do with anything up there? We came back Saturday night."

Pluman tapped on the pad and harrumpfed. Roberts continued, "Yes, we saw your vehicle. Serious damage to the front end."

"I think I hit a Bigfoot."

Roberts rubbed his nose. "You placed a call from Mogollon to the Catron County Sheriff's Department Saturday night."

Margo was looking at me as I responded, "I cannot confirm that."

"You don't have to. We want to look at the items you brought back from the town Saturday night."

Margo looked at me, "Can they do that, Rick?"

"Not legally, but they are from the federal government. Listen, Mr. Roberts, a man came into my house Monday night and ransacked my house looking for something. I don't think he found anything."

Roberts did not skip a beat. "Why don't you start by giving me the film from your cameras."

I stood up abruptly. "I can do that." We all stood up and I went to the darkroom area and retrieved the exposed, undeveloped film in a curled-up spiral. Pluman took the film for what it was worth.

After surveying clothes, camera equipment and other personal effects, including my pistol, the two agents looked at each other. Roberts explored his cheek with his tongue. "We notice that the .45 in the other room has been cleaned."

I couldn't let it go. "Yessir, it's like the laundry—it requires regular attention." He seemed to miss the sarcasm, so I challenged them, "Speaking of toxic spills, you should be investigating a fellow named Arthur Brunk and maybe a guy named Hiram Akeley, a couple named McCarty, and Dar—Matilda Brunk, the Petroskis, and….."

The agents double-teamed me. Roberts spoke through clenched teeth, "We have other people assisting victims in the town."

"That guy Brunk is not a victim."

Pluman spoke for the first time, looking at his partner. "We haven't found him yet."

Roberts relented, "Mrs. Brunk suffered from the toxic contagion, and she was taken to El Paso earlier today."

The interrogator's euphemisms infuriated me. We both knew that the conversation was subterfuge, and Roberts glared at me, "Do you have any objects taken from the mine?"

"I got nothing but myself out of that hole. How do you know I was even up there?" I was aching to tell them what I saw, but I knew that the well-being of Margo and myself depended upon our silence.

Roberts and Pluman looked at each other, and then Pluman concentrated on his note-pad. Roberts spoke. "Let me counsel you that it is not in your interest to spread unverified rumors about the toxic spill at the mine up there. Authorities investigated, and there is no unusual circumstance relating to the accident up in Moe-gullon. There were some unfortunate infections, but the victims are being cared for. The individuals and families you mention have been contacted and have all been safely evacuated until the site is cleaned up. If anyone asks you, you will be able to tell them what happened."

At that point, I was unable to hold my tongue. I blurted, "What about an alien ship and monstrous creatures at the mine?"

Both of the agents went rigid, and then they cocked their heads indulgently. Roberts did not smile, "Surely you know better than to believe wild stories like that. It was proved decades ago that there are no such things as flying saucers, UFOs, or aliens. When you spread that nonsense, you lose your credibility, and you won't get it back. Every one of those irresponsible UFO reports has been explained by the Air Force as atmospheric phenomena, misidentified astronomical bodies, weather balloons, aircraft, or hoaxes. You really do not want to be accused of trying to perpetrate some kind of hoax, do you? The publicity might have an unfortunate effect on your jobs and your financial well-being."

The warning was stark and unequivocal. We followed the AFOSI agents to the door and then, after the deadbolt clicked, spent time talking quietly as though the walls had ears.

Margo said, "I get the feeling that those men have done this kind of thing before."

"I think the federal government has been doing this for most of our lives."

As we sat on the couch, Margo put her face into her hands. "Those two were making sure we didn't have any proof of what happened to us."

"This is the second time our home has been violated in two days. Brunk took my notes, and I still don't know what else he was looking for…" I paused as I looked at Margo.

Suddenly I sat bolt upright and then sprang to my feet. Margo looked startled, but I was headed to the back door. I flicked the porchlight on and walked swiftly the 30 feet to the cyclone fence that bordered the alley behind our street. There was a clatter as I yanked the lid from the first galvanized metal garbage can—empty. The lid came off the second can, and the distasteful odor of our garbage was leaking from the plastic garbage bags therein.

THE WHISPERING DARKNESS

It had to be here! I ripped open the plastic and dug into the contents—a folded greasy pizza box, empty Miracle Whip jar, moldy flour tortillas, a cluster of damp paper, including editions of the local newspaper. The distant porchlight was little help, but I groped within the bag until I found it. My fingers recognized the plastic wrap, and I pulled out my hand, clutching the prize.

I almost ran into the house and went directly to the kitchen to turn on the hot water, letting it course over my hands and arm before I carefully scrubbed the tightly wrapped piece of shell that was suddenly more important than it was two weeks ago.

"Margo!" I almost shouted from the kitchen. "You know everybody. Who's that guy who's really in the Department of Health? You know, he works out of Las Cruces."

Her curiosity brought her into the kitchen. "Ahhhh, that's Dr. Jesse Monsevais. He visits the San Vicente office two or three days a week."

I held up the still-dripping parcel.

"Rick! I threw that nasty thing away. Only dogs and raccoons dig in the garbage."

"Margo, the Department of Health has a chemical analysis laboratory. I think it's in Albuquerque. We need to get an analysis of this…this, whatever it is. I have my suspicions."

Margo was shaking her head, "Not likely. They don't do private work. Everything is referred by doctors or law enforcement."

My face brightened, "But you are not only irresistible, you are very, very persuasive. Call him tomorrow and see if he will to do this, but nothing about Mogollon."

"I would argue, but after what happened to us, that thing looks so hateful. Put it into a paper grocery sack from under the sink, and I'll talk to him, and I'll tell him we're willing to pay for the analysis."

I prepared a label for the sample, typed out our names and contact numbers on a sheet of paper, then sighed with relief. The day was over, and my head was throbbing. I decided not to take any Aspirin unless the ache did not subside after bedtime.

In the middle of the night I was assailed for the first time by what I came to call "the red vision," that took me in a falling dream to unrelieved blackness beyond the rim of the galaxy. It was a vision that was to repeat unpredictably in the years that followed, and when I woke up gasping this night, my heart thudding, I could not fully describe what I had witnessed. Everything but the fear evaporated, and I did not even have time to get out of bed to seek writing materials before the memory disappeared, mocking me. All I could recall was a dim, crepuscular landscape dominated by a hellish red glow that penetrated me and pulsed in seething darkness. As I sat up in bed, breathing like a bellows, I touched my left arm—and I remembered a venomous touch and its assault on my psyche. Then, without disturbing Margo, I walked to the kitchen in the dark, this time taking Aspirin in hopes of sleeping until dawn.

As we departed for work Wednesday, Margo took the paper bag and said she we would check to see if Dr. Monsevais was present at the Public Health office. We both wondered when we would be able to return to the ghost town gallery, if ever. She took me to work, since the mini-bus was in the body shop.

Nine

Fate and Distance

That same Wednesday, I spent much of the day doing a reprise of the visit by the AFOSI agents and thinking of a dozen one-liners and comebacks that I should have thrown at them. One thing their visit had done was to heighten my concern and curiosity about our fellow ghost town colleagues. How had they survived, and were they also now refugees from Mogollon?

We were living in an ordinary American town with everyday concerns, and as we walked the streets, we were secretly privy to a horrific series of events that we could not even mention for fear of ridicule or of relentless suppression by government agents who were in our midst. The rumors I had heard about a flying saucer crash on a ranch near Roswell in 1947 must have left witnesses living not only in fear of an alien race, but also of their own government since their stories had yet to be revealed even after 30 years. I also discovered the discredited recovery of a similar craft near Aztec, N.M., in 1948, the story of which was savaged by government-sponsored disinformation that sought to destroy the characters of all who tried to inform the public at that time. Then too, as I went about my daily activities, I knew that the horror creatures were real, and their dehumanized agent, Arthur Brunk, was unaccounted for. The absence of personal safety still plagued me.

THE WHISPERING DARKNESS

In the stress of the Tuesday evening interrogation, I had forgotten the voice mail from Brub McCarty; so, one of my first priorities after a friend drove me home from work, was to call the McCartys. They lived in an upscale development just outside of San Vicente, and when Ouida answered the phone, I started apologizing as I asked how they were.

Her response took me aback, "Nice to hear from you. I hope you two can come over very soon. No time to talk on the phone." I confirmed with Ouida that Margo knew their address, and then hastily rung off. Her voice sounded strained.

When Margo walked in the door, I told her about the McCarty call while she still had her big key ring in her hand. Five minutes later we were on our way to the McCarty place. The well-kept yard was guarded at the corners of the property by mature spruce trees, and a five-foot tall decorative aluminum windmill was turning lazily to the right of the concrete sidewalk. A large front doormat read, "Welcome," as I pressed the doorbell.

From behind the four rectangular glass panes at the upper half of the door, I saw Ouida push aside the curtain to assure that it was us.

The spacious living room featured twin recliner chairs that faced a large television set against the far wall. Ouida hugged Margo, and Brub stuck his head out from the kitchen and asked if he could get us something. We waved him off as Ouida ushered us to the sofa under the front windows while she sank into the recliner, waiting for her husband to join her.

Brub came in with a beer in his hand, and I could see that they were different from when we had seen them Saturday night. They appeared older, haggard, faces drawn, eyes almost haunted. Brub raised the can, "I knew you made it out. I knew it."

"What happened to you?" Margo was direct.

McCarty glanced at his wife and then to me. "I can't even describe it. It was worse than what we saw in the mine—I think the worst night of our lives I thought we were going to die or worse. And I saw that ship! I know it was their ship as it lifted up from the mine."

Ouida broke in, "I looked out the door and saw those…" Her face twisted with revulsion, "…those demon things. I can't even describe them, but I never felt fear like that before. I saw one of them flying—like giant bats. It was coming toward our RV."

I asked, "Why couldn't you talk on the phone earlier? We were really worried about you."

Ouida stared at us, "Some government men came here yesterday. They told us bad things would happen if we talked about what happened. I'm afraid they are tapping the phone."

Margo briefly told them about the AFOSI visit to our house on Tuesday and then listened as the McCartys shared their story.

I knew we were partners in unthinkable terror, isolated from the thousands of residents in San Vicente. By turns the McCartys added the details of hearing my shots in the gallery, then looking out from the side door of their RV to see the nightmare spilling onto the street. He heard me yelling to him, but because it would be almost impossible to unhook the utilities and move the cumbersome vehicle, they backed into the vehicle and locked the metal door, turning out the lights. They heard our bus revving up and heading up the road while they held each other inside the RV, with only a .38-caliber revolver for protection.

We sat, rapt, as the McCartys described the sounds of the creatures gathering around the Winnebago. I felt the fear in the room and visualized arthropod aliens shambling to the vehicle. Brub described it: "It began quietly with just a hint of raindrops still falling on the metal ceiling, but then I heard—well, it sounded like whispering, and then it was a buzzing noise—godless sounds that almost sounded like words—like they were calling to us. That was before they attacked the door."

I felt the familiar icy chill as Brub described the rasp of horn appendages dragging with a screech along the aluminum wall, and the shaking of the vehicle as nameless horrors grabbed at the door handle and pushed their hideous bodies against the barrier, their sibilant buzzing alternating with clicks and pauses—voices from an alien primal ooze that had somehow mastered travel through a trackless void to the edge of the Milky Way galaxy—where our world is located.

"We heard your bus coming back down into town as we huddled together. The things momentarily stopped trying to get in. And then you came back down the street…" Ouida was reliving the night. "We didn't dare look out."

I said, "The road out was blocked at the hairpin, and we thought we could escape through the forest, but the Brunks' truck was blocking the road. We almost didn't make it, but we barely got through on the road in our second try." Now I waited to hear about the McCartys' escape.

As they described their seemingly endless night, we could sense the terror as the creatures rampaged through the ghost town with purposes unknown to them. I had seen what happened when these things came into contact with me and with Darouse Brunk. McCarty and I had seen what the alien arthropods had done to Art Brunk, and how they had reduced Hiram Akeley to near death.

The McCarty ordeal went on until the dawn. At times the rain poured down again, drumming on their Winnebago, and the horror creatures seemed to retreat only to return with a vengeance when the rain subsided. The powerful claws of the arthropods eventually penetrated the wall of the vehicle, and the night was rent with the sound of tortured aluminum being ripped.

Yet, Brub McCarty said the most frightening part of the ordeal was the sounds issuing from the beings as they conferred with each other in a hideous language not heard in a sane solar system. Because I had heard the guttural whispers and the buzzing challenges, I could almost hear the forms of the sounds they used with each other. I did not want to know what those non-words would mean if they could be translated into a human tongue.

Ouida sighed with relief, "The door lock held, and I thanked God as we sat in the dark with our arms around each other. We never slept."

As Ouida described the waning Mogollon night, I could almost hear the shuffling dispersion of the monstrosities, through the yawning doors of the Holland Store, into the hidden tunnel behind the back wall of the empty store, and through a labyrinth ending in the cavernous galleries of the Little Fanny mine. Others could have flown back to their nest in the mine buildings.

McCarty said he cautiously opened the door of the RV, pistol in hand, and he saw an

The Day After the Flood   *RickPhoto 1978*

abandoned town where the creek had rushed over its banks, cutting a cruel gash down the main street. The porch of the Holland Store was sagging and near collapse where the creek ran underneath it. Where the ground was soft, a forest of cloven tracks congregated in clusters where echoes of alien convocation still hovered in the morning air.

"Ouida and I looked around and began walking up the street. The door to your gallery was standing open just as the doors to the Holland Store. Funny thing—the doors to the museum were shut tight, but I didn't see Brunk's truck anywhere."

I broke in, "Maybe it's up at Akeley's place."

"Don't know and don't care after what we saw. Thank God the Chandlers and the Englishes were away…same with Frank Triolo. We walked all the way up to the Petroskis. The wooden bridge across the creek had collapsed, but we were able to find a shallow place to cross the creek. When we knocked on the door. Sarah peeked out from behind the curtains in their living room window."

It was Ouida's turn, "They looked so happy to see us. Poor dear Sarah said they spent the night the same way we did. She said she was sure that her loud praying kept those things at bay all night. She was still holding her Bible against her chest. Victor said he went out across the street to his car around dawn, but the things did something to disable it—battery was absolutely dead."

They asked the Petroskis if they knew the fate of any other residents, and the few others, such as the proprietors of the Old Kelly Store and the Chamber Por apparently did what the McCartys and Petroskis had done, hunkering down behind barred doors to survive the night assault. Then the four of them walked out to the middle of the street that was still littered from the overflow of Silver Creek.

Brub set the half-full beer can into the receptacle in the arm of his chair, and he stood up, arms extended. "I saw it. We were standing out there in the street, and I saw it. This giant ship—or whatever it was— seemed to just materialize above the Little Fanny Mine. Jesus, we were scared all over again, but the morning light was clear, and Sarah Petroski, still holdin' onto that Bible, pointed down the street. The air above the mine seemed to shimmer, like with heat waves, and this giant silver egg just appeared—like a mirage turning solid. It wasn't there, and then it was. It just came out of thin air. Giant—giant, like a flattened silver egg that seemed to be…I don't know how to explain it…wobbling, the skin slowly rippling as it gained altitude. Like it was a silver jellyfish. That's what it was—a giant silver jellyfish."

Ouida looked up at her husband, "You forgot to tell them that it didn't make any noise. No noise at all."

Brub described how they all ran back to the Petroski house, scrambling over the flood-scored creek bank as the strange craft arced over the town and gained speed as it vaulted into the heavens in a southward direction. The group did not come out of the house for almost an hour, deciding instead to allow Vic to make coffee for all of them. Stomachs were too unsettled to think about breakfast.

As Brub McCarty held court, Ouida got up out of her chair and went to the front window, looking out again. Margo and I looked at each other, puzzled.

When Ouida sat down again, Brub described what happened next. "We were still at the Petroskis, when we heard a rumble of engines on the road coming down into town. We argued about whether they came down the mountain or out of the forest. I don't know if we were relieved, or just bone tired."

As the McCartys described it, they all straggled out of the Petroskis' house and crossed the over the creek to watch a small convoy at the center of town. As they remembered it, there was a Jeep in the lead with a long radio antenna waving above it; following was a grey-painted Ford Bronco, and then two deuce-and-a-half military trucks with canvas covers on the back. The final vehicle was a yellow school bus possibly commandeered from a school system in the area, but they did not mention the name on the side of the bus.

The Jeep swung into the parking lot east of the museum, followed by one of the trucks and the school bus. A military officer in camouflage fatigue uniform vaulted out of the passenger side of the Jeep and walked in their direction, arms raised. As McCarty remembered, the officer spoke to them in parade ground command voice: "This area is quarantine. You are instructed to get your personal belongings and report to the bus. You have 15 minutes." When they stood there, the officer put his arms akimbo: "You have 14 minutes! How do we get to the mine?"

The residents pointed up the road and told him to take the left fork and go one mile to gain access to the mine property. At that, the officer sliced the air with his hand and the Ford Bronco led the second truck up the road, following the hand signal from the officer. As the truck passed, Brub said he saw armed troops inside the truck. A similar squad came out of the first truck and double-timed to the west end of town. As the two couples stared, the uniformed squad began going door to door.

"I think we were traumatized by the storm trooper attitude of that officer, and so we headed back to the Winnebago to get what we could carry." Ouida's mouth was a slit as she remembered, and then she got up and looked out the front window again.

Brub continued, "A lot of this was a blur, but I remember us grabbing what we could carry and getting onto the bus while some damn soldier stood by the door. Our arms were full of our belongings. The bus was half full, and I know I saw Mattie Brunk getting on—I think the soldiers found her when they searched the museum. She was the last to get on board. Her head was down, and she was wearing a scarf of some kind. I think she was hiding her face."

Margo and I did not ask any questions as we digested the McCartys' narrative. They described how the remainder of Sunday was spent shuttling the bus passengers to their homes or other places of refuge. The McCartys distinctly remembered the bus meeting an ambulance, and Mattie Brunk was transferred to it. Somebody on the bus heard that she was being taken to an El Paso hospital. I wondered if the troops who went to the mine were able to rescue Old Man Akeley. I knew where Arthur Brunk was on Monday night, but all else about him was a frightening mystery.

Margo stood up and walked over to Ouida, hugging her. "I hope we can get back to Mogollon very soon."

She replied, "I don't know if I want to go back there. I don't know if those things are really gone. Maybe they are setting up a colony in those tunnels." The way she said it made me shudder.

As Ouida spoke, I imagined the nucleus of a hideous invasion, and then the shock of an American military intervention cast an additional ominous light to it, with so many questions. How had the military learned of this horror? Where did the special unit come from? Why were AFOSI agents using veiled threats to cover up a horrific reality by using a lame story about a non-existent toxic spill? I smiled briefly as I thought with grim satisfaction about a flying monstrosity falling into the cyanide leaching pond.

Brub was stretching out in his recliner. "I admit I was scared on Saturday—lost my hat after all—but then your own government tells you that something bad will happen to you if you talk to the wrong people, or if you tell somebody what really happened last weekend. When that bus let us out in San Vicente Sunday evening, a guy in fatigues stood beside the bus at parade rest, and he didn't even look at us when he said in a low voice, 'We'll be watching you'."

Now I knew why Ouida didn't want to talk on the phone and why she was looking out her front window. The pall of paranoia was reinforcing the sense of cosmic fear that I was carrying into my nightmares. "Are you planning to go back?"

Brub sighed heavily, "That recreational vehicle is a heavy investment. We aren't going to abandon it, but there is no way of knowing when we can get back. I hear that the road is blocked. The official excuse is that the road is being rebuilt. All four of us know that's a lie."

I was now thinking about Arthur Brunk again. "I think Brunk was in closer contact with those things than anybody else. He came into our house Monday night. There's some kind of sickness in him that turned him into something horrible."

Ouida and Brub looked at each other, and she leaned toward him, "You think we should tell him about Ulibarri?"

McCarty squinted and rubbed his chin with thumb and forefinger; then he nodded.

Ouida told me a story I would never have suspected. "Rick, you say you were interested in flying saucers before all this happened. Well, our next-door neighbor told us a story several years ago that I thought was a fantasy until last weekend. He told us he could get in trouble. He even said that the government is still watching him after 30 years."

Even Margo was showing curiosity in the set of her face. I had no idea what they were talking about.

Brub interrupted his wife, "Tip Ulibarri is a great guy. He retired from the Air Force in '68 and bought the house next door. His kids are grown, and his wife divorced him about five years ago. We've had him over when we grill steaks in the back yard. I think he's kinda lonely. It was about a year ago that he drank three or four beers, and he started telling us about the government keeping tabs on him. Until those agents visited us this week, I thought Tip was getting paranoid."

"Tell me more. You think he is being monitored?"

Ouida picked it up, "We'll let you decide. I'm sure you read that old book by Frank Scully about a flying saucer crash near Aztec in the Four Corners area?"

I nodded, feeling a queasy curiosity beginning. "Most people wrote that off as a hoax—including the authorities on early flying saucer lore."

She nodded vigorously. "When Tip started talking, that's what I was thinking too. I can still see him—I think it was Labor Day last year, and he was wearing one of those gaudy

Hawaii flowered shirts and Bermuda shorts with white socks." She smirked at her own re-membrance. "He loved that shirt because he and his wife had gone there to celebrate his retirement from the Air Force."

Brub rotated his hand, trying to speed up his wife's narrative.

"Sorry, Honey. Anyhow, Tip is totally bald, but he wears one of those Army fatigue caps with his rank badge on it. I know he's read that book by Scully, but he swore to us that he was there when the Military found a giant flying saucer on a mesa outside of the town of Aztec. This was about the time when the Air Force was made separate from the Army."

I wasn't sure where Ouida was taking her story, but like most people, I thought the Az-tec saucer story was a fantasy and that it could not have happened.

"Well, you know how curious I am, and I didn't want to stop him, and he spilled the whole scary story. I'm only sorry that we believed he was making it all up back then." Ouida then cajoled us into refreshments before we sat and listened to the story Tip Ulibarri shared with the McCartys at their Labor Day cookout. Between the two McCartys, we were regaled with a story that would have changed public attitudes toward flying saucers in 1948 if it had been officially released, and it told of the relentless and detailed process of government cover-up, overlaid with the recovery of a craft and its occupants from another world. In retrospect, the couple now remembered the frightening consequences of that recovery as revealed by Ulibarri in his tipsy lapse.

"He was sitting in a lawn chair and telling us how this giant disc was disassembled into three pieces. They sent him from Roswell air field—he said the base had been re-named Walker Air Force Base in January of that year—and he didn't know any of the other guys they sent up with him. Rumors flew that there were 16 small bodies dead inside the ship, but Tip first denied seeing them; but then he said, with a shudder, that he had. He said every-body was scared to be there, and those guys who were inside the disc for more than a few minutes came out sick and vomiting. They had to be evacuated."

Ouida's husband completed the Ulibarri confession by saying that Ulibarri was debriefed and threatened after the mesa site was cleaned up. He was sworn to lifelong silence and told that he had been on temporary duty at Carswell air force base in Ft. Worth during that two weeks. "Here's a funny thing. Tip said that when he got back to the barracks at Walker, his sergeant asked him how the weather was in Texas. It was one helluva story."

Before we left, Ouida confided, "You know, the very next day, Tip came over and apolo-gized for telling us that story. He said it was all baloney…"

Brub interjected: "The word he used was 'bullshit'."

Ouida continued, "…anndddd, he asked us to forget that he had said it. Well, we said we would, and I didn't say a word to anyone about it until today."

On the McCartys' front porch, we promised to talk frequently and to share any Mo-gollon news we could get from Bob in Glenwood. As we went down the sidewalk past the slowly turning yard windmill, I found myself looking up and down the street to see if there were out-of-place vehicles with occupants. None seen.

We also looked across the fence to the house where former Airman Tip Ulibarri lived. It was a nice looking house with white stucco probably over concrete blocks. A fading pale green GMC pickup truck was parked in the concrete driveway, and the several windows I could see were uniform with drawn shades, and there were only three small panes in an echelon formation about eye level in the heavy looking front door. Of course the shades could have been protection against the sun.

On the way back to our huse, Margo got me up to date. "Dr. Monsevais was in the health office this morning, and I gave him that icky piece of shell. He'll get an analysis for us as a favor."

"Did he say how long?"

"Uh-uh. He said it depends of the work load. They do all the lab stuff in Albuquerque. I wonder if Mattie is in El Paso, or maybe at her brother's place here in town." In the organized chaos of the evacuation and a supposed transfer to an ambulance could have Mattie almost anywhere.

Just talking about the Brunks made me uncomfortable, and the image of an alien embrace inside the Mogollon museum flashed into my mind. I grimaced. "I just wish they would find Arthur Brunk. He's a danger." I was thinking of how the Ulibarri story established the reality that the government had known about alien invaders at least from the beginning of the Atomic Age.

Margo gave me a sidelong glance as we pulled up in front of the house. She was still trying to accept what I experienced during the Monday night invasion of our home. She had not seen me so disoriented and confused as on that night, but she seemed to resist the idea of Art Brunk being transformed into a semi-human monstrosity. She had not seen his face the way I saw him when McCarty and I fled the mine, and then when Brunk faced me in my living room, where his malevolent stare had blasted me almost in the same manner as when those worm-like cilia swept across my arm in the gallery.

For us, the prospects of the Memorial Day weekend seemed bleak. The gallery was out of bounds, even if we wanted to go there as we had long planned, and we did not feel like celebrating further than putting out the American flag in front of the house. When Thursday afternoon came, Margo picked me up at work, and we went to the Safeway grocery store on Hudson Street just as we did every gallery weekend, but this time we shopped without real appetite. The parking lot was half full as Margo steered the white 1977 Chevrolet Camaro into the lot.

The interior of the store was pleasantly cool as we took a cart and headed for the produce section. I grabbed a head of lettuce while Margo tried to decide between two bell peppers that were just a little too soft. I was waiting for her when I saw a familiar face.

The couple was selecting avocados, probably to use for guacamolé, or maybe it was my appetite that made me think of it. The man was tall—my height—with a tanned face, salt and pepper hair, and a narrow black mustache. He wore a checkered long-sleeved western style shirt with the top two snaps undone. He had his arm on the shoulder of a woman as he talked softly to her. It was Ofelia Armendariz. There were other shoppers in the produce section, but I was fixated on that couple. I nodded to Margo, my eyes flicking in the couple's direction. We pushed the cart toward the two shoppers.

Margo flashed her signature smile, "Ofelia! Do you recognize us? We were the ones…"

The man started to bristle, and then he relaxed, unsure of how to respond. Ofelia Armendariz was a handsome woman, full figured, and wearing a skirt and cream-colored silk blouse. Her full black hair was wavy and beautifully coiffed, but her eyes, as she looked at us, seemed haunted as though she were trying to place us.

"I'm Manuel." He extended his hand, and I took it, then returned to grip the handle of the shopping cart.

"I'm Rick. We were the ones …" I echoed Margo.

"Yes, the police told us about it. Ofelia hasn't been well."

I smiled at Ofelia as she looked back, almost vacantly. I tried not to notice that there were still gauze patches on her cheeks and a coating of Max Factor makeup elsewhere on her face. "Manuel, did you know about the guys in suits who visited your wife in the hospital?"

Manuel twisted his lip, "They came to the hospital, and they came to our house. Gringo bastards. They threatened us—said if we talked about this, we would be in trouble with the government."

Margo took a deep breath. "Oh no. We have to tell you that the same men treated us the same way just yesterday."

Manuel looked around, surveying other shoppers with his dark brown eyes under lowered brow, and then he turned back to us. "My wife has suffered more than I can tell you. You would not believe what she has been saying in her sleep." Mrs. Armendariz was standing, passive, as though trying to place us. She had said nothing, though the trace of a smile seemed to lengthen her lips.

I looked at him, then at Ofelia, "Yes, I would believe." We seemed to be instant conspirators, and I smiled broadly at him.

Suddenly, Ofelia Armendariz jerked and reached out to cover my hand with hers, her eyes alive, "I saw them. Iä…"

At that word, I felt vertigo and a red haze seemed to rise in my vision, the memory of evil, buzzing whispers crowding my consciousness. As I looked at Ofelia Armendariz, I knew she was in hell, and I was sharing her hideous red vision. That word…that word made my stomach lurch.

Manuel gently took Ofelia's wrist as Margo stared, and I shook my head, trying to regain my psychic balance. He said, "You have to understand. We don't know what terrible things happened to her out there outside of Glenwood."

Margo reached out and put her hand on Ofelia's shoulder, "No matter what those government officers say, we know that you have been through something nobody deserves."

Ofelia heaved a deep sigh and spoke for the first time, "I remember you, but I can't get this out of my head. I'm so afraid all the time, especially at night. Are they going to come after us?"

I looked at both of them. "I don't know. We have the same fear."

When we went to the next aisle, I suddenly felt tears in my eyes, and Margo looked at me because she had never seen me cry. She pulled tissue out of her purse for me. Women are very good that way. As we shopped, I wondered why the emotional reaction would come almost a week after the traumatic events in the Mogollon night.

As we dollied the cart, laden with groceries in brown paper bags, out into the hot afternoon sunshine, Margot was thinking out loud. "Poor Ofelia. I can't imagine. Do you think that the same thing happened to Art and Mattie Brunk?"

My answer was delayed, and I just said, "Something worse happened to Art, and I don't know about…about Mattie." Unbidden thoughts of Darouse as she was three weeks ago flashed into my mind, and I couldn't squelch the sudden fantasy image. I dismissed the thought by lifting grocery sacks into the trunk of the Camaro and trotting with the cart back to the collection point in front of the store. There are always people standing around outside the grocery store, but the two men loitering beside a grey four-door sedan near the entrance were too casual and too well dressed. I could tell at a glance they were not AFOSI agents Roberts and Pluman, and I wondered if the two loiterers were surveilling Ofelia Armendariz. It was a chilling possibility, and she was still traumatized by an encounter more hideous than a human should have to endure.

On the way home, Margo was talking about Ofelia, "Do you think those evil things carry diseases that we can't know about?"

"It can't be otherwise. They come from Hell, and they have to be seething with viruses and bacilli we can't imagine." I rubbed my left arm without thinking. "You know I got a glancing touch, and I've had those nightmares…" My voice trailed off.

Back home, we carried in the groceries and picked up the San Vicente Daily Enterprise lying rolled up on the sidewalk. After putting away the groceries, I went from the kitchen to sprawl on the sofa and begin my usual five-minute read of the local daily newspaper. Front page featured a story about summer activities for students who were now out of school until August. At the bottom of the page, below the fold, anchoring the lower corners of the front page were two news articles that caught my attention.

Gila forest travel limited for a week

Memorial Day travelers will be unable to access the Gila National Forest this weekend through N.M. Highway 78 through Mogollon.

The N.M. Highway Department reports that the highway into Mogollon is still being rebuilt, while reports from Catron County Sheriff's Office have revealed that recent flooding did result in the release of toxic chemicals from the inactive mine property.

Health officials say that residents of the ghost town will be able to return within a few days. The road into the forest will also be clear at that time.

Local break-ins top crime reports

SAN VICENTE—At least four home break-ins in the past three days have puzzled Police who found vandalism and missing food items, but valuables were not taken.

SVPD reports that four homes were entered in the North Swan Street area, during daylight hours Tuesday and Wednesday. Locks were forced and kitchen contents strewn in all four of the homes.

A local service station also filed a report of a drive-off, and Police are searching for a gray Ford crew cab pickup truck, recent model.

THE WHISPERING DARKNESS

When I read the first article, I wanted to yell at the reporter for her or his lack of curiosity. It was the biggest story in the city's history, and written off, just as the government wanted it to be. I shouted for Margo to come read the article for herself.

The second article was the usual must-read crime article meant to catch the attention of all residents, but when I saw the final paragraph, I sat back with renewed anxiety. He was here in San Vicente. I jumped up to throw the new deadbolt on the front door.

* * *

The Memorial Day weekend arrived with unremitting unsettled feelings in its train. I had not yet rewritten my account of the Mogollon horror, and I was constantly keeping watch against a visit from Arthur Brunk or the government agents. The subtle growth of distance between me and Margo filled me with guilt. I also had discovered a sad truth. The movies always showed people in love brought closer together by trauma and disaster, but it was not necessarily so in real life. Margo had not said anything, but I was sure that Darouse Brunk may have insinuated enough to verify my wife's intuition. My behavior could only confirm it to her. If it had not been for the ghost town battle, she might have confronted me. Now, we moved ahead uncertainly, still living in dread of an alien threat, and of our own government and its insidious operatives.

Friday evening found Margo out again, visiting with her friend Susan, planning to have dinner, drink wine, and probably do soul searching. Left alone, I turned again to the typewriter in hopes of resurrecting my narrative of the horror.

Inserting a sheet of paper into the Royal Portable, I began describing the brilliant light shining through the windows, when we had no idea what the next days would bring. It was only when I was getting lost in my narrative that the ringing of the telephone jarred me back from reverie.

The voice on the line created an instant visual of a woman embraced by an alien horror—a thing with writhing worm-like tentacles in place of a face, and she submitted to the infernal kiss. "Rick, I need to see you."

My first thought was wondering if she knew I would be alone. I wondered how she looked now. Unbidden, I was suddenly feeling the heat of desire, and I hated my weakness. "Hi, Darouse. I heard that you were in El Paso."

"I was taken to the hospital down there, but I was released after two days. I brought my son up here to my brother's house in San Vicente while we wait to find out what happened to Art."

I tried to terminate the conversation, but her voice turned querulous as though I was neglecting her. All the while I was trying to tell myself that I never wanted to see her again. Then, I turned the conversation to Art Brunk and his horrific transformation.

Darouse said, "I have not seen him. Nobody has. Some people from the government interviewed me and they're the ones that took me to the hospital. Now I'm staying at my brother's place for now. I must see you."

I protested, but knew I would give in as she described in rich detail what we had done together. There was an unnatural persuasiveness in her voice. It was still early in the evening, and I agreed to let her pick me up. Considering a town the size of San Vicente, it was a stupid decision, but curiosity and desire overcame whatever good judgment I had left.

The sky was still bright at 7 p.m. as I left the house in jeans and t-shirt with a Nikon camera around my neck. A black 1977 Lincoln Town Car slowed to a stop in front of the house, and I slid into the front seat as Darouse looked at me before heading down the street. She was wearing a skirt that reached mid-thigh and a tight blouse that was stretching the buttons where her breasts strained the fabric. Her hair framed her cheeks but could not hide the healing residue of cruel ringworm-like wounds that still showed the infection from her encounter.

Even with the damage to her face, she knew how to be desirable, but I asked her, "What happened to you that night?"

Her eyes were on the road as she steered out of town on the road that led to Mogollon. She drove to the entrance of the college football stadium and parked. She leaned against the door and faced me, "Rick, I'm not the same. When I think of that Saturday night—I don't even remember what time it was—it was getting dark when my husband stumbled into the museum. He wasn't Art any more. I felt dizzy. I can't think about the monster that entered behind him. I couldn't even scream. There was just a…a…thing…" She gesticulated as she talked, even as she resisted reliving the moment I had also seen. "It was like a nightmare, but I was awake. Oh my God, Rick, it attacked me and I could not even move." Her body was shaking. "My own husband was whispering and talking to the thing. He pointed at me, and he was grinning, Rick, the thing had no head! I think I fainted as it grabbed me."

I looked at her as she slid her hands on her legs. "I'm sorry for that. Did you see something when you passed out?"

"I had the worst dream ever. It was worse than a dream, but that's the only word I can use. I can't describe what I dreamed. It was all red and dark, and there were strange words I could almost understand. Those things came up from the mine, didn't they?" Darouse seemed to be silently weeping as though she were lost, but there were no tears.

"No, they were from somewhere else. What did the doctors say?"

She tried to smile, her face still comely even though showing those small but ugly wounds. "They said I wasn't assaulted—I think they meant sexually—and I seem to have recovered, except for the dreams, and sometimes I see terrible things—even during the day. Are they dreams?"

I shook my head. "I don't think so. I hope you will be OK. I think Art is beyond help."

"What if he comes for me?" She slid from under the wheel and across the seat, her thigh touching mine. Despite the trauma she had suffered and exhibited, Darouse seemed to have an assertive sexual confidence that I was unable to resist.

"I don't know. Nobody knows, I guess." I could feel her nearness and resisted reaching for her as I sensed the difference in her personality—something almost frightening that resonated with my nighttime visions of the days since our escape. She had experienced the infernal kiss, and the alien toxin was coursing through her veins.

"You could at least kiss me, Rick," And she leaned into me, her arms going around me. I felt an almost helpless arousal, and I kissed her as her tongue went into my mouth and her full breasts, jutting under the tight blouse met my chest. Her perfume was like a fog in front of my eyes. Her legs were on my lap, and she said, "Don't stop."

But I did, even as my breath came roughly. "Maybe I want to, but I won't do this."

She smiled faintly, her chest heaving as she put her hand on me. "I think you will." She pulled her hand back and unbuttoned the tight blouse until her breasts were free. She wasn't wearing a bra.

Awkward as it was, I was kissing her again, my hands on her breasts as she undid my jeans until somehow her dress was over her hips and I was doing something in the front seat of that Lincoln I swore to myself I would never do with her. But now, nothing could keep me from coupling with her.

When she finally unwound from me, and we adjusted our clothes, she slid back to the driver's seat. "I needed that, Rick. Let me take you back to your house." She did not call it my home.

As she drew the car up in front of my house, I put my hand on her thigh, "Mattie, if you hear anything from your husband, please call the police, or at least call Margo or me."

She nodded and looked at me as I got out of the car, her cleavage swelling where the top buttons of the blouse were still undone. I watched her drive down the street, certain that she knew I was in conflict between longing and revulsion. Then I went into the house, washed and changed my clothes, vainly hoping that I could erase the smell of Darouse from my body as I returned to my renewed guilt and sat down to once again resume typing my narrative.

During the Memorial Day weekend and into the next week, we seemed to be living in a separate reality from the rest of the community. Only those few who had experienced the terror in the ghost town walked through San Vicente with haunted eyes as though something frightening lurked just outside the back door or around the corner on Main Street.

Another complication was Margo's continued concern for her brother in St. Louis, who was recovering from his own encounter with very human thugs who were almost as frightening as alien beings, and perhaps more violent. It was only because of his ability to defend his home that Margo's brother and his family were not injured or worse. Still, Margo did call every day or two to speak with him.

I was now almost obsessed with my library of books on flying saucers and the documented cases of people who had interacted with occupants of UFOs. The works of former New Mexico residents Jim and Coral Lorenzen chronicled dozens of encounters where humans found themselves in contact with alien beings. Those contacts had a profound effect upon each person. The Lorenzens' A.P.R.O. Bulletin was the first to publish the complete facts about the 1975 abduction of Travis Walton in the forest outside Snowflake, Ariz., years after the now-verified abduction of the New Hampshire couple Betty and Barney Hill in 1961. The possible reality of flying saucer crashes and recoveries in 1947 and 1948 was still only rumors vehemently denied by the U.S. Military, whose minions now commanded us to accept the explanation of the Mogollon horror as a toxic mine spill.

Now I was part of this unhappy tangle of suppression and terror. I feared the hideous arthropod invaders, but the agents of my own government also gave me reason to fear, should I mistakenly talk about our experience in Mogollon.

There is no pattern nor logic to the encounters between humans and non-human entities. I knew it was not possible to know what they wanted as their ships descended to hidden places and where they seemed to treat humans as either their prey or their experimental subjects. As I read, I wanted to know why the monstrosities we encountered were injecting humans with a vile serum. Who could know what was even now working inside the bodies and minds of those luckless victims. Matilda Brunk was all too human, but she admitted that her mind was being tortured with uncontrollable images.

My momentary brush with the squirming tentacles that night in the gallery had knocked me temporarily unconscious, and the residual effects came to me unexpectedly in the hours of darkness, like a giant spider descending from the ceiling onto my face, projecting the vague, red-tinged visions I could not understand. I knew from our experience with Ofelia Armendariz, Hiram Akeley, Matilda Brunk, and her husband Art, that there seemed to be different degrees of infection, and we did not know the prognosis for any of them, or for myself.

Later Saturday night, Margo was trying to explain things to her father on the phone without mentioning "flying saucers" or "alien monsters." She was not having much luck since she was learning what I knew all along, that those who rejected the very idea of alien visitation held to their disbelief with religious tenacity, branding all others as poor fools. Her father revealed that he had been visited by the federal agents who were doing what they called "a background check" of Margo's recent history.

As I read the accounts in the Lorenzens' 1967 book *Flying Saucer Occupants*, I remembered a story from my Boy Scout days. The Boy Scouts of America published the magazine Boy's Life, and the only article I remembered down the years was the story of Scoutmaster Sonny DesVergers. He was taking three troop members to their homes after a meeting in 1952 when they all saw a light descending into a palmetto grove several miles south of West Palm Beach, Fla. Thinking it could be a plane crash, DesVergers had the scouts remain in his car while he took a flashlight and struck out through the darkness in the direction of the supposed crash. When he entered a clearing, he pointed the flashlight upward and found he was standing under a massive hovering metallic disc. The disc tilted as he tried to get out from beneath it, and from somewhere within the silent, hovering craft, a beam shot out and burned the scoutmaster, knocking him down.

When the incident was reported to Wright-Patterson Air Force Base in Ohio, the military took the encounter so seriously that the head of the U.S. Air Force Project Blue Book and an assistant flew to West Palm Beach to investigate and interrogate. The most important part to me was DesVergers firm oath that he saw one or more occupants of the massive ship, and that he refused to even talk about them. He said that what he saw was too terrible to describe.

As I sat, reading, the DesVergers story came back from memory in such detail, I now knew why he never spoke about what he saw when he looked into the hovering flying saucer. The combination of horror and the intimidation of the Air Force closed his mouth forever; though the rough details of his encounter were widely chronicled, he never revealed what he saw inside the craft that night.

The house was quiet. I could hear the muted cheerful tones of Margo's voice from the bedroom as she talked with a family member or one of her friends. I turned on the TV to watch a late-night weekend movie, the 1971 strange horror film "Let's Scare Jessica To Death," and I was half watching it as I read the Lorenzen documentation of flying saucer sightings and the documented interaction of humans with non-human visitors. I never dreamed I would be one of those who was drawn into the nightmare of encountering living beings so horrible that our minds are unable to process what we are experiencing.

I must have dozed, but I heard a noise and was instantly alert. Since the previous Saturday, I always kept my .45 close at hand. There was the noise again! It was the knob on the front door. A glance at my watch showed it was 11:37, and someone was at the door.

Without disturbing Margo, I reached over and switched off the floor lamp, stood up on my stockinged feet, and crept to the door. I stood with my back against the wall, pistol in hand as I watched the doorknob turn. We had installed the new double-key Schlage deadbolt early in the week, so I felt a sense of security, though I still had the impulse to shoot through the door.

The room was dark, the only light shining on the living room floor from the bedroom whose door was halfway open 25 feet away. My ear was on the door, and I could hear motion on the porch outside. It was a shuffling sound and then rasping breath.

He had come back! I knew it was him. Now he was whispering to the door. Was he talking to himself? No. His human throat was mimicking the whispering, buzzing, clicking sounds of the horror creatures. "Shub…Niggurath…Iä…Ftagn." Then came a hoarse, grating sound from deep in the throat as he rattled the knob once more.

I had a choice: I could open the door and empty the pistol magazine into Arthur Brunk's torso, or I could get help. Padding across the floor, I went to the bedroom and put my finger to my lips, whispering to Margo to call the Police. She nodded and swiftly hung up, going to the directory to find the police phone number while I tiptoed back to the front door, where the thing on the other side continued disjointed conversations as though trying to make the door open to whatever purpose his brain had concocted. He was an agent of the alien horror, and I knew he was speaking to me through the door, commanding me to keep silent. The thick wood of the oak door felt cold as my ear pressed against it.

Margo came to the bedroom door and nodded her head vigorously, so I stood by the front door hoping a police car would arrive in time to catch the intruder. Then there was a silence as I strove to hear the stertorous breathing, but it had stopped. As I leaned into the door, I heard the clatter from the back yard as something jostled the pair of garbage cans. I ran to the back door and turned on the porch light. One of the garbage can lids was on the ground, and the back gate was partially open.

Only minutes later a car door slammed in front of the house and a young SVPD officer in a pressed khaki uniform shirt with the metal name tag carrying the name "Brucker" knocked on the front door. For him it was just a prowler call, but then I saw the two men coming up the walk, and I stepped outside so that I would only have to tell the story once for the Police and for agents Roberts and Pluman. The agents only asked me about my whereabouts the past two days, while Officer Brucker took the few details related to our unwanted visitor. Before he said good night, he said. "There's a strange smell on this porch. Did you notice? Are you sure it wasn't a skunk?"

I then sensed the strange smell and shook my head, "I heard some mumbled words, and I think it could have been somebody we know."

Agent Roberts stared at me. "You mean Arthur Brunk? We talked to somebody else who saw him tonight."

"The McCartys?" I was unsettled at the way the government agents were involved in the lives of those of us who had been in Mogollon the week before.

The agents looked at each other but did not answer me. After Officer Brucker had us sign a statement, he went back to patrol, while the AFOSI agents conferred on the sidewalk. Roberts then intoned softly, "Remember—nobody would believe you." They walked into the night and I did not see their vehicle anywhere on the street in front of the house.

They were looking for Brunk, and I wondered if he was spreading his loathsome contagion to San Vicente residents who were susceptible. How could he avoid capture in a town this small? I thought about it as I fell asleep, never learning whether Jessica was scared to death in the movie. That night I was spared the fleeting red vision that was intermittently a part of my dream life.

Sunday morning I volunteered to do the laundry, and while I separated whites, colors, jeans—including what I had worn on Friday—I pecked at the typewriter and interspersed my thoughts of Mogollon with the strange story of Tip Ulibarri as Ouida McCarty had related it in great detail. That detail made his subsequent denial suspect at the very least. He had lived for 30 years as we might be destined to live.

With the thump, thump, thump of the Maytag in the background, I looked at the keyboard and thought about the second-hand telling of Ulibarri's harrowing story.

He was a corporal in the spring of 1948 during the transition from Army Air Corps to U.S. Air Force, and he was stationed at Roswell Army Airfield. He had only been on base since December 1947 and a supply NCO. His new fellow airmen told him that strange things had happened on the base, but he remembered being very proud of being associated with the only atomic bomb squadron in the world. One day in March, his senior Sergeant pulled him out of the breakfast—they called it the "Clipper"—chow line and told him to report to headquarters where he was told to get on a truck without any gear except web belt and canteen, for a mission. There were 15 other airmen in the truck that morning, but they were instructed to keep the flap down. The truck departed through the North Gate of the base, and the airmen spent several hours in jostling semi-darkness, mostly on paved roads, but finally along miles of gravel and unimproved roads.

When they debarked, Ulibarri found himself on a dirt road close to the middle of nowhere facing an officer who told them they were there to assist in the recovery of a secret military aircraft that had crashed. The officer pointed up a slope to what appeared to be a mesa and ordered them to follow him up. Though completely disoriented, Ulibarri went to the top of the mesa and saw a giant metal disc tilted on its edge and opened up as though someone had extracted a giant slice of pie out of the side.

THE WHISPERING DARKNESS

The men were ordered to go inside the craft and bring out anything that was not secured. Ulibarri went inside and, to his amazement, he could almost see through the wall of the craft that had two separate levels. Two or three other men came up from the bottom level carrying what looked like the body of a child in a blue cloth one piece uniform. Ulibarri said it was "almost human." Someone said there were 15 others but they had been removed from the site already.

He and the others followed the orders, removing peculiar items such as a book made of filmy metal parchment and what seemed to be a water container, three small black metal cubes, and some items he could not describe. Ulibarri told the McCartys he was in the craft for about 15 minutes all told and that the air inside was "hazy" but evenly illuminated as though the bulkheads of the craft emanated a soft, shadowless light.

Because he had not eaten all day, Ulibarri thought his vertigo was hunger-related, but when he emerged from the craft, he began vomiting and reeling. Three others who had been inside longer than he had been were in fetal positions on the hard bedrock of the mesa. He told the McCartys that he gradually recovered but that at least three others had suffered even worse complications and were taken to a hospital in Albuquerque. Rumor had it that they were suffering from internal bleeding and that at least two had died. It was cold and miserable on the mesa that day, as light snow had fallen. Strangely, no snow lingered on the surface of the disc.

The next morning, heavy equipment began arriving, and Ulibarri still did not know where they were. A massive operation was launched to dismantle the craft into three sections and haul it away. The airmen and others who joined the operation were sworn to secrecy and told to sign a document to that effect. They were reminded that this was a Top Secret U.S. Government aircraft, even though most knew it was a lie. Ulibarri kept the secret faithfully until that Labor Day afternoon in the McCartys' back yard.

When he returned to base the following week, he was told that he had been on temporary duty (TDY) at Carswell Air Force Base in Ft. Worth, Texas. It was only after the publication of Frank Scully's book Behind the Flying Saucers in 1950 that he figured out that he had been outside of Aztec, N.M., just before the end of March, 1948. He was quickly promoted to Sergeant, transferred within weeks to an airbase in England, and retired in 1969 as Airman 6th. He told the McCartys that he still had respiratory and stomach problems, but he attributes some of that to smoking, a habit that he only quit in 1975. He also told the McCartys that he believed his total hair loss early in his Air Force career was caused by his exposure inside the giant disc, a craft he said was probably 100 feet in diameter.

Somehow I knew that Ulibarri's story was legitimate and too detailed to be faked. The disinformation program from 1950 through 1953 showed that the U.S. Government would stop at nothing to squelch a story about a recovered flying saucer, and today they were covering up the events at Mogollon, with the terrorized victims treated as inconvenient survivors.

As another load of clothes went into the dryer, I thought I understood the few reliable accounts of alien abduction, because the stories of painful physical procedures performed upon human subjects seemed to make sense from a human viewpoint, despite those who held that alien visitors must, because of their advanced technology, hold benevolent motives. Yet, a survey of human science reveals a history of cynical exploitation of experimental subjects and sometimes inhuman procedures.

Margo and I folded clothes, and I suggested to her that I was certain the arthropods not only infected the subjects they attacked, but they must be extracting material from human consciousness or from the bloodstreams of their victims. Intellectualizing did not ease the constant sense of anxiety I felt.

The knock on the front door startled me, and when Margo opened it, she found the McCartys standing there, dressed as though they had just come from church. Margo had said they were Baptists but not strong churchgoers. Brub was sporting a brand new cowboy hat, and Ouida had obviously just had her hair done the day before.

"Sorry to bust in you like this, but we had a visitor last night." Brub said as Margo escorted them into the living room. She insisted on making sandwiches, microwaved French fries, and served them with sweet iced tea. She brought out packets of hoarded "emergency catsup" she kept in the cupboard.

"So, you're sure it was Art Brunk?" I was perplexed. "How is he getting around? The cops must have spotted him if he's still driving that truck."

Ouida shook her head. "We only saw a shape disappearing after he tried to get through the front door. Who else could it be? His wife?"

I winced at the mention. "Why did he run off?"

Ouida exhaled, "There was somebody coming up the walk almost as soon as he—if it was him—escaped. Now I know somebody is watching us."

Margo replied, "Yeah, and they seem to be watching all of us. It doesn't feel good, does it?"

After we sat at the kitchen table and ate, Brub volunteered, "You know, I was just thinking of poor old Tip and how he kept his secret for almost 30 years as the military kept checking on him. I know he is still terrified that he might lose his pension. He told me so."

I hadn't considered the financial coercion that enforced any and all career military who might have seen the evidence of interplanetary visitors. It was a powerful means of safeguarding the greatest secret ever kept by a government from its own people.

Brub McCarty looked at the three of us. "You know, the police haven't been able to locate Brunk. Do you think we might have more luck?"

Margo was shaking her head, but I said, "You never know. If he comes back to either of our houses, we might be able to track him." Then I was thinking about the hideous creatures and wondering if they had left Earth for good or if they were still manipulating their victims in some manner. The McCartys had seen their ship as it rose from the Mogollon mine, but I realized that I had never in my life seen a true UFO. I was convinced that seeing one was only likely to change one's life for the worse.

Ouida said, "Margo, can you get in touch with Mattie so we can all be ready if one of us sees or hears something. If we can just find Art and follow him, we can help capture him." I notice that she used "capture" instead of "apprehend" or "arrest." It was as though she didn't think of Arthur Brunk as fully human either.

"OK, I'm all for it. I think our VW bus will be ready on Tuesday." We at least had a plan.

Sitting around the table, it was obvious that we were avoiding any mention of other-worldly craft or of the monstrosities invading our world.

The rest of Sunday was nondescript except for learning that Al Unser had again won the Indianapolis 500. When I compared his performance to the straining 40 horsepower engine of my white bus, I had to smile at how the breadbox shape of my Volkswagen had become an icon of the counterculture era, even though I would never paint peace symbols on it or string curtains in the windows.

Monday was a typical Memorial Day, with the flag flying over the front porch, though we should have been at our gallery. I made a phone call to Glenwood to talk with Bob at the service station. He said that the road was still closed to Mogollon, and the residents were still not allowed to return to their homes. I wondered if Tip Ulibarri had joined his neighbors for a holiday cookout.

It was Tuesday when I again was behind the wheel of the VW bus that would get me to work, the restored front end skillfully matched in paint color to the rest of the vehicle. The repairs had not been too difficult. Margo phoned me at work Wednesday after lunch and said that Dr. Monsevais wanted to talk to us. I had almost forgotten about him, and now my curiosity was renewed with the news that our peculiar sample was worth the time of the public health officer.

Margo and I pulled into the Public Health office parking lot on N. Silver Street, almost simultaneously, at 3:45 p.m., and we walked in together to be ushered immediately to the doctor's modest office down a short hallway from the reception desk. A framed 11x14 black and white photograph of popular Governor Jerry Apodaca joined framed diplomas on the beige south wall of the office, and behind the doctor were blinds drawn against the afternoon sun coming through the doctor's office window.

Jesse Monsevais stood to greet us, obviously glad to see Margo, as are most people. He had no stethoscope around his neck and was wearing short sleeves, a silver-and-turquoise bolo string tie around his neck. In his late 30's, he presented a spare figure with a pleasant, narrow face behind his glasses. He gestured to the metal chairs in front of his desk before he sat down. His gilt-trimmed leather briefcase stood open at the side of his desk.

Smiling, he put his palms together and brought his fingers to his lips. A turquoise ring was on his right ring finger but no ring on the left hand. "Well, your sample did get our lab's attention, and I wanted to give you what I learned before something else gets our attention."

Margo returned his smile. "Thanks for taking the time." She scrunched her lips in an expression of disapproval. "I am sure it is something ordinary, but I really don't like it—sort of like something left over from a fish fry."

Dr. Monsevais chuckled, and I joined him. "No, Margo—quite the contrary. I don't know exactly where to start." He took out a yellow legal pad closely written from top to bottom with very few gaps. He adjusted his glasses and scanned his precise handwriting.

"I had a long talk with Consuela Lucero in the Albuquerque office this morning. She's our primary lab tech up there. She was really excited about your sample. It wasn't anything that she expected. She even sent a report to the Centers for Disease Control in D.C. last Friday."

Margo seemed distressed. "Disease control? You mean that thing was infected?"

Dr. Monsevais waved her off, "No, no, it's just that the better labs are organized by the feds under that umbrella. Let me tell you what we learned from the sample."

Using a ballpoint pen, he touched the page of notes, sometimes shaking his head. "One side of the 'shell', if I can call it that, is a silicon compound, but it is organic…"

He went on to give the standard discussion we all learned in our college chemistry courses about the similarity of silicon to carbon, with its many congeners—almost as many as carbon, and often put forward as a possible platform for life. Silicon is hard, almost metallic, and was the major material used in the development of the transistor in 1947.

I remembered the sound when I fired into the monstrosity in the gallery, the bullets sounding as though they were entering the densest wood. I was linking the fragment now to those hideous arthropods.

Dr. Monsevais continued, "Like carbon, silicon can form organic as well as inorganic molecules, and there is a strong bar between the silicon molecule and the carbon molecule, but silicon is remarkably resistant to temperature and pressure variations. Anyhow, the piece you submitted seems part of a tessellated larger whole."

I was imagining how Sparky must have obtained that sample with a courageous attack as the doctor described that the pattern was like that of a tortoise shell, only in modified squares connected at the edge of each unit by a very thin cord-like rubbery substance that was impossible to cut but which was flexible to some degree, and perhaps allowed for growth. I was visualizing the thin solder seam in a stained glass pattern.

"So this was something alive?" Like me, Margo did not want to mention the horror as we remembered it.

"Yes, the tests point in that direction. It is a complex silicon molecule that is extremely strong. Because silicon is tetravalent, it can form extremely hard surfaces. But with a Silicon-carbon bond, the molecule can adapt to a silicon-hydrogen bond. In short, we know it is an organosilicon material, but we don't have a clue what it is."

The analysis was even more bizarre for the sticky, foam-like material adhering to the reverse of the brownish fragment. The doctor continued, "Such a mixture of amino acids and peptides seems to defy our reality. When I did my master's degree in organic chemistry, I wrote a paper on dissolving acidic peptides and extracting protein from the human stomach."

The good doctor was starting to leave me behind, as I had barely made it through basic chemistry in college. He then described how the material seemed to be a form of material that could actually process protein and convert it into energy.

So, from what I had seen, perhaps what was inside that exoskeleton could substitute for what we call the digestive tract, and from what I had seen in Mogollon, it meant that there were no normal interior organs in a hellish creature like that—only seething mass of animating proteins. I was thinking of it as a soft interior mass like a semi-liquid Styrofoam. It was a revolting thought. I had shot holes into it, but the effect seemed minimal.

"Anyhow, Consuelo and I agreed that this fragment was part of a larger form, and even though the silicon molecule seemed to be almost metallic, it was still organic. I don't know any creature on Earth or in the ocean that has this kind of makeup. I don't know where the hell you found it." Dr. Monsevais leaned back in the swivel chair and put his hands behind his head.

I took a chance. "So, if this is from something living, it would be some kind of monstrosity?"

His grin was tight-lipped. "I couldn't say it better myself. I don't know what you had there."

I asked a further question, "Did Dr. Lucero describe the molecule?"

Dr. Monsevais nodded, hands still behind his head, "Ummhmm. She put samples under the electron microscope and plotted them. You probably aren't interested in the difference between single and double bonds and the other terminology."

Margo shrugged. "Probably not. I guess we should just take our icky fragment and go home." She was grinning.

Dr. Monsevais leaned forward now, his elbows on the desk. "Uh, that's going to be a problem. A strange thing happened up there in Albuquerque. Consuela told me yesterday that she was visited by federal officials Tuesday, and they confiscated your sample as well as all the documents and lab test printouts. I assure you that your names were not associated with the sample. What she told me on the phone this morning was strictly from memory, and she was almost whispering when said she was violating their warning by talking to me. I think somebody really scared her."

Margo said it best. "She's not alone, Jesse." Meanwhile I had images of an army of Roberts and Pluman agents intimidating every person who experienced a UFO sighting in the United States.

Dr. Monsevais closed his briefcase and walked out with us into the afternoon sunshine. Margo gave him a brief hug before he went to his white Ford Explorer and we two went to our separate vehicles. The normalcy of San Vicente was not comforting this Wednesday, and tomorrow would be June. My other concern had me wondering what we would cook for dinner that evening.

The dinner problem was solved as we made burritos from ground beef, potato chunks, chopped onions, green chile, and cheese, wrapped in warm flour tortillas. What came after an early dinner was what I later thought of as the most unlikely phone call I could remember.

Margo answered the phone, pausing, then, "Yes, this is she…Oh, yes, I DO remember you…well, I'm so glad you are happy. That's a great home.…uh-huh…I remember that… that's right…I think he did…"

From the kitchen, I began to eavesdrop on the conversation and wonder whom Margo was speaking with. Now she was beckoning to me, and I walked into the living room.

"Y'know, that is a very strange coincidence…yes, I know that we were concerned…why don't you give Rick all the details."

I said "Hello," and was suddenly talking with Nurse Diaz from the San Vicente Hospital. Margo lifted her eyes and went to her office area to look at some material she had brought home from her office downtown.

Nurse Diaz began by telling me that, after the agents hovered around Ofelia Armendariz, she was not interested in contacting any authorities concerning what was obviously a bad situation, and she had read the same newspaper stories we had read.

I was glad she had no idea what had happened to us in Mogollon.

She explained that she had a nephew who lived in a trailer park south of town. Actually, she called him her "drug-dealing nephew." Her long-suffering sister told her the story, and she said what happened smelled "like a dead skunk in the middle of the road."

As I listened, my stomach began to get that uncomfortable feeling. Her nephew's name was Jorgé Maldonado, and when Diaz's sister went to see the 23-year-old Maldonado at his mobile home, she found him severely ill and vomiting from something more than the smell of marijuana and cigarettes inside his cluttered and dirty residence. She was alarmed and telephoned Nurse Diaz, who called for an ambulance before driving to the trailer park. According to Diaz, the young man had some unusual wounds that made her think of Ofelia Armendariz.

At that point, I began to listen more intently as she said, "There is something wrong at his place. He has been driving a grey 1973 Honda Accord with a faded paint job and a cracked windshield. His car was gone when I went out there, and now there is a nice new Ford pickup parked behind the trailer. It has no license plates."

While that was compelling news, what she said next turned my skin to gooseflesh as though I had come full circle. I remembered her every word.

"We took him to the hospital in restraints. I thought he was taking LSD or something, but he kept saying that he had the mark of the Devil on him."

"The Devil?"

"He used the words over and over—said the Devil came to his door with a face so evil he could not describe it. He was crying, saying 'he breathed on me, *mi tia*, and he whispered to me in a buzzing voice, making me see the vision of Hell'."

"That's horrific. Did he say anything else?"

"Oh yes, he said this 'devil' put a spell on him and on his friend Anastacio—said the devil made him sign his name. He said the Devil attacked him and put his mark on him, and when he woke up again, Anastacio was gone and the kitchen area was trashed. He found his own car keys gone, his wallet empty, and a set of new car keys in his hand. He said the Devil took his shotgun. I can't tell that to the police or those government agents who talked to you in the hospital. Public Health Department? Ha!"

"Has your nephew come back to normal yet?"

"Of course not. He is still delirious, and I saw a terrible mark on his chest, black with bruising and infection. It is a dangerous wound that is not responding to antibiotics."

I felt my chest tighten. "Poor guy. Could I talk to him?" In truth, I had little sympathy for those involved in the drug world, but here was validation of what I had read over the years about demonic attacks and pacts with the Devil.

Nurse Diaz said that Jorgé was in isolation, and she mentioned that he disliked gringos, but she did give me directions to the address of the mobile home, just as she emphasized that she was not going to call the police until her nephew was lucid again. I thanked her for the information and said we would call to check on her nephew's progress.

I sat with my hand on the phone after hanging up. I knew that Brunk's contact with the creatures had given him an uncanny power of influencing humans, and I knew that he had rendered me helpless when he invaded my home that Monday evening. I wondered how the hapless young drug dealer had been attacked, but I now knew why police had been unable to find Brunk's new Ford 250 crew cab pickup. It was a chilling moment.

Ten

A Final Horror

Margo looked up as I walked into her home office area and told her what Nurse Diaz had revealed. I also told her where I thought Arthur Brunk might have gone. She said, "We really should call the Sheriff. That place is way outside of town."

I disagreed. "I don't want to do that. I don't want to call the authorities until I can check this out. Do you think I should get McCarty involved?"

Margo stared up at the gold filigree framed modern oil painting on the wall depicting the Tenney Mogollon Freight wagon train coming toward the viewer up Broadway Avenue in San Vicente in 1900. It was painted from the well-known San Vicente Museum photo taken back in the day. Then she tapped her pen on the desk pad and nodded. "Maybe you should call Mattie and tell her as well." There was something in her tone that knifed me in the stomach.

As I dialed the McCartys' number I was thinking about the connection between Mogollon and San Vicente, visualizing that single telephone wire that ran between the two towns in 1908. I wondered how many town residents had a sense of that historic connection that remained in 1978.

Ouida answered the phone, and I asked to speak to her husband. If there was something dangerous south of town, I didn't want her or Margo to be involved.

The Wagon Train to Mogollon circa 1900   Courtesy Silver City Museum

When I explained the situation to Brub, he said he would pick me up in his truck in 20 minutes. Margo made me promise to be careful and that I should not approach Brunk, even if we did find him.

Her parting comment as she hugged me was, "If you see him, you come back and get the sheriff." I assured her that I would, but mentally I had my fingers crossed.

It was too late to change my mind, and there was still plenty of daylight when McCarty braked his white 4x4 pickup in front of the house. The windows were down, and his new hat seemed to fill the space on the driver's side. I was wearing my Levi's and the sleeves of my Wrangler shirt were rolled up to the elbows. I saw McCarty's Winchester 30 30 in the rifle rack against the rear window, his .38 in the hip holster on his right side.

I had the loaded .45 in my right pocket, with two spare magazines in the back pocket, a little uncomfortable to sit on, while McCarty drove south on Hudson Street, accelerated up the hill, and turned left onto the Ridge Road, while Highway 90 continued southwest on to Lordsburg. He hunched over the steering wheel as we followed Nurse Diaz's directions to turn left again and down Mountainview Drive into the nest of mobile homes. It was not difficult to spot the single-wide trailer that Jorgé and his friend were using as a base for their drug operation. It would not be long before the jackals would descend on the unit and ransack it, but for now it appeared to be waiting for somebody to pick up the rubbish littering the yard, and the charcoal grill leaning precariously on a weak leg. A cardboard carton filled with empty beer cans and bottles stood beside the raised plywood stoop with three weathered unpainted wooden steps.

We got out of the truck and went over to a sagging aluminum-roofed carport. Underneath was a vehicle covered by sheets of cardboard with "Kelvinator Refrigerator" printed on them. The truck certainly belonged to Arthur Brunk. I shoved aside one of the cardboard sheets and peered into the driving compartment. The truck was almost new, but the interior of the cab was littered with food and drink containers, possibly stolen in house break-ins, while the seat was stained and aged. We were certainly now looking for a nondescript Honda Civic whose best miles were behind it and whose paint job was fading down to the primer.

We were back in McCarty's truck, roaring up the hill and back to the Ridge Road, headed south to where the road became dirt and gravel as it veered east as the back road to several ranches, and finally to the county airport served by Frontier Airlines with its workhorse DC-3 passenger planes.

Headed down the road at 40 mph, a dust cloud roiled up behind us, creating a dirty orange haze in the late afternoon sky. Traffic was almost non-existent. "You sure about this, Rick?" McCarty's eyes were nailed to the road ahead.

"It's just a hunch." We shot over a cattle guard with a Brrrrrp sound, and I looked for the dirt road turnoff. "There has always been something about the old Smith Place that made me think of it. Here! Take a right."

Brub hit the brakes, making the tires growl on the dirt as he swung the wheel and headed south down a rutted road. "Wait a minute. There's a ranch house down there."

"Yeah, it looks that way, doesn't it? It has been abandoned for years. It was flooded out, and the family never did come back to clean up the mess. The barn is intact, and there's a windmill, so there are usually cattle hanging around the corral and the pasture."

The rough, eroded dirt road led down the hill before giving way to a 15-yard expanse of deep sand where the sandy wash overwhelmed the road. Tracks in the sand showed the passage of other vehicles, probably 4-wheel drive trucks, before us. McCarty gunned the engine and we ground through the sand that almost stalled the engine, and then we rose up again to the hardpan dirt. A hundred yards farther another cattle guard loomed, and just beyond it, at the right side of the road, stood the five-foot high iron water tank fed by a creaking windmill. The breeze turned the windmill, and the water was flowing over the edge of the tank, making a dark path across the road, trickling down toward the pasture. Its path was bordered by ragweed and nettles.

McCarty pulled the truck up beside the tank, and we got out, stretching. The rocky hillside rose steeply behind the tank and sloped down across the road to the front of what remained of the ranch house. If it were not for the empty window frames and the absence of doors, it would look habitable. Much of the roof had collapsed. I didn't see a vehicle parked anywhere around the abandoned building.

As I remembered from exploring the ruin more than one time, there was a front room just inside the now-absent front door, and a bedroom to the left and to the right. Beyond the front room was a small kitchen and a bathroom, the fixtures of which had been pillaged long ago. Flooding had destroyed the hardwood floor that was twisted and sunken. Nothing of value remained inside the shell of the house. Outside, there were three tall and dying trees, one on each side of the house, and the tallest in front of the entrance.

My watch read 7:12, and we had an hour of daylight remaining. McCarty lifted the brim of his hat with his forefinger, "Nobody home."

"Maybe not. Let's circle around in the pasture to be sure." The "pasture" was baked clay, cracking in the May sunshine. Close to the corral fence that ended by the northeast corner of the grey stucco wall of the house, prickly pear cactus and creosote bushes had staked their claim.

We walked across the road and down into the field. The smell of manure dominated in the still-warm air. Dust was already tinting the waning sun, and the aridity of the air sharpened my sinuses. I put my hand on the butt of the pistol as we walked slowly, trying to avoid the minefield of deep brown cow pies dotting the field, our boots tramping on the hard clay. Flies swarmed around the fresher heaps of ordure, and McCarty waved away a pair of yellow jacket wasps that were no doubt sustained by the trickle of water descending from the windmill tank.

I stopped and watched a swift Cnemidophorous whiptail lizard scooting across the field, his yellowish stripes adding to his streamlined appearance. McCarty had walked around the northwest corner of the rear of the house and past a gaping window frame. I was behind him and approaching the same corner when we were both taken by surprise.

A noise from the front of the house caught my attention as a young Hispanic male came racing around the corner toward us, head down. He must have seen McCarty through that back window, and he did not even seem to see me. Unlike a movie scenario, I was unable to move for a few seconds, and the young man was almost eight feet away from me when he suddenly leveled a sawed-off shotgun underhanded toward McCarty. The man's back was toward me.

I shouted, "MCCARTY!" as the shotgun went off, its characteristic hollow boom shattering the peace of the afternoon.

It is often said that you can't miss with a shotgun, but he did. Instead of peppering Brub McCarty, the entire load struck the side of the house and the pellets ricocheted directly back in our direction.

I felt the stinging heat of pellets, one hitting my thigh and another striking my forehead. The gunner was not so lucky. He yelled and grabbed his chest as the shotgun fell into the dirt.

Suddenly regaining my senses, I drew my .45 and did something much smarter than I might have done. I drew back and slammed the side of the pistol against the side of the young man's head, knocking him to the ground, where he lay moaning and crying. Glancing to my left I saw Brub McCarty with his .38 aimed directly at the assailant, but he was also wise enough not to pull the trigger.

I felt a trickle of blood on my eyebrow, but luck was with me. The pellets were probably #6 birdshot and had lost much of their energy hitting the stucco patch on the house wall. I reached up and felt the pellet lodged under the skin of my forehead. The other pellet had penetrated my jeans but was no worse than a bee sting in my upper thigh. The blood was already drying.

We picked up the old 20-gauge pump shotgun with a sawed-off barrel and a stock that had been chopped off to make a pistol grip. He had started to recycle the gun to get another shell into the chamber, but instant karma changed his mind. He was closer to the wall than I was, and he was bleeding from at least three pellet wounds in his face. His dirty t-shirt was also showing blood in three more places on his torso.

McCarty squinted, "What the hell is he doing?" I was certain this was Jorgé's friend, Anastacio, but I could tell from his pained and vacant stare that he was feeling something worse than physical pain. What had Brunk done to him? Were all those bleeding wounds from shotgun pellets? The side of his face was swelling up from the pistol blow I had dealt him.

"More importantly, what are we going to do with him? Art Brunk is out here. I know he is. He's more dangerous than this poor kid—not that he wasn't trying to kill you."

McCarty looked the young man, who was trying to sit up now. "How old are you, Son?" He got a blank and hostile stare.

I looked down at him. "Do you have the Devil's mark?"

Now his eyes glazed, and his whimper turned into a quiet laugh. He touched his chest.

"I think we'd better get him into the truck and get the hell out of here." McCarty was echoing my thoughts, but then I looked around, listening to the creak of the windmill and the warm breeze soughing through the tree branches.

"Brub, if Arthur Brunk gets away, we'll be cowering behind our doors again. You haven't seen what he looks like now."

"And I sure don't want to see him now." He squared his shoulders and smiled with one corner of his mouth. "Let's make sure this guy doesn't give us any problems." With that, McCarty walked back to his truck, threw the shotgun into the bed, and opened the tool box inside the truck bed. I could hear the clank of tools and a grunt as he came up with a length of ½" diameter cotton rope. We tied Anastacio's hands securely behind him and wrapped the rope around a fencepost with its top strand of barbed wire. The sullen kid had gone back to whimpering, his wounds appearing more serious than they actually were.

We entered the ruins of the ranch house, now shadowed in the coming evening. The back room was obviously where Jorgé's friend had been holed up. There were three empty Coors long-neck beer bottles and food wrappers scattered on the sunken and splintered flooring. Looking out the rear-window frame, I could see what Anastacio saw as McCarty came around the back corner of the house. I was thankful that he didn't fire that shotgun through the open window.

After we searched the house, we returned to the field and approached the corral, whose gates were all yawning wide open. The pellet wound in my thigh was uncomfortable, but the next sight caused my stomach to jump and made McCarty mutter curses under his breath.

In the center of the corral or stock pen was a dead bull lying amidst manure pies that almost filled the enclosure, some of them still wet as the flies swarmed over them.

Living in New Mexico, I had seen dead livestock over the years and in various stages of decomposition, even demonstrating the action of predators, but what I saw here instilled fear inside of me. Yes, I had read occasional stories of cattle mutilation, and I know that

Margo had reported on such a case several years ago when she was working as a newswriter for the Daily Enterprise, but that was before I met her.

McCarty and I approached the carcass tentatively as though its loathsome appearance was toxic. While glossy bluebottle flies were already settling on the steer, it was obviously still fresh. There was no blood, and it showed an evil surgery that removed the lower jaw and tongue, the flesh still glistening. As we gingerly sidled around to see the backside of the bull, we saw a precise cylinder extracted from the anus, as though removed by a cookie cutter. The male organs were sliced off, leaving a bloodless crater. As we looked closer, we could see that the hide of the animal was seared along the incised areas as though some kind of heated instrument had cauterized each wound.

McCarty pointed out that the eye had been removed, cut out and leaving a perfect circle around the orbit. Whatever had killed the bull had probably stopped the heart before beginning an ungodly dissection. We looked at each other, feeling the horror of something we could not explain. I did not like the stillness that was settling over the Smith place as the sun settled in the west, turning the horizon a salmon pink.

McCarty pointed to the ground around the steer, and we both saw the strange imprints in the dirt and the manure that we had seen in only one other place—Mogollon during the nightmare time.

We were looking east toward the gate leading to the dark wood frame of the large barn, still used for storing hay. The road passing east in front of the house went through another cattle guard, past the barn and down into a second depression that followed the wash southward. The barn was at a higher elevation, and we took a few halting steps toward the gate leading to it.

We stopped, McCarty's arm stretched across my chest. I saw two bare legs, bare human feet extending into the path on the far side of the corral fence, whose gate was opened in our direction. I swallowed, but my mouth was as dry as the sandy wash we had just driven through. I could also see the bumper and trunk area of a car parked at the south side of the barn, close to the road.

I now wanted to run back to the truck, but something drove me forward, step by step, gun in hand, bolstered by the company of the tall man on my right. The horror of the mutilated steer was only the precursor to what we saw next.

The naked body was spread-eagled on its face, the head turned grotesquely to the left. At one time it had been Arthur Brunk, car salesman, family man, husband of Matilda. Now it was barely recognizable as a human being, its bloodless shape instilling a sense of cosmic horror inside me.

The pale legs were spread, and the contents of the entire pelvic area—rectum, sexual organs, gonads—was gone, surgically sliced open and extracted, the edges cauterized, and not a drop of blood to be seen on the dirt, rocks, and cattle excrement on the ground around the body.

Emblazoned on my retinas was the image of an alien transformation. Though his eyes had been removed, the face was inhuman, its cheeks sprouting tubercules, like limp pink cotton swabs. The lower jaw, tongue, and throat were gone from the bottom of the head.

The skin on his back was horribly deformed and seemed to form a vague pattern of horn-like plates that were smooth and greyish-brown in color. The arms were extended, thumb and fingers pinched together like lobster claws.

Whatever happened here was fresh enough that it had to have occurred within hours, not days. Perhaps even the blowflies would stay away from this hideous corpse. This was Brunk's reward for becoming an agent of an alien race.

"I think we should get the hell out of here." McCarty made perfect sense. As he said that, I looked toward the barn, which was about 150 feet east of the fence. I blinked and shook my head, wondering if fatigue was affecting my vision. The outline of the barn roof seemed unsteady, wavering like a heat mirage in the late afternoon light. As the air grew even more quiet, I imagined hearing those too-familiar, hateful, buzzing words that I had heard so many times. I hoped it was the whine of a cicada. I fought mindless terror, but as I looked at the remains of Arthur Brunk, I remembered how he mimicked those sounds.

I stared at the corpse, and my paranoia imagined sounds that seemed all too real.

McCarty adjusted his hat, still staring at the mutilated body on the ground. Perhaps it was exhaustion and shock that was affecting my mind, but he said, "Got to admit that this place feels really spooky." He grabbed my arm and started us walking back through the yawning corral gate, past the mutilated bull, and even faster to the fence where we untied the semi-conscious young man and half-carried him to the truck, Anastacio's hands still tied behind him. The entire left side of his face was swollen, and his eye was blackened.

As we reached the pickup, I was stricken with a throbbing headache, but it could have been a reaction to the shotgun pellet that hit my forehead. I did not know what we were going to do with Anastcio. As McCarty backed the truck onto the road and started back the way we had come, we discussed what to do with the adolescent sandwiched between us in the cab of the truck. We decided not to deliver him to the county sheriff, and so we were bound for my house in hopes that Margo could reach Nurse Diaz.

The other problem was how to report the body. Should we call the Sheriff immediately? As soon as we did that, government agents would take charge, and we would be unquestionably discredited, intimidated, and even threatened. We came up with a plan that again would require Margo's assistance, but it just might be the best plan.

As we reached the Ridge Road, the sun had set, and the pain in my head strangely subsided. We were headed into the sunset and back to San Vicente filled with adrenaline and anxiety, our prisoner sitting between us in the cab. I leaned against the passenger side door, pushing into the restraining seat belt for comfort, and I let waves of fatigue wash over me, the acrid smell of fear soaking my armpits.

We talked little as we drove the several miles back to town, and the silence was only broken by occasional muttering of the young man sitting between us, his head hanging onto his chest, the blood on his face forming a crust.

McCarty drove through town, making the turns and pulling onto Arizona Street, slowing to a stop in front of the house. As planned, Brub would remain in the truck with the captive while I went inside. Before I opened the truck door, I saw the vertical, unique tail-lights of a Lincoln braking at the stop sign down the block. Had it been parked in front of the house? I was too tired to worry about Darouse Brunk revealing all to my wife, even if Margo instigated the meeting. The urgency of events trumped everything.

Margo was standing inside the front door as I came up the walk, and she started to say something but saw my face and the words came out differently. "What happened?"

It was then that I felt the blood on my cheek and looked down to the dried droplets on my unsnapped shirt. Margo reached out and started to lead me to the bathroom when I resisted. "No, I'm OK, but there's something we have to do—fast." I led her to the front door and pointed to the two occupants of the truck.

"Get to your rolodex and find Nurse Diaz right now!" I described the visit to the nephew's trailer, the discovery of Brunk's truck, and the combat at the abandoned Smith ranch house. I was certain that Diaz would be willing to take Anastacio to the hospital rather than seeing him turned over to the Sheriff. "In case somebody's listening on the line, just say that a friend of her nephew came to see us and wants to talk to her about important family business."

It worked, and Margo said Nurse Diaz was on her way to our house. It was better that Margo did not see the young man's face, so I went out to the truck to update McCarty. He had put a toothpick into his mouth, chewing nervously, and explained what we were going to do. Then I went back inside and tell Margo about Arthur Brunk.

Her face was slightly flushed with the look that said she was about to tell me something, but I stopped whatever she was thinking, when I blurted out, "Art Brunk is dead—horribly mutilated."

"God, no!" She let me hug her.

"I don't think God had anything to do with it." We stood under the front porch light, and I tried to explain why we had not alerted law enforcement and why I wanted somebody else to see the proof of what we experienced. I then asked her if she could contact Dr. Monsevais in Las Cruces to see if he would make a special trip in the morning to see for himself what I had witnessed in the manure-littered corral. When I described the mutilated bull, she made the decision and went inside and called 411 to get Jesse Monsevais's home phone number in Las Cruces. I followed her and again wondered if our phone line was being monitored. Margo was showing excitement now, and she volunteered to drive downtown to her office and make the call from there.

Twenty minutes later, she was back, having succeeded in getting Dr. Monsevais on the phone, using the description of the body as I had given to her, especially the condition of the transformation of the skin on Brunk's back. She reminded the doctor that the original sample we gave him had been confiscated, and that if government officials got wind of the scene south of San Vicente, we would never be able to prove the reality of a praeternatural event. We owed it to the residents of Mogollon and especially Ofelia Armendariz to follow this to the end.

Shortly after Margo returned, I heard a car door slam outside the house, and I rushed out onto the sidewalk to meet the nurse from San Vicente Hospital. Her grey hair was more unkempt than when I first saw her. "What's this about Jorgé's friend?" She was wearing a black jacket and loose-fitting pants and a headband as though she had been working out.

"He says he has the mark of the Devil on him. He shot at us, and he hasn't said much since we brought him along with us. It was a decision to either turn him over to the cops or to you. From what you say, whatever happened to your nephew—happened to him. Can you help him?"

She went to the truck and looked inside. "Let me use your phone."

I escorted Nurse Diaz into the house so that she could call for an ambulance.

While we were waiting, we bundled Anastacio out of the truck and untied his hands. Diaz took him by the chin and examined his lopsided face, the left side now swollen and bruised. She looked at the other wounds and turned around with a quizzical expression, "Did you shoot him?"

McCarty shook his head, "He was such a bad shot that he shot a wall and the pellets bounced back onto him. We both could have shot him, but we didn't."

Nurse Diaz nodded, her mouth tightly closed to a wry slit before turning to me and seeing the blood on my forehead. "You need any care?" I just shook my head as I wondered whether the nurse's call for an ambulance would get some kind of response if somebody was tapping the line.

We were very careful not to mention the details of our discovery or even what we knew about Ofelia Armendariz's purgatory. The EMTs put Anastacio on a gurney and wheeled him into the ambulance, and Diaz said she would follow them to the hospital.

When the two of us walked into the house, Margo gave me a wet wash cloth to wipe my face as she relayed the information from Dr. Monsevais. "He said he wants to be here before 7 in the morning. He's more excited than I thought he would be."

"And he doesn't know the half of it." McCarty was understating, and all three of us knew it. We plotted our tactics and decided that we would go out to the abandoned ranch at dawn, and make sure that Ouida called the Sheriff's Department when she thought we would already be well out of town. It would be a standard "rumor of a dead body" call. If government agents picked up the message, they would have to follow the sheriff's deputies since they did not know San Vicente or the county roads. Too bad for them.

McCarty said he would be back before dawn, and he was certain Ouida would not want to go along. I went back into the house with Margo. I cleared my .45 but was too tired to clean it. I stripped down to my shorts and grabbed tweezers from the bathroom. I was able to pluck the shotgun pellet from just under the skin of my thigh, and the pellet had not done anything to my forehead except break the skin. Head wounds were always dramatic. Margo came in and applied some antiseptic to my wounds, but she was not very talkative. I thought about the Lincoln taillights.

Margo knew where we had been earlier, and I asked if she as going out with us in the morning. She said, "Maybe. Let's see what Jesse has in mind. I don't know if I'm up to seeing another mutilated cow."

I passed a fitful night and once, when I did fall asleep, I was assailed by that cursed red haze, and through it, a figure came walking toward me. As the figure drew closer, I recognized the ghastly naked shape of Arthur Brunk, no longer human, his face erupting with pustules, his inhuman voice issuing its buzzing whisper "Iä…Iä…Shub…Niggurath…," and I knew it was commanding me to join him and the legions of misshapen entities.

Another voice joined him, and it was Nurse Diaz's nephew standing in the reddish shadow, proudly baring his chest and pointing to the black wound. He said, "You must sign. You must sign," and I awoke in confusion but with my heart hammering in my chest.

I was up well before dawn, doing exercises and leaving a voice mail message at work saying that I would not be in before noon. Margo also awakened early and was drinking coffee as we waited for the arrival of McCarty and Dr. Monsevais. She was wearing jeans, and was obviously deciding to go on the expedition to see Arthur Brunk's body. As she explained it, she could be useful in guiding the doctor on the dirt roads south of San Vicente.

As it was, McCarty's truck was in front of the house before 6, and Margo brought him in for coffee, the fragrance in the kitchen reminding me that coffee smells better than it tastes.

Even though the doctor had to drive two hours from Las Cruces, he was still able to arrive before 6:30, having followed Margo's directions to find our address. By then, Margo had served coffee to both of the vehicle drivers as I prepared my Nikon F camera, determined to get some photographic proof this time. It was grey in the east as all four of us went to the vehicles. The final phone call was from Brub to Ouida, telling her not to forget to make a phone call in about 20 minutes. She knew what to do.

It was still chilly in the San Vicente morning, and I was glad to be wearing the blue denim cowboy shirt, despite two drops of dried blood on the right breast pocket. Traffic was sparse as we drove through town headed south up the hill and left onto the Ridge Road. After passing the mobile home division and another upscale subdivision down from the ridge, the pavement ended, and we were headed East toward the dawn and the abandoned ranch we called the Smith Place. We would probably have the place to ourselves for a half hour or so before the Sheriff's Department arrived. Whether the federal watchdogs would be along behind them was anybody's guess.

With Dr. Monsevais and Margo following close behind in the Health Department Ford Explorer, Brub McCarty jolted us in his truck as we followed the rutted access road we had taken 12 hours earlier, taking care to blast though the broad sandy wash that presented a ridge of sand in the middle, requiring a vehicle with high clearance. It was no problem for either of our vehicles. Soon we clattered over the cattle guard and pulled in beside the stock tank where the windmill was turning lazily.

We were all out of the two vehicles quickly, and Dr. Monsevais seemed eager to find the confirmation of the astonishing analysis from the fragment that had been confiscated by federal authorities from the Albuquerque lab. He was carrying a small valise, and a cellophane packet containing a pair of latex gloves protruded from his back pocket.

My camera was around my neck, .45 in my pocket, and McCarty was wearing his hip holster with the .38 revolver. I beckoned to the doctor and pointed down past the shell of the house and toward the corral. Perhaps I had not gotten enough sleep the night before, because I was now aware of a beginning headache in my right temple.

McCarty reminded us, "We'd better get moving. I don't think we have more than about 20 minutes before we have company."

Margo was walking beside me, with Jesse Monsevais on her left. McCarty was on the left, slightly ahead of all three of us. Margo wrinkled her nose, "It stinks out here."

I added, "And it's gonna get worse."

She grinned and pushed my arm. It was the first smile I'd seen from her since the day before. As we passed the northwest corner of the ruined ranch house, I pointed out the blast pattern on the wall where Maldonado had fired the worst shot on record.

Walking through the cattle dung-littered pasture, we could see the corral gates still hanging open. Our steps quickened as the sun emerged on the eastern horizon. Inside the corral, the mutilated bulk of the dead bull was still unmolested by predators, though its odor was almost overpowering. The light was now strong enough that I could shoot available light photos. I walked around the carcass, shooting photos that even today are chilling enough as they show the precise cauterized circular wounds and gaps where the tongue, sexual organs and anus had been removed.

"This looks the same as the cow I saw years ago before I met you, Rick." Margo was visibly uncomfortable.

"I remember you showed me your story in the Daily Enterprise, and if we didn't have worse things on our minds, this would be scary enough in itself."

Dr. Monsevais seemed impressed, as though he recognized some unnatural process at work. We then headed across the corral interior toward the gate leading to the two-storey hulk of the barn whose black shingled roof jutted above the horizon in the pre-dawn.

I stopped Margo momentarily. "Are you sure you want to see this? I know you hate things like this." I remembered being with Margo on this same ground on a cloudy day just one year ago, watching and photographing a gentle 20-inch-long Western Hognose snake as he went through his mediocre performance of feigning death, despite not having been touched. As we backed off a few feet, he recovered quickly and went back to searching for toads, his favorite food.

She replied as we all paused, "Thanks, but after that Saturday in Mogollon, I just want to see the end of it." We then approached the other open gate.

As with the night before, the first thing I saw were the two extended bare feet, pale against the dark rocky ground. The destruction of Arthur Brunk was even more horrific to me 12 hours later, and it told me of a heartless science or possibly even a hideous appetite. I knew not which. Oddly, there was still no evidence of earthly predators anywhere in the vicinity. Only the flies communed with the sprawled remains of Arthur Brunk.

Margo gasped and turned her head into my shoulder, but Dr. Monsevais put on the latex gloves and opened the valise to extract several clear plastic vials and two or three plastic bags. There was no integrity to the corpse, and he put on a cloth mask before approaching Brunk's body. Another strange thing I noticed was Monsevais pulling out a small blue jar of Vick's Vaporub, and he put a dab of ointment in each nostril so that he had to breathe through his mouth.

As the three of us watched intensely, the doctor cut out a small section of Brunk's cheek and small pieces of flesh from other parts of his body, or at least what was left of it. With some difficulty, he cut a chunk of the tough greyish-brown material from Brunk's back. He remarked that the small portion he successfully removed was tough as leather, yet toward the center of the back, toward the shoulders, he was unable to penetrate the dense substance that he said reminded him of the now-lost sample he sent to Albuquerque. Arthur Brunk was in the process of being transformed into something alien.

The doctor turned his head toward us and pointed with his scalpel to a pair of fleshy bumps near the top of the dead man's shoulders. He was able to slice one of the protuberances and place it in a bag. From the cored rectum, he scraped pulpy material into a vial, and I felt my stomach lurch despite my robust constitution.

Dr. Monsevais stood up abruptly and backed away from the corpse. He adjusted his glasses with a gloved hand. "Come look at this!" He walked toward the three of us who were watching in discomfort. He held up the transparent vial that was covered by a hard plastic cap.

Margo was the first to peer inside the vial being held up by the doctor. "Oh, God!" was all she said as she spun around.

McCarty and I looked closely, and I took a closeup photo with my 55mm Micro-Nikkor lens. That was before I realized what I was looking at. The piece of tissue taken from what was Arthur Brunk's cheek was approximately almost an inch long and less than a quarter inch in diameter. It was like a small grey cut worm, visibly twitching inside the vial—it was a living thing!

I was so shocked at what I saw inside that vial that I forgot to photograph the ruined body of Arthur Brunk. Now Dr. Monsevais was placing the samples into his black leather valise. He was looking toward the western horizon as we heard the sound of a vehicle speeding noisily up the dirt road, its engine revving and its suspension constantly scraping on the brush growing in the center of the road.

We all stood, watching as the Grant County Sheriff's Department cruiser came over the cattle guard, past our parked vehicles and along the road past the front of house, coming into view just up from the corral where we were standing. The car doors opened, even before the vehicle came to a complete stop, and the driver keyed the microphone he was holding. Two large deputies struggled out of the car and walked down toward us, hitching up their equipment belts as they walked. A third man emerged from the back seat of the vehicle, and he was wearing U.S. Air Force uniform, with captain's bars on his collar, his light blue shirt clean pressed, his dark blue visor cap shading his eyes against the sun that had just now risen at the horizon.

Deputies Archuleta and Combs, according to their name tags, looked at our driver's licenses and Dr. Monsevais's State of New Mexico credentials, and then the three officials walked down to the corral as I thought with some satisfaction that the Air Force officer's sparkling shoe shine was doomed. None of the three showed concern about our weapons. The captain did not look at my face, but he focused on my camera as he surveyed the four of us. My headache was growing in intensity

The sound of retching came from Deputy Combs as his partner told him to go retrieve the evidence kit from the trunk of their cruiser. As Combs almost staggered up the slope while wiping his mouth, Archuleta shouted after him, "Call it in."

Combs waved back to his partner as the rising sun cast a looming shadow of the barn all the way to the edge of the corral. The doctor was talking to Deputy Archuleta, gesticulating, while the captain stared down at the remains of Arthur Brunk. We three were also looking at the grisly remains but not quite close enough to hear what Dr. Monsevais was saying to the deputy. My head was throbbing, and I rubbed my eyes to clear my vision. As it turned out, I did not have time to wish for relief.

The USAF captain shouted, "My God!" and pointed in the direction of the barn. All of our eyes snapped in that direction. They were there!

The shroud of dread settled over every human in this sunbaked cattle pen as horrid entities seemed to emerge through the wall of the barn, shambling, their hideous faceless mien enough to freeze the blood and paralyze the mind. It was as though they were advancing toward us. One of the arthropod aliens held what appeared to be a two-foot cylinder gripped with all four of the alien's segmented appendages and clamped by those frightening claw-like nippers.

Deputy Combs was halfway to the cruiser when he saw them, and he appeared to be frozen in place, fumbling with the retaining strap on his pistol holster.

Almost like radio static, the wave of buzzing whispers drifted eerily on the morning breeze, insinuating itself into the ears of the stricken human observers. My head was pounding, and I struggled to ignore the alien words that I did not want to comprehend. As I feared, the sounds from the monstrosities created hideous images in my mind. My God, anything but that! I do not want to see into the black core of a hellish vacuum.

Deputy Combs issued a piercing scream as he stood, paralyzed. "I'm on fire. I'm burning…burning."

I now saw the alien thing was pointing the tube in the direction of the deputy. A glance showed that the deputy was not on fire, but a light grey haze seemed to surround his torso. I could not hesitate. I drew the .45, slammed back the slide and aimed at the monster with the tube. The explosion of the pistol firing broke the morning into pieces, and Deputy Archuleta also drew his gun.

Everything seemed to happen simultaneously as worlds went to war. Margo screamed and squatted, her hands over her ears. The boom of the .45 and the lighter crack of the deputy's .38 service revolver sent bullets at the creatures while the Captain waved his arms, shouting, "No, no, no."

The shambling horrors kept advancing, but I knew I had struck one of them at least twice. Now I could hear a high-pitched hum that certainly came from the wicked cylinder in the claws of the one alien. The tube swept across our group, just as McCarty put his own .38 pistol into play.

Deputy Combs dropped to the ground in a heap, immobile, and I heard the high-pitched hum and felt a searing heat as the tube pointed briefly at me before sweeping to the doctor, the captain, and Deputy Archuleta. I knew we had to escape—somehow, as we had done before, or we would be doomed to be the repast of those unthinkable creatures and their worm-like tentacles that would suck our humanity and leave us with an infection from the merciless depths of space.

THE WHISPERING DARKNESS

The captain yelled as he wrapped his arms around his chest and twisted his torso. Archuleta suddenly ducked and began running toward his partner as McCarty and I fired again at the arthropod with the cylinder. Aiming just above its head, I knew the 230-grain bullet would strike its center mass.

At that moment the buzzing horrors faltered and turned away. McCarty's final shot struck one of them on its carapace, and the bullet ricocheted from the nearly impervious glossy surface.

Everybody backed away, seeking to put the boarded fence of the corral between us and whatever still lurked within and beyond that barn. I reached down and took Margo's hand, lifting her up as the creatures disappeared around the corner of the barn. Before we struck out for the vehicles, I looked again across the fence. It was not an illusion! The ridgepole of the barn seemed to ripple in the sharp clear light of the rising sun.

McCarty squinted and looked in the same direction. I was certain he saw what I saw. "Rick…Margo…we need to get out of here."

Deputy Archuleta half-carried his partner, and they had reached the cruiser just as the captain recovered his senses and sprinted to join them. Dr. Monsevais joined us, holding his valise in both arms as though it was a baby. He said, "That Air Force guy was telling me he would have to confiscate my samples, and he was going to take your film as well. He's forgotten all that."

McCarty was backpedaling before we turned and headed for our two vehicles. We rounded the back of the ruined house and followed the algae-bordered trickle running down from the cattle tank overflow soaking into a small weed patch in a corner of the pasture. As we reached McCarty's truck, I felt a hammer blow in my temple, causing me to lean against the truck door, my ears thick with pressure. I felt confusion until McCarty shouted to Margo and the doctor. "Get moving!"

They were both looking back, open-mouthed, and I turned to follow their eyes

Still leaning against the door of the truck, I was gripped by mindless terror as I looked back toward the barn. At first it seemed the structure was melting before my eyes but it was obviously some kind of optical illusion.

But then…the very air above the barn seemed to swirl with a luminous current as a massive object materialized before my eyes. It was rising silently as it took the shape of a dull, aluminum-colored disc almost 100 feet in diameter and with a cupola on the top and the bottom.

Though it was silent, it pulsated and waves of energy made me tingle with a praeternatural heat. As the craft rose vertically, it began to undulate very much like the ghastly ripples of a stomach that was digesting a nameless meal. The sheer size of the craft left us all open-mouthed, but as it rose, it began to drift in our direction.

The deputies and their passenger scrambled into their cruiser that was so much closer to the alien disc than we were. I could see Archuleta working the shifter while the Captain appeared to be waving his arms from the back seat. The cruiser backed up against the rising slope on the south side of the road, striking the barbed wired fence, and then he floored it, shooting forward and past us as we were all climbing into our vehicles. We were not far behind him.

McCarty was driving like a wild man, gaining on the doctor's Ford Explorer ahead of us. We were abandoning the mutilated corpses at the Smith Place to Beelzebub's minions as three vehicles tore down the rutted dirt track to escape the alien craft. I rolled down the truck window and looked out. The craft was now rising vertically at a dizzying speed. As I watched, it dwindled until it was a shiny silver dime high in the morning sky, and I urged McCarty to slow down.

Ahead of us the Ford Explorer was braking, and the Sheriff's Department cruiser was stopped ahead, its lights flashing red. As we rounded the bend to full visibility I saw a medium blue 1977 Chevrolet Caprice sedan bottomed out in the sand-filled wash. AFOSI agents Roberts and Pluman, in shirt sleeves, were standing beside the vehicle, the trunk open. If I wasn't still terrified, I would have been laughing.

The Explorer went into four-wheel drive and skirted the stranded agents, with McCarty following suit. Agent Roberts stuck out his arm, walking in the deep sand in our direciotn, struggling to get our attention as we passed, but I just waved. McCarty pulled down the brim of his cowboy hat and pressed the accelerator in low gear, the wheels grinding and growling through deep sand and out the other side of the wash onto the rutted track, leaving the agents and the USAF Captain behind, dependent on the deputies who were on their radio as we passed.

Knowing what we all saw, I was certain none of them would go back to the abandoned ranch for fear of the alien monstrosities that might still be hidden in the dark hulk of the barn, their insidious buzzing whispers conspiring to infect human prey. Arthur Brunk was hideous proof of what they could do—merciless, emotionless, alien beyond human conception.

As we jolted up the primitive road, I struggled to attach the seat belt. Looking out the windshield, I could see Margo in the Explorer ahead of us, and she was looking back in our direction.

A few minutes later, we were on the graded and improved dirt and gravel of the Ridge Road, headed for San Vicente as though pursued by the Devil. Only a half-minute later we saw a cloud of dust approaching on the road in our direction. The Explorer pulled onto a wide spot, and we followed as the brownish cloud drew near.

Three vehicles thundered past us, the dust boiling over our vehicles, and we saw what had to be a command vehicle, a field ambulance without a red cross insignia, and a 2 ½ ton truck, all painted Army olive drab. My first thought was that they were from the National Guard Armory vehicle park in town, and the men we saw in the cab seemed to be dressed for combat. I snapped four photos of the convoy as it passed. McCarty and I looked at each other, and he said, "It's getting deep out there." I knew he was not talking about water.

I saw Dr. Monsevais wave us forward from the open window of the Explorer, and we got back on the road, eager to return to my house in town. It was not yet 8:30 a.m., though it seemed as though an entire day had passed.

It was a relief to be back on the blacktop and to be at the end of Ridge Road, turning right and down U.S. 90 into San Vicente. We followed the Explorer through town and finally to my house, where Margo and I debarked from the separate vehicles.

THE WHISPERING DARKNESS

McCarty wasted no time putting his truck in gear and departing for his own home, just as the doctor's Ford Explorer was no doubt headed either for the local Public Health office or back to Las Cruces. I was sure Dr. Monsevais was now very conscious of how sensitive his samples were likely to be. Margo and I were left standing together on the sidewalk in front of our house, and we knew we would have visitors before the day was over. While I felt the terror of the creatures from beyond, there was also a very distinct and palpable fear of our own government whose major mission has always been to ridicule and suppress the stories of anyone who might offer credible testimony to alien encounters.

We walked inside and stood in our living room. Margo looked at the floor and fluffed her hair. "I'm going over to Mattie's brother's place. Somebody has to tell her. Are you going to work?" She didn't look up.

I fumbled with the Nikon slung around my neck and then nodded, looking at her. "I think I'm going to develop this film before I do anything else. It's important."

Margo responded with a slight smile before she turned away to go to the bathroom. She was there while I rewound the Kodak Plus-X film, dropped the camera back and pulled the canister from the spool. As I usually did, I immediately inserted a fresh roll of 24 exposures into the camera and closed the back, but did not advance the film. Margo was still in the bathroom as I went to the darkroom area and got the stainless steel metal 35mm developing tank and the black changing bag that made it easy to load film even in daylight. With my hands in the elastic sleeves of the bag, I threaded the film into the reel and inserted it into the tank with a muffled clink before putting the lid on the tank.

While I was unzipping the bag and removing the developing tank, Margo came out of the bathroom dabbing at her face with a tissue, and she said over her shoulder, "I'll go on to my office after I'm done."

"Are you sure you want to go?" I knew I was still in a mild state of shock, and Margo certainly was still filled with horror from what we saw at the Smith place.

"No, but I'm going. Maybe we can have lunch later." Then she was out the door and gone.

I went back to the sink and prepared the Agfa Rodinal developer in the beaker before beginning the developing process. It was close to 45 minutes before the negatives were fixed and rinsed. I hung the long strip of exposed negatives from the string I had stretched from the ceiling light fixture. I left the negative strip to dry and closed the door to the darkroom area.

I placed the Nikon on the kitchen counter, grabbed a bag of peanuts from the pantry and went to the refrigerator to get a Pepsi for a mid-morning snack, and that was when the agents pounded on the front door. Because the door was not locked, they entered without an invitation.

Roberts and Pluman looked slightly rumpled, dress shirts limp with perspiration, and the same could be said of the USAF Captain in shirtsleeves order who was now with them. They took a flanking stance, with the Captain standing back, his eyes shadowed by Ray-Ban aviator sun glasses. Roberts did the talking.

"We saw you a little while ago outside of San Vicente at a dead body site. Every time we see you, it is in an inappropriate situation."

"Look, Agent, these 'situations' as you call them are more than inappropriate. We saw things out there…"

He cut me off. "You saw a dead cow and a dead man. That's all. It could be a crime scene that you might have contaminated."

I realized that nothing I said was of interest to the three Air Force men. "You were stuck in the sand, but you had to see that…that ship going up into the sky."

"What you saw was a DC-3 Frontier Airlines regular flight taking off from the Grant County Airport four miles away and flying over that barn, headed for Tucson." Roberts was officially serious. Agent Pluman's hands were akimbo, and the Captain's hands were in the parade rest position.

I should have been aghast, but standing before me was the entire relationship between the U.S. Government and the American public regarding flying saucers since 1947 and perhaps even earlier. At that moment, I flashed back to the story blurted out by Tip Ulibarri at the McCarty cookout and how he must have been looking over his shoulder for thirty years.

"I think you guys are as frightening as those things I saw in Mogollon and again this morning. You should have seen the body of Arthur Brunk."

Roberts advanced a half step. "We expect you to be reasonable. How many people in this town would believe that fantasy? What about your employer? Your wife's clients? You realize that her father is a retired Air Force Lt. Colonel, with a pension?" His voice was officious and vaguely threatening.

The Captain now broke his own silence. "We will have the film in your camera. The details of that scene are not for public consumption."

They were not joking, and Pluman's arms were now at his side, his eyes cold.

My stomach was doing flip-flops, but I shrugged and walked into the kitchen where the camera lay on the counter. I picked it up and pretended to rewind the film into the cassette. I popped off the back and removed the film container, tossing it across the room to Pluman.

Agent Roberts closed the interview. "You saw a dead cow, damaged by predators. You saw a dead man who may have committed suicide, and you saw an airliner flying low over the barn from the Grant County Airport a few miles away. It will be better for you if you do not say much about this now or in the future. Now, where is your wife?"

"She is probably at her office." For once I enjoyed dissembling.

As the three left, the Captain said, "Thank you for your cooperation." He paused at the door, "You will someday forget all of this. Consider it a gift from 4602."

"What is 4602?" I shouted after them, but they were gone.

When they left, I bolted the door and went immediately to the darkroom. The negatives were not completely dry, but I took the strip from where it was hanging and cut it into four 6-frame units, put them into glassine negative protectors, and then into a white letter size envelope that I labeled as "Christmas Decorations/December 1975," burying the envelope within my old grey metal filing cabinet, with dozens of other envelopes containing hundreds of negatives. The drawer always stuck upon closing, so I always had to gently slam it. I was gambling that the AFOSI would be satisfied with extracting the film in the cassette and exposing it to erase the images they assumed were there.

Never before had the pressure of circumstance prevented me from moving intently from hour to hour. I planned to get out of the jeans I was wearing. I sniffed the redolent odor of manure and death that had permeated the clothes I was wearing. I was going to change clothes, wash, and go to work. I walked to the bedroom and pulled off the dust-covered engineer boots and stripped out of my shirt and pants. It was my intent to get fresh clothes and get back to a normal morning.

I sat on the edge of the bed, immobile. A hot wave of fatigue washed over me, and I felt the fear, horror, and revulsion that I had held at bay for two weeks. My mind filled with a deepening reservoir of horrific images. I rubbed my left forearm and thought fearfully of the red mist that invaded my dreams on three separate nights as though it could be the result of some loathsome venom injected into my body. Behind the shifting cloud of crimson was a lurking vision that I feared might manifest fully if I slept too soundly.

As I sat there, head in my hands, I saw the face of Ofelia Armendariz when we first met her, and then again at the grocery store, haunted by some hideous memory. And I had seen those beings, whose mien was so horrible that the mind could not accept their hideous forms. Though I tried to reject the image, I then saw Darouse Brunk, irresistible in her kimono, and then, that erotic image shattered by the succeeding sight of a faceless horror creature embracing her in the museum, its writhing worm-like cilia attached to her face in the infernal kiss.

My thoughts were a tumult, and I lived again the terrifying night escape from Mogollon, and from the back of my mind the satanic image of Arthur Brunk seemed to stare at me from oblivion, his inhuman appearance challenging every vestige of sanity. I imagined the terror Brub and Ouida McCarty must have felt as they huddled in their darkened Winnebago while vile creatures surrounded their refuge and the whispering sibilance sought to drive them mad.

I again heard the voice of the AFOSI agent telling me that we had experienced a toxic mine spill. Of course he had not seen Hiram Akeley brought to the point of death by the monstrous creatures infesting the abandoned mine.

A half hour later I still had not moved, I sensed the horror of Mogollon but also felt the knife of fear instilled by agents of the U.S. Government. Again and again, I thought about the reclusive Tip Ulibarri who had lived with government threats since 1948, just because he had been part of the recovery of a crashed flying saucer on a mesa near Aztec, N. M. I thought about how he was silenced by his Air Force masters who showed him proof in his 201 File that he was not even in the state when the incident allegedly happened.

From this day on, Margo and I would walk among friends and family completely alienated from the normal society of humans who would never believe the horror we experienced. Even as I sat there, a military team was at the site south of San Vicente cleaning up the mess to make certain that there was no evidence of an event there. The mutilated bull would vanish, and the corpse of Arthur Brunk would disappear as though he never existed. Any inhuman tracks near the barn would be completely raked over, and the vehicle Brunk commandeered would be taken away to be compacted at some undisclosed location.

I was still sitting, half-dressed when Margo unlocked the front door and came inside. Her face was drawn and pensive as she came and sat down beside me. She hugged me. "Mattie is going back to El Paso today. She…she doesn't look well. The marks on her face are not healing very fast."

My turmoil must have been evident, but Margo continued, "When she was evacuated from Mogollon, some military guy on the bus was very harsh with her, and she is still very scared."

"She joins our club." I said to steer Margo away from Matilda Brunk, so I told her about the Air Force visitors to our house while she was gone.

"Rick, I am worried about Jesse. He's driving to Las Cruces, and he has those samples."

"It's never more than a two-hour drive. He's probably almost there by now." This was not the time to exaggerate conspiracy fantasies.

She sighed. "Hope you're right. You know, I need to talk to my dad. He always talks sense about this Air Force stuff. I still have a bad feeling."

I looked at the blue-grey carpet on the bedroom floor. "I have a bad feeling about everything right now." I felt Margo's hand on my shoulder as she stood up.

When I finally cleaned up and dressed for work, Margo finished talking with her father on the telephone. "Daddy says that he thinks 4602 is an important number—he calls it the 4602nd, whatever that means. He will do some checking. By the way, he said one of his friends who's still in the service telephoned him and told him that you and I should be careful when it comes to national security." She emphasized those last words.

"That doesn't make me feel any better."

"Me neither. Do you think we will go back to Mogollon?"

"Yes, I think we have to. Don't you? I'll call Bob in Glenwood later today to find out what he has heard." As I prepared to leave the house, Margo told me that Mattie was turning the museum over to the Chandlers and that she was ready to return home to El Paso. She had not decided whether to sell the family Ford franchise, but she was never going back to Mogollon.

We both went on to our jobs and did not return to the house until close to 6 p.m. I arrived home first and felt that the house didn't smell right. There is something about the subtle placement of items and general array in a home that is instantly recognizable to us. The door lock was secure, but somebody had been there, and I went immediately to the darkroom.

The negative sleeves on the print easel underneath the Beseler enlarger were obviously in a different order, and the file cabinet drawer was not quite shut. I swallowed hard and opened it. The envelopes had been disturbed, but there were too many for anyone to review inside of several hours. The December 1975 envelope seemed untouched, but the 1978 dated envelopes labeled "Mogollon" had obviously been tampered with. A quick review showed that nothing had been taken.

I was still in the darkroom looking at the negative strips in their translucent sleeves when I heard the front door open and close. When I went out, I found Margo standing just inside the door with tears in her eyes.

"What happened?" I put my arms around her and she talked into my shoulder.

"There was an accident…"

I waited.

"Jesse Monsevais is in the hospital in Las Cruces. There was a wreck somewhere outside of Deming on I-10 late this morning." As I listened, I could not help but feel a finger of dread punching me in the chest.

All I said was, "It will be called an accident." It turned out I was prophetic.

As the evening progressed, Margo was able to locate Dr. Monsevais's parents in Las Cruces. It was a harrowing account. The doctor told them he was driving on Interstate 10, bound for his office in Las Cruces, when there was a break in the traffic and an older SUV, with two occupants, came along beside him at 70 mph and ran into the side of his car, pushing him off the highway into the ditch, where his Explorer turned over twice. The other vehicle stopped and the two men ran to the overturned SUV and cut off his seat belt, pulling him out, leaving him dazed behind a mesquite bush. One of them told him, "You are very lucky," as though they did not care one way or another. One of them ran to the wrecked car as other cars were slowing behind. They took items from the car, and one of the men threw something into the wrecked Explorer before they raced to their vehicle and accelerated away from the scene. Monsevais said the license plate on the SUV was obscured, but he had no time to reflect on it, because suddenly there was a flash of thermite, and the Ford Explorer burst into flames just as a State Police cruiser arrived.

"Is he OK?" As I asked Margo, I somehow knew that this was almost as frightening as the horror creatures in Mogollon.

Margo shrugged. "His mother says he has a fracture of his left arm, but he will be back in circulation within a day or two. She says he is more scared than hurt."

Before we went to the local Grinder Mill takeout restaurant on College Avenue for meat burritos and French fries, I called the Texaco station in Glenwood, where I found Bob still on duty. He reported that the road to Mogollon was open and that he had talked to two travelers who had gone through there on Wednesday.

We almost decided on impulse to go there but then thought better of it. It was another week before we were able to load up the VW bus and steel ourselves for the trek. We told the McCartys that we would do the trial run to determine whether it was possible to return in safety.

It was 9 June when we left San Vicente in the late afternoon summer heat, taking the so-familiar two-lane highway to Glenwood. I admit that my trepidations had me constantly looking out the windows, sometimes looking up to the skies. Traffic was light, and the small hills and long valleys were deceptively neutral and typical of New Mexico with its creosote, mesquite, scrub juniper, and dry grasses. As we entered the valley of the San Francisco river, the emergence of green trees surrounded the village of Glenwood. Past the Blue Front Bar on the right, we pulled to the left into the service bay of the Texaco Station where we were pleased to see Bob coming out to pump gas for us.

Wearing a Texaco shirt with red star insignia on the left breast and his embroidered "Bob" name in yellow thread on the right breast, he seemed pleased to see us. We talked

The Mogollon Gallery   RickPhoto 1978

about the strange road closures of previous weeks. He asked about the lady who owned the brown Toronado, and told us his story of the men who interrogated him.

"Never saw anything quite like this. There were all sorts of guys staying back in the guest ranch," Bob pointed to the Los Olmos Guest Ranch complex behind the service station. "Sold a lot of gasoline, but nobody wanted to talk much. They kept to themselves and drank beer over at the Blue Front. Then, a week ago, they just up and left. Strangest thing that has happened here this century."

We thanked Bob and departed Glenwood to quickly find the turn onto the Mogollon road. As the engine strained, we wound upward on the paved road, not seeing any signs of major repairs, although there was new black asphalt where the sinkhole had been, and obvious scars where the collapsed bank was cleared all around the hairpin turn we knew so well. It was impossible to traverse this road without remembering the wild ride we took to escape Mogollon a lifetime ago.

The serpentine road led to the summit and followed the steep slopes down until we emerged into Silver Creek Canyon. The town seemed unchanged in the June afternoon sunshine, and we parked beside our gallery.

Our first impression was that nothing ever happened, although I did notice an acidic odor on the breeze. As we stepped out of the bus, the first thing I noticed that the ground everywhere was scored by heavy equipment tracks and even some marks around the gallery door that appeared to be made by a rake of some kind.

Margo pointed back up the road to the leveled area at the far west end of town. "It's gone!" She was talking about the McCarty's Winnebago, and it was, indeed, missing. We would not be able to verify Brub and Ouida's account of the scoring, rips, and mangled metal they had endured while they were being sought by the horror creatures. The word "sanitized" came to my mind as we looked up and down the paved street that was clear, the asphalt patched where the flooding had created potholes in May. "Rick, they don't know that somebody stole their RV!"

I just shook my head as we went to the now-closed gallery door. The key still fit the lock, but I remembered leaving the door ajar when we fled. The air inside the gallery was stale, but the smell of paint or varnish drew my attention to the floor. In the center of the gallery floor a three-foot square section had been removed and replaced with new pine board, hastily stained but not quite matching the original worn flooring of the rest of the gallery. I closed my eyes, and I saw again the arthropod monstrosity dripping some kind of odious fluid onto the floor just before it came for me.

Nothing else seemed out of place, and when we went outside and up the stairs, the makeshift living quarters seemed to be much as we left them. I wondered how well we would sleep after what had happened.

We spent at least an hour reconnecting with the Chandlers, the Englishes, and with Sparky, who was blissfully unaware of the contribution he had made to revealing the make up of the aliens' bodies. Those residents were not present in town the weekend when the aliens ravaged Mogollon, and Frank Triolo was still at the VA Hospital in El Paso even now.

We walked up the street past the Old Kelly Store and across the hastily repaired foot bridge to visit Vic and Sarah Petroski. They were not so talkative as they were when I had last seen them. They admitted that they had seen the saucer-like craft rise up from the mine, but they were not as definite as the McCartys had been.

Vic recounted how the officers on the bus had instructed them on the toxic mine dump story until it seemed almost believable, and Sarah was adamant that a demon had visited Mogollon. She was certain that prayers had saved the both of them. Perhaps she was right.

Before we left, Vic mentioned the persistent acidic odor hovering in the canyon. "Y'know, when they brought us back to town, there was this smell coming up the canyon. I saw a yellowish stream that had spilled down the mine dump—about 15 feet wide and going down a third of the way to the bottom. Really peculiar. I know it had to be put there after we was evacuated, but the story is the story. You understand?"

I just shrugged and then asked if they had heard anything about Hiram Akeley.

Sarah shook her head and clutched her rosary, "There were some stories on the bus. Somebody even said 'they' took him." It was a chilling piece of gossip—the tough old survivor of Mogollon carried into the depths of the mine or even taken aboard an alien craft and subjected to unthinkable experiments, perhaps never to be heard from again.

I asked, "Has anybody gone up to the mine this week?"

Sarah fidgeted, wringing her hands. "Nobody's gone there except tourists, and they all come back and say there are barriers and 'keep out' signs on the road."

Vic said, "Maybe Akeley was evacuated separately." All four of us knew that was unlikely.

We took our leave of the Petroskis and walked back to the gallery. There were still a few visitors walking on the street in town, casting long shadows as they stepped into the open doors of the museum, where the Chandlers were already putting displays into different order.

The front lights were already shining on the 1915 theater building, even though the sky was still bright, and I knew one of the movies they always showed to visitors was the 1973 film "My Name is Nobody," starring Henry Fonda and Terence Hill, not because it was a good movie, but because the first segment was filmed on the street and at the mine in Mogollon. There had been a rumor that the Italian producer Sergio Leone had personally arranged for Bill and Nikki English to have a complete 16mm print of the film.

As we put the gallery in order and greeted the few Friday evening browsers, I felt a permanent sense of unease about what had happened to us and how the town seemed to be hiding its secrets. What were we to say when visitors asked why the town was shut down for weeks?

That night we dozed in the upstairs apartment but did not sleep. Margo brought a snack up with her and was not disappointed, because our ringtail cat made his appearance, skittering along the rafters as part of the allure that characterized this unique community living under the pall of a horror difficult for the outside world to imagine.

The next morning, I took time to walk down the canyon toward the base of the mine dump and looked up the pallid, gritty, tailings slope toward the forbidding buildings where McCarty and I had run for our lives. What I saw was the pale yellow residue of what must have been hundreds of gallons of acid. From the smell I suspected it could have been glacial acetic acid, but the dye being used wasn't identifiable. I suspected that weather would gradually reduce it to the color of the surrounding pile.

It would not be long before the new mining company would move in and begin its operation. As I walked back up the canyon toward the town, I suddenly thought, with a flash of fear, of the cyanide pool. Did the military cleaning crews find a mouldering monstrosity floating in its shallow fatal waters? Then again, it is possible that the thing from beyond space was immune even to that toxic soup. I did not like even the thought of an obscene liquescent horror decaying so close to Mogollon.

Almost as unsettling was the thought that the Air Force recovered the corpse of that alien thing and had somehow transported it to a research facility in Ohio or at Los Alamos or some unnamed desert base unknown to the American public where its frightening ontogeny could be explored. I was struck with the terrifying thought: what if it could not die, and even though rendered immobile, the cilia in that faceless dome would continue to writhe like a nest of worms that could infect anything it touched with an otherworldly virus, capable of lodging in the brain communicating vile images of cosmic horror. Compared to that venom, the earthly viruses such as herpes simplex and hepatitis seemed almost benign.

As I walked the street of Mogollon in the bright daylight, I could see signs of meticulous raking, and attempts at sanitizing the community before people were allowed to return. The parking areas for the gallery and on the other side of the museum had been carefully cleaned, leveled by bulldozer and with much of the familiar debris removed. There was even evidence of paint applied to buildings and the residue of sandblasting as though to erase even the suggestion that an alien visitation had come to Mogollon. I wondered if the U.S. Government had applied equal attention to other flying saucer landing and recovery sites in order to gain plausible deniability. Even those of us who had seen the arthropods and battled them would begin to doubt our own senses, falling back on the simpler story of a minor flood and a toxic mine spill.

Yet they had not seen what Arthur Brunk had become, and they could not explain away the disappearance of Hiram Akeley up at the mine. I looked up at the bright blue of the morning sky and sensed that behind it was a cosmos both splendid and horrific. Could there be a fate worse than to be taken from this planet to be experimented upon by unnamable horrors without heart or sympathy? It was a fate that Arizona resident Travis Walton had been subjected to and who had somehow been returned with his personality untainted. By Walton's account those creatures were at least humanoid, though alien in most other respects.

As I walked the warming pavement in Mogollon toward the boarded up church on the hillside, where the turnoff to the left went up, doubling back to the cemetery, I could not help but remember the 1953 story of Scoutmaster DesVergers who had glimpsed a horrible creature inside a hovering disc, so frightening that he was never willing to describe what he had seen. Could he have seen in 1952 what we experienced in this Year of Our Lord 1978? My reverie was interrupted by the seeming normalcy of vehicles coming down from the mountain and treating Mogollon as a pleasant tourist stop. It was the best form of convalescence. Margo and I would be the last to start rumors of an alien visitation, and so we showed photographs and talked to visitors about the rugged history of a tough mining town whose buildings survived fire and flood for almost a century.

Some visitors were well-informed and curious about the "mine spill" and the number of days that the road was closed. When they questioned us, we found ourselves just repeating what we were supposed to say, even though we knew so many things we were warned never to tell.

As the day progressed, I occasionally I looked across the street to the empty Holland General Store, remembering the dark tunnel accessed from the back of the building and running into blackness behind its iconic façade, going down into darkness north under the massive hillside toward the mine. Who knew its cloistered warrens and its branches? I was one of the few who knew how it had vomited alien horror that we had barely escaped. Today the three sets of doors were locked, and the broad wooden porch that spanned the front of the building was still sagging drunkenly from the effects of the flooded creek that had run underneath the porch since the store's construction in a previous century.

Some residents stopped at the Old Kelly Store to retrieve the mail that came up the mountain from Glenwood or to purchase a few staples so that they would not have to drive over the mountains and down for the drive to the Catron County seat of Reserve.

As we finished the weekend, we packed up and drove back to San Vicente. The trip carried the undertones of discomfort because we could not help but look anxiously upward through the windshield and side windows as the lonely road wound back to the main highway and, and then south to San Vicente and home. I knew that others had been terrorized on this stretch of highway. Even the comforting conversation with Bob at the service station did not absolve us from an undercurrent of fright.

We were reconstructing our lives as we were lulled by the 40-horsepower thrashing rattle of the VW bus engine, mile upon mile. Life might never be whole again, and we joined a segment of the population that had been pummeled by traumatic events, unable to explain why we, and they, would always be separated from the normal human condition. I wanted to take out a full-page newspaper advertisement, or sell a frightening documentary—maybe even present the story to a metropolitan investigative reporter, but it was not to be. We would have to live in the shadow of the malevolent alien presence for the remainder of our lives, and I would be visited at night with visions of a place of horror beyond human conception in the vastness of the cosmos, and I knew there were at least two others who would be plagued with virulent dreams that would shake personalities to their core. This was the legacy of the Mogollon horror.

That night back in San Vicente, I once again was awakened, my heart pounding, the fear sweat soaking my underarms. The red vision had come to me again, and it was more familiar, better defined than when I first experienced it—the images were of infernal heat and a dim reddish glow—twisted strands of alien vegetation bordered by a sluggish flowing black stream—and in the dark distance the unnatural outline of massive structures. Wavering in the heat waves emanating from the surface where I stood, a hellish shape materialized, its bulbous body glistening in the red twilight, its segmented arms beckoning, and the mass of cilia that served as a face squirming as though eager to embrace me. As I came awake, I shuddered and tried not to scream. You cannot know the relief I felt, knowing that I was still in my San Vicente home.

Mogollon Winter   RickPhoto 1978

Eleven

Epilogue 2018

"In the face of the unknown we are all children. Our reactions are those of children; we seek parental authoritarian reassurance."—Coral and Jim Lorenzen 1969

I returned to Mogollon in 2018, and it has been almost forty years since those early days of happiness and horror. I can only say that nothing was the same in my life after the events of May and June 1978, and I must explain by recalling the Roman stoic Seneca's famous saying, "Fate makes playthings of men." I have always simplified it to read, "Fate makes fools of us all," and that with a nod to Puck.

After 1978, the days of our Mogollon gallery were numbered, though many of the hardy residents maintained the traditions of the town. So many memories crowd my mind as I think of that era.

Though I first thought that Tip Ulibarri's reclusive nature was an affectation, I underestimated the power of intimidation in shaping the human personality. Here was a former Airman who had touched and worked on an alien craft but could never reveal what he knew for fear of losing his pension or even being taken into custody to make sure the general public could never know the truth. The mission of the CIA-sponsored Robertson Panel in 1953 was to suppress reports of flying saucers, and the government-funded Condon Committee at the Universitiy of Colorado issued its report in 1968 confirming that there was nothing to support any reports of UFOs. Thus, the thousands of truly unknown sightings and encounters were rendered null and void because the government so decreed. Now I knew that Ulibarri had lived a haunted life, as we were now also condemned.

I remembered my final visit to Mogollon in those days and a chance meeting with Vic and Sarah Petroski. When I broached the subject of the alien craft, they both demurred, saying that they did not remember anything except the toxic mine spill. How many other people had adjusted their memories under pressure from government agents and academics who used their expert status as cudgels.

The last thing I remember Vic Petroski saying before my last weekend at the gallery in 1982 was, "You know, I don't remember nuthin'." The narrowness of his eyes and the grim set of his mouth told me everything.

Perhaps it was a fitting closure to the Mogollon experience that the Venture Mining Company did bring in an ore crusher and use the cyanide leaching process to extract quantities of gold from the Fanny Hill mine. The miners and their overseers had no knowledge of the events that preceded their occupation of the site, though the manager was heard to have questioned residents as to the absence of Hiram Akeley, who had even left in his house a display of valuable gold dust and nugget samples. An abandoned Chevrolet Blazer sat beside the house for several years after 1978.

I was not in Mogollon to record the eventual fate of that mining operation, but they hired me to photograph the operation at its inception. I was not willing to go into the mine buildings, even on contract.

We remained friends with the McCartys, and the one positive outcome for them was a brand new Winnebago Chieftain motor home, after their RV was spirited away and taken somewhere for study. Ouida never forgave the government for the loss of her favorite chair with the floral cushions. I noted in our visits with the pair that Brub became increasingly reticent to talk about the things we experienced, especially after the arrival of the new RV in front of their house. I suspected I might have made the same accommodation had I been in their situation. They returned to the ghost town and resumed their retirement activities, even purchasing a new Honda three-wheeler. I do not think McCarty ever drove it past the cemetery in his rambles around town. For us, the mine and the Akeley house were off limits.

While many of the residents of Mogollon were not touched by the horror, aside from the inconvenience of being evacuated for two weeks as a result of a "toxis spill," it took time to clean up the damage that was the legacy of the minor flood that had collapsed the Holland Store porch and at least two of the wooden foot bridges crossing Silver Creek as access to residences. The face of the ghost town remained unchanged to visitors and to most residents.

The impact on the Armendariz family was a reminder of how real the terror had been for Ofelia Armendariz. She survived the unthinkable, but I heard that she had occasional periods of hospitalization for a condition that doctors were unable to properly diagnose. My own bouts of night visions gave me sympathy for what she struggled with. On the few occasions I saw Manuel and Ofelia at Safeway, Manuel confided that they received regular "welfare visits" from government emissaries who always said they were there to help her.

He never revealed whether Ofelia had ever told him about her experiences and whether the AFOSI agents had extracted any information from her in the hospital. He said her life had returned to normal, but that she sometimes woke up screaming and disoriented. Her physical wounds healed eventually but the damage to her spirit was not so easily repaired.

As for Arthur Brunk, he was effectively erased, and his commonplace obituary appeared in the El Paso Times a week after the incident south of San Vicente: "husband to Matilda, father of…" and of course mentioning his successful ownership of the Lone Star Ford Agency through which he was considered a prominent El Paso resident. The newspaper story recorded that his ashes were interred in the cemetery there, but I knew that the body was probably taken to an unknown location for dissection and study. There was no inquiry into the obituary statement that described how Arthur Brunk had died "after a short illness," but they did not add that the illness followed contact with vile entities from the nexus of chaos.

As Margo reported to me, Matilda Brunk returned to El Paso with her son, where she took charge of the Ford dealership. I never learned whether she remained in control or if she sold the dealership to a new cadre. I never saw her again, but the damage had already caused an irreparable rift between Margo and me.

Though I occasionally remembered Darouse Brunk lustfully, I always tried to suppress the irrational impulse, despite the memory of her blatant sexuality after her minor surgery. Thus it was unsettling at 5:30 one evening when the living room TV set was broadcasting Action 7 News from El Paso, and a lead item focused on an upscale home in El Paso, with the pert TV reporter announcing a domestic dispute that ended with a murder-suicide the night before. I wasn't paying attention until Margo shouted, "Rick, look at this."

When I looked at the screen, the camera was focused on an officer interviewing a woman standing with her arms crossed over a silk kimono. My heart was in my throat. The reporter with perfect blond hair was holding a microphone, "Police say that a love triangle ended in tragedy for two men who were allegedly involved with the same woman. The dead men were both local car salesmen at an El Paso Ford dealership. Police are talking with a woman who says she knew the men but did not know why they had both come to her home tonight." Margo's sidelong glance at me was to confirm that I knew why the men were there, and at least I had escaped that particular fate.

It was Margo's grace not to mention what she knew I had done in Mogollon, and I was certain that Darouse could have revealed details to her that I would never have confessed to. When I think of Darouse, I know that she too has to be plagued with hellish dreams, and her personal magnetism has become a curse for her. I would try to remember her as Mattie.

One of the stranger outcomes was more uplifting when Nurse Diaz came by the house on a Friday afternoon to tell us that her nephew Jorgé Maldonado had been dismissed from the hospital. His friend Anastacio was still in isolation, suffering from a psychotic dissociation the doctors thought was similar to what they had diagnosed in another recent patient.

Jorgé underwent a cathartic change in the hospital and asked to come live with his aunt. She accepted him so long as he attended Mass with her and went to Confession. Then there was the issue of the 1978 Ford 250 pickup truck. As fate would have it, Arthur Brunk had signed the title to Jorgé, trading it for the youth's worn out 1973 Honda Accord. It seemed fitting that the young man could make use of the truck, and the Department of Motor Vehicles agreed with that disposition.

It was only then that I learned that Nurse Diaz was actually "Norma," not just "Nurse." She asked both of us why government agents were in San Vicente. While I started to explain the unbelievable, Margo caught my eye, and I hesitated. The agents' warnings came back to me, and I knew that Nurse Diaz would be unable to digest the reality of what we had experienced, and she should not have to bear the curse of knowing the horrors that had touched so many lives.

After Mogollon came the hovering spectre of government intrusion. Margo's father visited one weekend and solved the mystery of "4602." He discovered that the 4602nd Air Intelligence Squadron formalized what was a clandestine USAF organization known under the innocuous name of The Air Force Special Activities Center. They never admitted to investigating UFO cases, but it was the primary mission they were trained for. They were masters of clean-up, disinformation, and silencing of those who witnessed things that are not allowed to exist.

As time went by I learned how thoroughly UFO landing sites were "salted" by cleanup crews who replanted vegetation, scooped up contaminated soil, and even left mundane evidence to be discovered by the curious who would be led to conclude that the event was ordinary, with fragments of weather balloon scattered at the sites, or perhaps even toxic chemicals dumped at a mine site.

Margo's father related the anecdote of how a top secret USAF plane rumored to have radar-defeating design had crashed a hundred miles from its secret Nevada base. When the curious located the crash site, they found identifiable pieces of a Vietnam era Republic F-105 Thunderchief, and so, keep moving—nothing to see here. If the government goes to this length of sanitize an aircraft crash, what would they do to make sure a real flying saucer event could be plausibly denied. It was done with a vengeance near Aztec, N.M., and in 1978 we were just learning about another crash and recovery outside of Corona, N.M., that would later be famous as the Roswell Incident. As Margo's father told the story, I was thinking about Tip Ulibarri, next door to the McCartys and how he was condemned to keep a massive secret for the remainder of his life or risk losing his Air Force pension.

Tall, balding, and affable, Margo's father also had a commanding presence. After telling us about the clandestine USAF UFO hunters, he hesitated before looking at both of us. "I don't know exactly what happened to upset your life in that godforsaken ghost town, but let me suggest something. I've seen strange things too, but the officers in command told us that we are the protectors of public opinion. It would be a disaster if the public ever gets the wrong idea about what we call 'peculiar phenomena.' I know Rick may not agree, but I'm saying that people have no choice but to trust authority, and it is best that we accept what our military and our government tells us. That's all I want to say on that subject."

He looked at his daughter and at me, shook my hand firmly as though we had a contract, and then gave his daughter a kiss before leaving.

After he left, I sat in the living room, looking at the furniture, the framed photographs and art pieces on the wall. They were anchors for what we accept as reality. Perhaps the Lorenzens were right when they wrote about the human reaction to arrivals from elsewhere: "we seek parental authoritarian reassurance." This flaw must be a worm that has gnawed at us throughout human history.

With that authoritarian reassurance in mind, it was fear-inducing to hear from Dr. Monsevais, who dropped by the house two weeks later. He and Margo were in conversation when I arrived from work. He said he did not trust the telephone anymore and was sure his office and home phone were tapped, with peculiar noises, clicks, and static on the line. He also warned us that his supervisors in Santa Fe had told him his career was dependent upon abandoning irresponsible comments about his experience south of San Vicente that day in June. His director confided that he was informed by an anonymous representative from the Department of Health, Education, and Welfare in Washington, D.C. He was told to forget any biological samples he might remember, because they were destroyed in a vehicle fire outside of Las Cruces.

In the years that followed, after my departure from San Vicente, the trauma of my encounter with the horror creatures in Mogollon drove me further into the study of flying saucers and UFOs. I read the books of Coral and Jim Lorenzens, Donald Keyhoe, Frank Scully, William Steinman, Stanton Friedman, Scott and Suzanne Ramsey, Frank Feschino, Travis Walton, and many others. Through these responsible writers, I was deluged by verified worldwide stories of encounters with flying saucers and UFOs. The long covered-up accounts of what is now known as the Roswell Incident and the Aztec saucer recovery became familiar and proved beyond a reasonable doubt.

For decades the architects of authoritarian reassurance had suppressed the stories of contact between humans and alien invaders. From the cynical disinformation of Dr. Donald Menzel, who invented the swamp gas explanation and the daytime planet Venus observations and who brilliantly discounted the radar tracking of the overflight of the U.S. Capitol by flying saucers in the summer of 1952 as "temperature inversion" that had not happened before or ever again on those scopes. I studied the government's Robertson Panel findings of 1953 that sought to allay the fears of the public by saying that all flying saucer sightings had been explained away as balloons, hoaxes, hallucinations, birds, or astronomical phenomena. If that was not enough affront to those who had experienced genuine encounters, there was the creation of Project Blue Book as a USAF body whose job was primarily to explain away all UFO sightings. The term "explain away" became the mantra and the goal of all governmental interaction with the public. Then came the Air Force-sponsored Condon Committee whose a priori findings paved the way for the closing of Blue Book. After all there was no such thing as a flying saucer or a UFO. One of that committee's panel later actually admitted that he had many times visited the site of the Aztec flying saucer recovery that supposedly never happened.

The majority of the public knew almost nothing about the reality of flying saucers. I met one of the executives in control of The Associated Press who was speaking at New Mexico

State University in Las Cruces. When I asked her why, since the 1950s, the AP did not report the multitude of UFO incidents that occur regularly. She said it was the wire service's policy not to report UFO stories unless they were whimsical and obviously explainable in nature and always included an obligatory dismissive quote from the Air Force, an astronomer, or a hothouse academic. The authoritarian reassurance reached back into the 1950s and became an institution for all journalism beyond level of local newspapers.

What I learned over all the years of study was that all manner of unearthly flying vehicles had been reported by reputable observers, and frightening encounters were far more common than anyone ever imagined, not only in the United States, but worldwide. Governments worldwide continue to hold the reality of alien invaders as above Top Secret. From my experience, I understand that it is best to deny the existence of that over which we have no control, almost as though we are helpless in the face of that which preys upon this world from the blackness of space.

It was not by accident that I also read the praeternatural fiction of H.P. Lovecraft who, long before I was born imagined other world horrors lurking in the forests of New England. It seems his eerie fiction was prescient in more ways than I had once thought. We saw things in 1978 befitting the author's nightmare visions.

* * *

It is now May 2018 as I drive from my current residence in Las Cruces, New Mexico, 100 miles up through the old hometown of San Vicente and then another 78 miles on the still-familiar blacktop past Cliff, Buckhorn, Pleasanton, and finally, into Glenwood.

It does not seem that forty years have passed, but everything has changed, as things always do. Margo and I separated four years after the Mogollon encounter. I never overcame my guilt, despite Margo's fidelity and forgiveness. I moved to Las Cruces and pursued advanced degrees in order to pursue another career. I abandoned ownership of the gallery, the San Vicente house and most other financial assets when I decided to begin again.

Over the years I often came back to the creed I learned in church when I was young, and page 6 of *The Book of Common Prayer*, "…we have left undone those things which we ought to have done; and we have done those things which we ought not to have done; and there is no health in us." Not only was it true of me, but I believed that we must own our transgressions in order to live with our limitations.

I also was increasingly aware that I was infected with a horrific venom that created visions becoming increasingly more real as years passed, ever more frightening, even as I sought to reject the mocking images as I awakened, sweating, from the nightmares they ingendered.

It was ony to be expected that Margo would eventually find love again, and she found it with Dr. Jesse Monsevais, who moved to San Vicente as the public health officer when the state department expanded its role in the ever-growing San Vicente community where growing family disintegration and substance abuse problems seemed to be addressed mainly by governmental programs. The couple married, and they had a son in the following year. They remain together to the time of this writing. As I drive to Mogollon today, the nostalgia for an earlier time was at least as strong as the memory of horror that had ultimately destroyed the idyllic era of the gallery. It is fortunate that most of the residents of the town remain oblivious to the terror in the night and that others have been able to forget whatever they saw or experienced

As I rounded the bend into Glenwood, I remember the 1978 conversations with Bob and his characteristic head dip

The Glenwood Service Station   RickPhoto 2018

when he was about to say something humorous. It was almost a shock to see the service station I remembered so well now closed and fallen into disrepair. I felt guilt that I had lost touch with Bob in the years after the long-ago horror that had disrupted all of our lives. Also closed was the elegant Los Olmos Guest Ranch behind the station; even the regionally well-known Blue Front Bar across the street apparently had grilled its final cheeseburger.

In the clear mid-morning air, I stopped and photographed the abandoned service station, remembering all those conversations with Bob and also the mysterious disappearance and rescue of Ofelia Armendariz. Was the decline of Glenwood somehow related

Turn-off to Mogollon   RickPhoto 2018

to the disturbing events of May 1978, or was it the changing habits of tourists and hunters that made the town businesses unnecessary? I pondered all that as I drove on up the highway almost three miles to the Mogollon turnoff.

The road into the mountains and Mogollon was now named New Mexico 159, and those who instead remained on U.S. 180

into Arizona would find that the old north-south U.S. Highway 666 was long ago re-designated to appease those squeamish Americans who had dubbed it "the devil's highway."

Driving a powerful new 2018 Volkswagen Golf-R, I began the climb easily into the mountains on a road that I knew would top out above the 7,500-foot level and then wind down into Silver Creek Canyon 1,000 feet below the summit. Beyond Mogollon, mountains such as Mogollon Baldy were as high as 10,000 feet. The hairpin turn was broader than I remembered it and far less precarious. Looking into the deep gash of the canyon, there was no forlorn wreck near the bottom as the one I so clearly remembered from those years. It was difficult not to think of that night when the bank collapsed and almost prevented us from escaping in 1978.

Mountain Road to Mogollon   RickPhoto 2018

As I topped out and began the long descent on well-maintained blacktop, I seemed to shed years as though peeling an onion. The road was becoming familiar once again as I wound down past the shell of the old powder magazine on the right side of the road and, before making the final turn down into Silver Creek Canyon, I recognized the dark forest road still beckoning darkly off to the right. There was no sign of the cyanide pool location, because substantial reconstruction had been done on the roadsides.

Many things had indeed changed. There was reinforcement to the sides of the road as though an expensive public works project had come to Mogollon in recent years. This was only a preparation for driving down into town.

The old Mogollon was very much still there,

The Fannnie Hill Vista   RickPhoto 2018

View of Mogollon Street West to East   RickPhoto 2018

View of Mogollon Street West   RickPhoto 2018

yet gone, and Silver Creek was now a deep concrete-sided gulch, with metal bridges. I stopped where we once parked a 1971 Volkswagen bus loaded with art work and photographs, but the remnants of the former town were not easy to find. The grand J.P. Holland Store had been refurbished, re-roofed in expensive Spanish tile and open as a bed and breakfast. The classic broad porch was long gone, and the creek that had been at street level for more than a century was now trickling 15 feet down in a reinforced modernistic channel.

The friendly owners of the store across the expensive metal bridge described the "100-year flood" that had roared through Mogollon in 2013, completely taking out the main street. When I looked across the street at our old gallery that was originally the Coats and Moore mercantile in the early

20th Century, then over to the museum, I was surprised that the gallery building appeared much the same, but the old rock museum building was now stuccoed over and fronted with thick iron plates over the windows and doors to protect the valuable exhibits therein. It was nothing like my vintage photographs of the place from 1978. The current museum proprietors described how their building had been buried in a wall of mud during the day of the roaring 2013 flood.

The Mogollon Museum   RickPhoto 2018

I knew that Margo sold the gallery many years before, and it now exhibited no commercial signs, no stairs on the outside, and where the outhouse had been, there was an overgrown pile of junk. The building appeared unoccupied but somebody had installed a doorbell button where the door stood padlocked. The pangs of memory struck me as I stood on the threshold, but it took more than a flood to wash away the past.

When I looked north across the canyon, it was apparent that the mine dump was all that remained of the Fanny Hill. The ghostly buildings had been razed, and I could not help but wonder if the federal government might have had a hand in sanitizing the site. Decades of weather had bleached the government-applied yellowish acid, and the massive dump was pale and colorless, like a giant's beard flowing down the mountainside. I remembered Hiram Akeley with sadness.

When I glanced to the left, I could see no trace of the bulldozed space where the Mc-Carty recreational vehicle had once looked across at the townsite. All that remained was a bare spot, but no wires were connected to the Arizona Cooperative lines supplying the residents of Mogollon.

It was probably 15 years ago, in 2003, that I received an email from Margo letting me know that Pablo "Brub" McCarty had died in San Vicente. It seemed so unlikely, but then he was already retired in 1978 despite his size and his vigor. He was survived by his daughter Kathy and two grandchildren. Kathy was married to San Vicente High School Principal Vance Koger. In the same message from Margo, I learned that Air Force veteran Tip Ulibarri had left San Vicente, selling the house next door to the McCartys and supposedly moving to live with his daughter in Denton, Texas, but when Margo asked Ouida about it, Mrs. McCarty said that Ulibarri left no forwarding address. She suggested to Margo that his indiscreet remarks about his role in the recovery of the Aztec, N.M. saucer may have made his situation unstable. I thought of Ulibarri as one of the early victims of authoritarian reassurance.

As I began my first walk down the main street in almost 40 years, I could see that some other buildings I remembered were destroyed or damaged beyond repair in the flood, and the old movie set General Store front had been moved north across the street and placed as a front to another vacant wood structure. The movie set saloon was long gone, and the 1915 theater building belonging to Bill and Nikki English had

The Mogollon Theater   RickPhoto 2018

been put back together but was showing age and disuse. Current residents explained that the federal government had poured millions of dollars into repairing the flood damage, building a deep reinforced channel, altering the antique and rustic charm of Silver Creek and the community in the process.

One real survivor after the 2013 flood was the Old Kelly Store that seemed to have changed little since the 1970s. Its porch still presented a rack of mailboxes, even though the post office at Glenwood no longer made official daily deliveries up the mountain. Residents still get mail, but mail sent to Mogollon addresses are required to use Glenwood as its destination.

As I walked up the street past the modern steel bridges connecting to such houses as the Petroskis once occupied, I could see surviving dwellings that had been up on the hillside where the

The Mogollon Church   RickPhoto 2018

166

The Road to Fanny Mine   RickPhoto 2018

raging floodwaters of 2013 did not reach.

High on the hill at the east end of town, the small Mogollon church stood out like a jewel on the mountainside, no longer vacant with galvanized sheeting nailed across the front doors. To my surprise, it was now beautifully restored, painted, and renewed, ready for services and weddings.

I started walking up the road toward the cemetery and the mine road, but I changed my mind and turned around under the mid-day sun and returned past what had been a gallery in some other lifetime and then past the pile of junk where the VW bus had parked in 1978 and on to my car. Perhaps the ghosts of Mogollon were laid to rest, and the horror that visited the town was now only a legend that none would believe, even if I were foolish enough to talk out of turn.

It was only two weeks ago that I made the mistake of answering a phone call when the phone screen read "Name Unavailable," and an unknown voice called me by name, saying only, "Remember the toxic spill," before hanging up. What remained of the day would be lunch at the roadside restaurant in the wide spot in the road called Alma just north of the Mogollon turnoff, and then a long and uneventful drive alone back to Las Cruces.

* * *

Then comes a summer night of rolling thunder and flashing lightning. I can feel the turmoil in my brain as though the final revelation is coming. Alone in my bedroom I feel the heat and humidity of stifling darkness, but I fight against falling asleep. For many years I have feared the nightmare vision that grows ever closer, ever more distinct, and so unthinkable that my entire being resists what lurks just beyond the wall of sleep that I now delay with reading, music, eating, and yet feeling the molasses drag of fatigue that will pull me into an abyss if I relax for even a moment.

As I maintain wakefulness by writing, I describe the dilemma of the hidden alien substance inside me. The nightmare visions were never common in the years since 1978, but hey progressed inexorably in detail as the years progressed as did the strange neurological ailments that have plagued me since the Mogollon years. I hesitate to think about what this subtle venom has done to Matilda Brunk, to Ofelia Armendariz and to the nephew of Nurse Norma Diaz. There must be a difference as to how the toxin affects each individual. When I think of Darouse Brunk, I wonder why I never again contacted her, though I was long ago divorced by Margo. Humans are perhaps inscrutable after all. At times I think of the irony that Darouse was attacked by the horror creature whose entire being was organic silicon, and she had chosen breast enlargement based upon the same element.

There are those who have decided that beings from outside must be humanoid and benevolent—unlike many humans. By "outside," they must mean from other planets or solar systems, but this position is absurd on its face. The universe must be multi-dimensional, both material and spiritual. It is a place of infinite wonder and infinite horror. The demons of uncounted centuries must be as real as the documented visitors visiting from outer space. The horror of outside beings is beyond the descriptive power of humans. When confronted with the unnameable, humans desperately seek to normalize, to equate with something—anything—that is known to them.

It is now close to 2 a.m. and my face is slack with exhaustion. I finish my blog on the computer by commenting that there is a sublime order in the cosmos, but along with it is a bubbling heart of chaos. In the ordered universe, there is a symphony of integration, leading from ideation to form, in the dance of celestial mechanics, with the perfect progression of the periodic table, and the ordered diversity of forms.

In direct and opposite reaction to cosmic order is the heart of madness. From somewhere in my lifetime of reading, I found the name to describe this darkness: Azathoth. From that source pours out the spawn of chaos, interfering not only with divine order in the vastness of interstellar space, but manifesting in the affairs of men as well. The Hubble telescope has seen the evidence of a galaxy 13.2 billion light years distant, and I have seen the horrors that must exist crawling out from between the girders of the universe.

I was never given to visions, but in that horrific moment of struggle in the dim lamplight of the Mogollon gallery, when I felt the touch of those venomous cilia on my arm, a rush of carrion and sulfurous odor shot through me with the power of an electrical current. Over the years, I came to the conclusion that, circulating within the rugose bodies of those other-world horrors coursed a fluid—a vile serum that dripped from the cilia writhing on their faceless protuberances, and it carried within its molecular structure the history of the dark planet and replete with their own grotesque evolution.

My writing had given way to introspection, and I was sliding away from consciousness, even though my eyes were still open. The room with all its familiar objects was crumbling as I slumped in the chair, sleep overcoming my desperate attempts to rise from the chair. I was lost.

Now I tumbled through the vastness of midnight galactic space into a void whose stars were unrecognizable to me. I was in the center of featureless midnight, tumbling toward a red pulsing dot that grew with such rapidity that I would have screamed had there been air to breath or someone to listen. I was plunging through space towad a celestial body whose immensity as I neared it filled the universe, blotting out the faint pinpoints of any other object in space. I was in the presence of a monstrous star—a red giant sun of incalculable size, whose heat far exceeded its light. For indeed, heat is the lowest order of energy. Two hundred million miles from that pulsing giant, I was falling toward a dark planet that careered in oblate orbit about the monstrous sun.. In the dim reddish luminescence, I was now witness to a dark and seething landscape. Unspeakable things emerged from within the spongey soil of the planet—white, misshapen larvae reared slimy bodies upward to worship the soul of darkness.

Under an ebony vault tinged with crimson, the planet rolled in its blind orbit, endlessly spawning obscene forms, their mindless mouths devouring each other through millennia, until the heart of chaos spawned merciless creatures absent sympathy, remorse, or pity, but given the festering chemicals within their chitinous shells, they became masters of an evil, non-Euclidian geometry, and in their poisonous thoraxes they distilled random impulses into a mathematical brilliance born of that silicon/carbon double bond through which they began the inexorable march to master dark sciences under the dim and foreboding red skies. Impervious to heat and pressure, the creatures dominated a blighted landscape punctuated by geysers of dirty steam in a soil sprouting twisted fungoid growths in the shadow of towering black volcanic cones from which spewed streams of molten metal and deadly ash. The veins in the vile bloodstream of this planet are three massive, turgid rivers of pitch that could well be named Styx, Lethe, Acheron—death, forgetfulness, and hopelessness. In the swarming welter of horrific larval forms and the fungi that sustains them arose those monstrous arthropods that became masters of the twilight planet. Their two pair of segmented arms terminated in opposable jointed nippers of horn gave them the power to manipulate matter and to create a technology as twisted as the fungus nourishing the squirming larvae they preyed upon.. The acherontic night of a blighted world, the nighted planet shuddering with skies alive with electrical discharge, and the steam geysers turning into ghastly fluorescent fountains under moonless skies. In that airless night an acidic deluge descends to nourish the mass of wriggling abominations that crawl upon the floor of hell to become prey to the silicon horrors.

In countless revolutions about the pulsing red giant, these creatures shambled, sightless and yet satanically wise. Cyclopean cities arose on the pitiless plain, fashioned by many thousands of faceless beings employing clawlike, segmented tentacles and becoming artificers of a dark mechanical science as they communicated with the buzzing coded sounds as their facial cilia wriggled and waved under dark skies. Vast windowless towers sprang up and reached into the threatening sky, hewn and shaped of igneous rock, the lightless interiors bordered by winding stairs leading from underground charnel houses, and then up, up, to dizzying heights, with obsidian floors as platforms to their dark science. From the summits of those towers extended giant metal rods perhaps 100 meters tall and with the diameter of tree trunks. These conductors were conduits for the lightning and generated an endless surge of current to power machines undreamt of on Earth. The soulless horrors learned the secrets of gravity and constructed flying machines sophisticated beyond the imaginations of the sons of Earth. Imprisoned in my waking dream, I was forced to watch columns of the horrors entering their monstrous ships, determined to spread their contagion throughout the cosmos. Even in my comatose state, I seemed to realize that these creatures from the center of chaos, spawn of the god Azathoth, were the seed of a real war in heaven as the beings beyond evil became the enemy of the organizing principle of cosmic evolution.

As one trying to rise up in deep water to reach the surface, desperate for breath, I sought to escape the mad vision, only to find myself looking into the hideous face of Arthur Brunk and suddenly realizing that he was the avatar of a mutant race. Herein was the stillborn motive for the alien invasion of Mogollon. The cosmic terror of this possibility had never occurred to me until this moment, and yet the missionary fluid inside the cilia of the alien horrors contained within it the seed for transforming humans, and Arthur Brunk was to be the prototype. I wondered if Hiram Akeley was now weightless in interplanetary space being injected with a noxious serum that was inexorably stealing his humanity as the faceless monstrosities destroyed him without pity.

When I finally came back to consciousness, I was soaked with perspiration and panting with exhaustion. I had seen the center of chaos countless billions of light years away, and I remembered Sarah Petroski who was saved by prayers. At that realization, I turned within and sought the divine spark that would save me from the evil of the Mogollon horror.

* * *

The last time I spoke with Margo on the phone, she told me she was beginning to doubt that our 1978 experiences actually happened. As she said, "I think I remember what happened, but Susan asked me the other day if I exaggerated the things I told her after we came back that weekend in 1978. I told her I wasn't sure any more." This is a warning that memories are fragile, and if were not for the abominations inside my head, I would long ago have denied my senses, assisted by mass media and the occasional threatening anonymous message on the telephone. I would allow the merciful filters that cleanse the memories and leave only nostalgia and pleasant residue to soothe my awareness. Yet I know the vision could return at any time, and I could never communicate the unspeakable reality to another living person.

At this late stage in my life, I am caught between the unquestionable reality of cosmic horror that makes me shrink when I look at the open, malevolent night sky, and the alternative of accepting the parental authoritarian reassurance forcefully telling all of us there is no such thing as a flying saucer. And there never was.

The J.P. Holland General Store, Mogollon   RickPhoto 2018

THE AUTHOR'S STORY

For most of his life, the author has ventured into the twilight realm of supernatural horror, both as a reader, and as a writer. Now he brings his stories home to the desert Southwest. Born in the mining district of southern New Mexico in 1939, Frank Thayer grew up exploring the country that now becomes the setting for a set of supernatural horror tales.

Frank Thayer

Thayer was in the cadet corps at Texas A&M University for three years before transferring to New Mexico State University, where he graduated with a degree in journalism. He worked as a reporter, photographer, weekly newspaper editor in Las Cruces, N.M., before serving with the National Guard.

On his return from active duty, he was writing stories for men's magazines in the early 1960s, Thayer was mentored by August Derleth of Arkham House Publishers. Derleth was a member of the original Lovecraft circle of writers and became the publisher of all Lovecraft's work in the decades after his death. Derleth subsequently selected one of Thayer's stories to be anthologized in a Derleth collection Travellers By Night, and Thayer since considered himself part of the secondary level of that august circle. Later in this period, he traveled to Canada, searching for work in journalism, and he served as a college journalism instructor and department head at the first community college in Ontario, Centennial College of Applied Arts and Technology in Scarborough (Toronto), Ontario, remaining from 1966 to 1977.

After his return to New Mexico in 1977, Thayer wrote stories and did photography in locations that now are part of the fiction in this volume. He went back to NMSU to earn his advanced degrees and to spend 30 years as a journalism professor and department head at that university. Today he is professor emeritus and still teaches in the department while devoting much of his energy to his fiction writing. Contiguous to the writing of horror fiction, Thayer has also published three journalism textbooks and is a co-author with Scott and Suzanne Ramsey, of North Carolina, in two ground-breaking books confirming the crash and recovery of a flying saucer near Aztec, N.M., in 1948. Their books The Aztec Incident: Recovery at Hart Canyon in 2012, and The Aztec UFO Incident, released in 2015 have sold thousands of copies and are complimented as being the best researched flying saucer books ever published.

Born and reared in southwestern New Mexico, the author takes his part as a guerrilla warrior against the ordinary world, keeping one foot in everyday reality, and the other in the realm of cosmic horror. A lifetime of devotion to the literature of supernatural horror culminated in his 2017 book Terror Tales of the Southwest. Frank Thayer has walked the places where these stories unfold, and now the horror novel The Whispering Darkness set in an actual New Mexico ghost town and illustrated with many vintage black and white photos from 1978 as well as an epilogue with photos of the town as it appears in 2018.

For more unique horror tales of the Southwest, order *Terror Tales of the Southwest*, richly illustrated at $29.95 from Amazon.com or signed from the author at the address below. Add $3.82 for domestic media mail.

Order the illustrated *Terror Tales of the Southwest* Today!
    $29.95 from Amazon.com
       author-signed copies add $3.82 domestic media mail

Consider also a cosmic abomination from the Old World that festers underneath an unsuspecting Canadian town, rising to afflict four generations of its residents — a trilogy of horror tales in an illustrated volume that includes the facsimile of a 1679 dissertation from the British Library in London that documents the dead who chew in their graves.

Order *Cobston Trilogy: The Ontario Horror* Today!
    $19.95 plus $3.82 domestic media mail postage
    $12 shipment to Canada and the UK
    PayPal payment to: gticruiser@aim.com
    Check or Money Order by regular mail

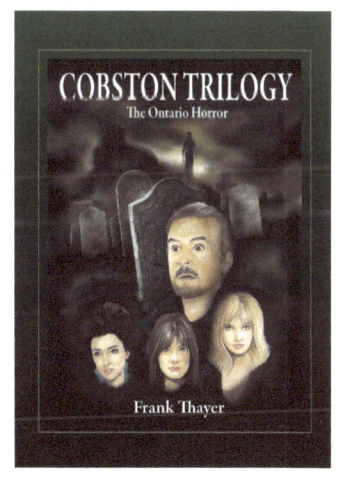

Both books available from:
Frank Thayer
Sun Cross Publications
P.O. Box 3136
Las Cruces, NM 88003
USA